HEALING the DOCTOR'S Heart

Other Books By Lorin Grace

American Homespun Series
Waking Lucy
Remembering Anna
Reforming Elizabeth
Healing Sarah

Artists & Billionaires
Mending Fences
Mending Christmas
Mending Walls
Mending Images
Mending Words
Mending Hearts

Hastings Security
Not the Bodyguard's Baby
Not the Bodyguard's Widow
Not the Bodyguard's Boss
Not the Bodyguard's Princess
Not the Bodyguard's Bride

Misadventures in Love
Miss Guided
Miss Oriented

Spellbound in Hawthorne
(with Maria Hoagland)
Taste of Memory
Sprinkle of Snow
Hint of Charm
Dash of Destiny
Stir of Wind
Essence of Gravity

Bradford Brides
Rescuing the Sheriff's Heart
Bending the Blacksmith's Heart
Converting the Preacher's Heart
Healing the Doctor's Heart

Hastings Legacy
Too Much in Common

Stand Alone Titles
A Little Clean Fun
Love in the Valley

BRADFORD BRIDES No. FOUR

HEALING the DOCTOR'S Heart

Lorin Grace

CURRANT
CREEK PRESS

Healing the Doctor's Heart© 2023 by Lorin Grace

Cover design © 2023 by LJP Creative Cover photos: Midjourney AI enhanced

Formatting by LJP Creative

Edits by Eschler Editing

Published by Currant Creek Press

Utah, United States

ISBN: 978-1-970148-25-1

Printed in the United States of America

FOR ALL DOCTORS

THANKS FOR ALL YOU DO.

wo chimes.

The echo of the courthouse clock confirmed it was the middle of the night. The crossed legs of the old cot groaned beneath Aiden as he swung his legs over the side and sat up. His army-issue bed was no more comfortable than the day he left Chimborazo Hospital at the end of the Civil War fifteen years ago. He never thought he would sleep on it again. Aiden hadn't imagined most of the circumstances of his life. *Texas*, *widower*, *lonely*, and *exhausted* were four words he hadn't planned on describing his life when the war ended and he went to medical school to complete his training.

Stretching, he stood. As long as he was awake, he should check on his two—no—three patients. For the first time in years, his office housed someone for more than just one night. Since two of them were female, he pulled on a shirt and buttoned it. Not wanting to wake anyone who slept, he left his shoes and socks under the chair in the broom closet that had become his bedroom for the last two weeks.

Jax, an injured Texas Ranger, occupied the smaller of the two rooms. In the dark, the shadows of the traction ropes resembled those of a hangman's scaffold.

"Hey, Doc."

Aiden moved farther into the room. "Can't sleep?"

"A mosquito crawled into my cast. My leg itches something fierce." Jax slapped his bare chest with a bandaged hand. "Twenty-three. It's a sad thing when a man has to count his worth in bug kills."

"If you'd let me put up the netting…" Clearly, the mesh on the window did little good.

"What fun would that be?" Jax's voice lacked humor.

Aiden poured a glass of water for Jax. Between the injury to his left shoulder and the amputation of the fingers on his right hand, drinking and eating required aid. "I can't figure out why Miss Lavender isn't bothered by the bugs."

"It's that flowery salve she wears."

"Lavender."

"That's what I said. Miss Lavender wears that flowery stuff."

"No, the flower is lavender." Aiden helped Jax take a long drink.

"Oh, I knew that. Sometimes it's confusing with all those women renaming themselves after flowers."

"New life, new names." He wasn't sure which of the women living at Rose's Rescue started the tradition of choosing a new name as they found their way out of life in the brothels. "Reverend Green says it's like Jacob in the Bible having his name changed to Israel."

"Even if they want to honor Rose, they could choose something other than a flower. I feel like I'm walking in one of those severely pruned flower gardens whenever I'm around them."

Aiden chuckled at the description. "It could be worse. They could use the Latin names. *Lavandula angustifolia* is way too pretentious."

"She is American lavender, not English, even if she is as proper as they come."

"You know Latin?"

"Don't tell the other rangers."

"I won't. Try to get some sleep. It'll help you heal."

Jax held up his bandaged hand and dropped it.

Aiden wasn't sure if the ranger meant the gesture as a farewell or to mock his words. The amputated fingers would never grow back.

In the other room, moonlight streamed through the open window. Miss Lavender appeared to be sleeping, as did his newest arrival, Miss Catherine Taylor. If her twin sister, Clara, could have taken her in, Aiden likely wouldn't have Miss Taylor here. However, the arson that destroyed Rose's Rescue had created a shortage of available rooms in town, and Clara was currently sharing hers with two other women. The shortage hadn't affected Aiden until now. There simply wasn't another place to shelter the mother-to-be. Since the injuries Jax and Lavender sustained that night required they stay here, it was simplest to add Miss Taylor to his care.

Having arrived in Hiramsville on the afternoon train, Miss Taylor was an entirely different problem. Allowing the expectant young woman to stay in the hotel after stitching her forehead closed would have been unwise. Assuming she was of the same stature as her twin, she'd lost weight with the pregnancy. The chances of her fainting again were high. Unwed as Miss Taylor was, Mrs. Forsythe, the town's prudish midwife, would likely refuse to take her as a patient, leaving her to Aiden's care.

Aiden wasn't eager to take her as a patient either. While he could deliver children, he rarely had the opportunity and didn't feel confident about his skills. So the only maternity cases he took were those Mrs. Forsythe refused. He already had one patient in the family way. Only his long-standing friendship with TJ, the sheriff, had convinced him to see Emily through her pregnancy. And the midwife's disapproval of Emily founding Rose's Rescue made the situation uncomfortable for all.

Miss Taylor muttered something and tossed off her sheets. She didn't need him. Food, rest, and time were the best medicine.

Wide awake now, Aiden went downstairs to his office and lit a gas lamp. Three days' worth of mail sat in a box at the corner of his desk. He combed through the stack, thinking a new medical journal might help him sleep. Aiden pulled out his leather chair, setting aside the journal. A letter from one of his teachers in Ohio caught his attention. Maybe they'd found someone willing to join his practice. Ever since Dr. Jones left, the town had grown and was in desperate need of another doctor. And given the number of patients Aiden had upstairs, they could also use a hospital. One doctor could only do so much.

How long could he go on, fueled by coffee and his convictions?

—◆—

The predawn light filtered through the lace curtains fluttering in the window, shedding light on the shadows Catherine had been studying since she woke up and counted five peels of the bell. It may have been six. Why did such a small town have a clock tower, and who'd decided it should ring all night long? As light filled the room, a ghostly form took shape on the wall; her stained traveling dress hung on a peg where the nurse had left it the night before.

She'd worn it every moment of the last four days as she traveled to the one person who could save her from herself— her twin. The long days and nights on the wooden bench of the third-class car left her filthy, odoriferous, grumpy, and, if she remembered last night properly, stupid. The memories of her arrival and the conversation with her sister were a little fuzzy. Clara was supposed to be married but wasn't. Then her sister had left her alone at the hotel. The food Clara ordered for her twin had come back up, any shred of sense Catherine had left with it. She'd gone to Lewis. Oh no. She really had, hadn't she?

Please, please, please be a nightmare. Lewis and Clara must think her unhinged. As for the rest of the town…everyone must believe her horrid. Her sister had been here for weeks. Those close to Clara would have formed opinions of the situation, and every member of Lewis's congregation knew Catherine had jilted the preacher. Coming here was a bad idea. The contract she signed didn't specify she had to go to Texas. On the train, she'd hoped Clara and Lewis would adopt her child, but when she arrived and discovered they weren't married, she'd acted rashly again.

Mother always chided her for not being one to look before she leaped. Usually, things solved themselves. But ever since she'd tricked Lewis into proposing to her, nothing had gone right. Even her attempt to fix the mess with Lewis and Clara hadn't worked. They weren't even engaged. Every thought and action led her deeper into trouble. What was wrong with her? Was she losing her mind like the woman in the novel she'd read who had to be put in an asylum?

Catherine closed her eyes and reopened them; her soiled traveling gown still hung there. She should put it on, tiptoe down the stairs, and leave town. She would as soon as—

The baby inside her kicked.

Pressured with need, Catherine looked around the room. The nurse had helped her to an indoor bathroom last night. She sat up and swung her legs over the side of the bed, the metal frame groaning. Catherine stood, the room swaying slightly. She put one hand on the wall to steady herself, the other where her back ached.

No one told her pregnancy would be so uncomfortable or that a woman could feel the child moving inside her. Not that anyone would. Mothers passed information regarding childbirth to their daughters as needed, usually in the days before a wedding. The class on basic midwifery and nursing taught at Bradford College had been short on many of the details regarding impending motherhood and the act that led to such a condition.

Still, Catherine knew enough about human interactions to not plead ignorance. She'd known what could happen when she followed the man who'd willingly walked down the lustful path to ruin with her, his promise of marriage an illusion meant to lead her on and on and on. Clara would think her a fool if she told all. The embellished version she'd given her sister had been meant to … to … What did it matter? It hadn't worked. Her sister hadn't married and now pitied her.

Of course, when they'd left Boston, she believed she would be married by now and living in New York among the cream of society. Everything she said and did when she left Clara on the train was to force her sister to marry Lewis. Perhaps if she had pleaded and begged. Or told her sister earlier. Clara had seen Bernard more clearly. Her sister would have accompanied Catherine to the elopement to ensure it happened.

Catherine twisted her nightgown in her hands. If only she'd understood then what she did now. Bernard never felt anything for her, never intended to wed her, engaged as he was to another woman the entire time. The promised elopement was nothing but a ruse to provide him with a diversion while stuck in Massachusetts. He wasn't even a student at the nearby college, as she'd assumed. He'd been overseeing a merger for Fairlane Shipping, his father's company.

She'd told her sister most of the truth about the elopement.

When Catherine had switched trains for Niagara Falls, she expected to be married. After a week of Bernard putting her off, then leaving, she'd followed him to New York City and learned the truth. According to the paper, this month, he would marry the New York socialite and daughter of a successful Boston businessman. The woman had a far better pedigree than Catherine. She could never compete with the bride Bernard and his family had chosen for him—a bride who insisted Bernard wait until after the wedding, a bride not stupid enough to believe in happy endings.

Bernard taught her one truth: most men were philanderers. And Mr. Fairlane, Bernard's father, made that clear when he offered to pay Catherine an absurd sum of money to disappear from his son's life. Desperate for funds and not daring to return to her parents' home near Boston, Catherine signed the papers and was escorted to the train, where she received a paltry sum, a slew of papers, and a ticket "befitting her fallen state." The wealthy shipping magnate must not have realized that a first-class Pullman ticket would have been more embarrassing in her condition. On board, she'd read the papers she'd signed. Never again was she to cross the Mississippi. She must remain in the West. Since Clara lived in Texas, that was no hardship. Mother and Father wouldn't welcome her back anyway. Once she arrived, she was to send a telegram to the attorney, which she did yesterday before leaving the train station. When the child was born, she was to send proof through an attorney in Dallas that they had not listed Bernard on the birth records. Then she would have the $2,000—enough to care for herself and the child for some time. Maybe once it was born, she would feel more herself.

The baby kicked again, making her gasp. Catherine covered her mouth so as not to disturb her roommate. She had a flower name. Lilly…Lilac…Oh yes, Lavender. From The

Rescue. The victim of a fire, Lavender was still under the doctor's care.

"Bathroom is out the door to your right. The doctor is downstairs, and Jax can't leave his room. No one will see you." The scratchy voice from the other bed startled Catherine.

"Sorry, I didn't mean to wake you." Catherine took a step forward. "How did you know what I needed?"

"Easy. Any woman in her eighth month—"

"Sixth," Catherine corrected. The midwifery class had taught her how to calculate gestation.

"My apologies. Even women not in your condition need the necessary first thing in the morning," said Lavender.

"I'll hurry so you can—"

Lavender pointed to her bound feet. "I'm not to walk. Someone will be along to help me."

Catherine hurried to the bathroom and back, afraid the doctor would come upstairs and scold her for being out of bed. During her quick trip, she realized her escape plan wouldn't work; she had no money. Even a third-class ticket required funds.

She slipped into her bed just as soft footfalls sounded on the stairs. The doctor paused at the door but didn't enter. He then crossed the hall and looked into the other room, his shoulders slumped as he entered it and closed the door behind him.

A few minutes later, he crossed the hall to the room she shared with Lavender.

As Dr. Palmer approached her bedside, he spoke in a hushed voice. "How are you feeling?"

Like a burden, a problem, so tired, and so awake. Not able to answer truthfully, Catherine answered politely. "Better."

His eyes narrowed, and the lips below his mustache thinned. "I have asked the midwife to come."

"Is something wrong?"

"I'm not sure. Most women in your condition prefer the midwife. And honestly, she knows more about pregnancy than I ever will."

Lavender muttered something, and the doctor turned to her. "I didn't mean to wake you, Miss Lavender. What did you say?"

"You didn't wake me, Dr. Palmer. I said she's carrying twins."

wins? Impossible.

Catherine stared at her rounded belly. No. She could not do this.

The doctor turned to face the other woman. "How do you know?"

Catherine glanced across the room and took a deep breath. The woman was from the place that rescued soiled doves—the one Clara went on and on about. She couldn't possibly know anything the doctor didn't.

Lavender pushed up on her elbows and leveled her gaze at him. "I was in here when the nurse helped her dress last night, and when she was out of bed a few minutes ago. Either she's mistaken about the date or there is more than one baby."

Twins? Like her and Clara? Lavender had to be wrong. She was in the fire that had burned down Rose's Rescue. She couldn't be a doctor. She was a former prostitute.

The doctor looked from Lavender to Catherine's rounded stomach. "I hadn't thought of that. How can I be certain?"

Lavender winced as she sat up. "You may be able to tell with your stethoscope or by gently feeling the positions of the fetuses."

"I am not sure what to look for."

What kind of doctor was this, asking for help from a woman more experienced in the ways of creating children than birthing them?

"If you will help me get into that chair, I can show you." Lavender swung her bandaged legs and feet over the side of her bed. She adjusted her nightgown to cover herself, pulled a wrapper off the headboard, and knotted the belt around her waist. Who would have thought a woman in her profession would be so modest?

The doctor left Catherine's side, scooped Lavender up, and set her in the ladder-back chair next to the bed.

"Can you scoot me closer?" asked Lavender.

The doctor did.

Lavender turned to Catherine. "This will be easier if we don't have your nightgown in the way. Can we pull it up?"

Catherine clutched the sheet so hard her knuckles turned white. "No. I won't be exposed. It isn't proper."

"If you help me arrange the sheet while the doctor turns his back…"

"Why? You're not a doctor. You're a—"

The doctor cut Catherine off. "Miss Taylor, be very careful what you call Miss Lavender."

"She's not a physician." Catherine crossed her arms. Few women were, and one would never choose a life of prostitution over the medical field.

Dr. Palmer shook his head. "Miss Catherine, I don't have time to explain Miss Lavender's qualifications, but she is qualified to assess your condition. Please do as she asks. I'll be back in a moment."

The door shut behind him, and Catherine stared after it, her mind in a muddle. The doctor had scolded her.

He'd talked about Lavender with respect, not just charity. After all, the woman had chosen to leave the brothels and make a new life. She deserved some pity.

Lavender pointed to Catherine's sheet. "I will not force you to do this, but it will make it easier on all of us. We cover your above parts with your nightgown and your below with the sheet. All the doctor will see is your abdomen."

Keeping one eye on the door, Catherine pulled up the nightgown. Lavender used her unbandaged hand to arrange the sheet. "Hey, Doc, we are ready."

Ready? Catherine would never be prepared to be a mother. And, if Lavender was correct, which was impossible since the woman wasn't a doctor or midwife, a mother of two.

⟨•◇•⟩

Aiden opened the door to the women's room. Lavender had arranged the bedclothes as he hoped. "I brought a second stethoscope."

Miss Lavender took the wooden stethoscope from him. "You haven't taken my advice about a binaural scope."

"On the contrary." Aiden pulled out his new Codman & Shurtleff stethoscope and put the ends in his ears. He agreed it was a vast improvement over his monaural, which was nothing more than a wooden straw with two cupped ends. "I like it very much."

Miss Lavender huffed. "So, I get your old one? I won't be able to reach the other side with it."

"You have a point." Aiden switched stethoscopes with her, aware that Miss Taylor watched the exchange with interest. "While Miss Lavender lacks a medical degree, her training is extensive."

Or so he'd observed. Miss Lavender had delivered little Scotty last January when the midwife refused to attend to any of the women at The Rescue. Miss Petunia wouldn't allow

Aiden or any man in the room for the breech birth, a sentiment many of the women of Rose's Rescue shared. It was that day Miss Lavender revealed she had studied at the Woman's Medical College of Pennsylvania and completed her obstetrics courses.

Miss Taylor studied the woman for a long moment. "Can you do whatever you need to quickly? I don't enjoy lying here…"

"Yes, sorry. Do you mind if we touch you?" asked Lavender.

Miss Taylor shrugged and lay back, eyes on the ceiling.

Miss Lavender set her hand on Catherine's midsection and pressed lightly. "I am trying to feel the child, or children. This would work so much better if I could stand." She palpated the midsection. "Ah, here is a rather large lump, and here is another. Likely, this one is a head, and this one is the posterior."

Stretching as far as possible, Miss Lavender continued. "This lump is the same size as the other one I thought was a head. That's three. Your turn, Doctor. See if you can find a fourth."

Miss Taylor's abdomen stiffened when Aiden's hands replaced Miss Lavender's. He waited for her to relax before lightly feeling for the child.

"Press a little harder. You won't hurt the baby or mother." Miss Lavender pressed on his hand until Aiden felt a rounded resistance he recognized as the baby's head.

In moments, Aiden located all three lumps, as Lavender called them. "Should I be able to find a fourth?"

"Not necessarily. The pelvic bone could hide the fourth. It doesn't matter since there are more than two, which is all you'll ever find when a mother is carrying a single child."

"So I am having twins?" Fear colored Miss Taylor's voice.

Aiden looked to Miss Lavender for confirmation before answering. She nodded ever so slightly. "We believe so."

Miss Lavender placed the stethoscope on Miss Taylor's abdomen and listened, her head bobbing slightly as she appeared to count. "A nice strong heartbeat." She slid the end over and then smiled. "And here is a different one. It is a bit slower but still strong."

Miss Lavender removed the stethoscope from her ears, then handed it to Aiden. "It is easier with this one."

Aiden bent over to make his stethoscope reach and mimicked Miss Lavender's actions. Sure enough, the faint thumping changed rhythm slightly as he moved from one side to the other. "How did I miss that?"

"You weren't looking for it. Also, you were more concerned about Miss Taylor's fall last night. We are done." Lavender raised the sheet. "You may lower your nightgown."

Faster than lighting, Miss Taylor covered herself. "Twins? I can't have twins."

Aiden tried to reassure her. "According to the timeline you gave your sister, you have weeks to prepare."

"But I'm not married. I don't have a place to live. I can't do this." Miss Taylor's eyes grew wide with panic.

Aiden wished he could give her something to calm her. However, he did not prescribe laudanum merely to reduce anxiety, and opium was more dangerous than many of his colleagues believed.

Miss Lavender patted her hand. "It will amaze you what you can do. Women are much stronger than society credits us."

Miss Taylor's breathing slowed. "So the reason I fainted was twins?"

Aiden shook his head. "Probably not. It may have had something to do with heat and exhaustion. Last night, you said you traveled second class. What did you eat during your journey?"

"Bread and cheese mostly. Now that I'm here, I promise to eat more. Clara will see to it, anyway. May I leave?"

"I'd like you to stay for the day at least. I am not sure if it was the heat, fatigue from your journey, or something else that caused you to faint. You said last night you had problems holding down your food. This has been the case for a while, I presume?"

Miss Taylor nodded.

"I'd like you to stay until you can keep your food down." He contemplated saying more. Miss Taylor wasn't the type one could tell that she was skin and bones and possibly a danger to herself. She needed someplace safe to stay, and that left very few options. Mrs. Reese's was full to bursting with the women the fire left homeless. Clara originally put her twin in the hotel for the night, but that wasn't safe if she were to faint in her room. His clinic was the best place for her. "Is there anything you need?"

Miss Taylor laid a hand over her stomach and winced. "I wish they wouldn't kick so much."

Miss Lavender put her hand on top of Miss Taylor's. "Try turning on your left side. It may help."

Miss Taylor awkwardly rotated on the narrow bed but managed to accomplish turning onto her side. She let out a sigh of relief.

Miss Lavender's eyebrows furrowed. "Doctor, would you mind carrying me to the washroom? I can't wait for Mrs. Bickford to arrive today."

"My apologies, Miss Lavender. I should have offered." Aiden lifted her off the chair and carried her out into the hall. "I need a wheeled chair to give you and Jax some freedom."

"Without an elevator, we can't go far."

"True. I don't want to pry." Aiden slowed his step, hoping he wasn't meddling too much. "Exactly how much schooling did you complete at Woman's Medical College?"

"They abducted me two weeks before graduation."

Aiden hoped his mustache hid his shock. "So you completed your schooling?"

"I was to deliver my thesis the next day, so not completely."

"More education than many doctors have, especially since the glut of fraudulent medical schools after the war has turned out all sorts of charlatans."

"I do not have the degree to prove I am not one of those poorly educated quacks."

"A few letters should solve that."

Miss Lavender stiffened. "No! You may not contact them."

Aiden paused. "Let me be more direct. I need help with Miss Taylor. We both know Mrs. Forsythe's views on unmarried mothers. Would you be willing to work as my assistant?"

"How would that work?" Miss Lavender pointed to her feet. "I won't be walking for a few weeks yet. Which reminds me—I think my hand is sufficiently healed to remove my bandage." She was correct, of course.

"We can bargain about your hand later. As for Miss Taylor, I need to keep an eye on her. I can't put my finger on it, but something seems off. Granted, I don't see many of the expectant women in Hiramsville. The midwife and I have an agreement, more or less." Mostly less. He simply stayed out of her way.

"Mrs. Forsythe is rather narrow-minded in her views and doesn't give her best care to those she sees as unworthy."

"So, will you help me?"

"As much as I can. Least I can do since we both know I am in no position to pay your fee."

"I wasn't expecting you to pay since you lost everything. The trade is more than fair on my end. Consider working for me full-time when you are well. For pay, of course." As long as she was happy to take her fee in the form of eggs or a fresh beef roast.

"Doc, you must be more tired than you look. No one is going to allow me to do any nursing or doctoring around here. People would rather die than have a soiled dove touching their family members."

Narrow-minded people—more a danger to themselves than a jar of leeches. The recent letters published in the newspaper and the arson proved just how backward-thinking his fellow citizens were. Didn't they grasp that the women at The Rescue sought refuge from a profession forced upon them? Aiden set Miss Lavender on the stool Mrs. Bickford had placed next to the toilet to help her be as independent as possible. "Call when you're done."

Miss Lavender pointed to the string that went up the wall and through a small hole, where it connected to a bell in the hallway. "I'll ring the bell."

"A rather useful invention. I keep forgetting to thank Peony. I'm going to help Jax, so don't worry if I don't come right away."

"You mean don't keep ringing the bell and drive you crazy?"

"That too."

<>◆<>

"Good morning." Aiden's greeting was met with the usual grunt, but he pasted on his brightest smile and opened the curtain.

"I told you I don't like the light."

"And I told you the fresh air will do you good. Best get some in before the day grows too hot." The light from the window spilled across the bed. Even four days of beard growth couldn't hide the hollow in Jax's cheeks. Despite Aiden plying him with food, the former ranger was losing weight, though his burns and bones were healing. The gamble to only amputate three fingers instead of the whole of Jax's right hand was paying off, and there were no signs of gangrene. But it wasn't Jax's body that worried Aiden.

"Suppose you came in to tend to my needs since I can't get off this bed."

"Would you like a shave today?"

"No point in taking up your time."

"Wouldn't be taking up my time. Miss Peony said she used to give shaves. Volunteered her skills."

Jax grumbled. "I won't let her shave me for free. But it would be worth two bits if she would let me pay her. Those women lost everything. Isn't right for me not to pay."

"You might have a hard fight paying her. They can't do enough for you since you saved Lavender's life."

Jax grunted but sat a bit straighter. "You tell her she either lets me pay her or she can leave."

Smiling inwardly, Aiden maintained a straight face. His ploy to get Jax to do something other than lay in the dark had worked.

Clara's voice carried into the room from the stairway. Not ready to talk, Catherine closed her eyes.

"Good morning. We brought breakfast." Her sister's singsong voice greeted them.

How could Clara be so cheerful? Oh, that's right, the perfect twin never made any mistakes.

"Your sister had a difficult night," whispered Lavender.

The woman had to know Catherine only feigned sleep. Only moments ago, they had discussed when food would arrive.

Clara whispered back. "Oh, sorry. I'd thought she'd be awake by now. I'll leave yours and take Jax's to him."

On the other side of the room, something clanked on the bedside table.

Catherine couldn't hear Lavender's response before footsteps crossed the hallway.

"I don't know what you are playing at," Lavender spoke in a clipped tone, "but if you want to eat, you'd better wake up."

Catherine opened her eyes and sat up, the room swaying for a second before righting itself. "I'm up."

"If you're curious," Lavender continued, "aside from your being Clara's twin and with child, I know very little about you. No one does. We all know you didn't marry the preacher, but he didn't talk about you much." Lavender finished her statement as Clara returned with another woman with hair clipped close to her scalp.

"Good. You're awake. I didn't want to miss you this morning." Clara set a bed tray laden with breakfast across Catherine's lap. "I assume you've met Lavender. And this is Peony."

Peony smiled. "The girls all say I'll have my hair back in no time. The fire singed it so much there was no point in trying to salvage it."

"Pleased to make your acquaintance." The obligatory comment rolled off Catherine's lips.

Peony settled into the chair beside Lavender's bed. "Don't mind us. We will have our own conversation."

Clara smiled at the two women and turned to Catherine. "Privacy is scarce in Hiramsville at the moment. Ever since the fire, Mrs. Reese's home has been overflowing. Everyone willing is boarding someone. Still two women are rooming at the hotel."

"Is that why you insisted I stay at the hotel?" Yesterday she'd assumed it was because her sister was ashamed of her state. However, comments from the doctor and Lavender made her question if there might be a more practical reason.

"Partly. I was so astounded you were here, and I didn't know what I ought to do." Clara folded her hands in her lap.

"Then, the moment you depart, I go off and make another poor decision. I'm not sure what I was thinking." The entire conversation with Lewis was a bit of a blur in her mind. She remembered insisting that he marry her. And failing to flirt. There had been another preacher there too. Maybe. Catherine peeled the shell of her hard-boiled egg. "Obviously, I wasn't, since I ended up fainting on my way back. I haven't been thinking much these last few months. What's wrong with me?"

Dismissing the conversation Catherine desired to engage in, Clara gestured toward the bandage on Catherine's head. "Does it hurt?"

Catherine reached up to touch it. "Oh, I'd forgotten about that. So, no, it doesn't. Do you think it will scar?"

"Most likely."

"Then people won't struggle as much to tell us apart." It was fitting that she would be the scarred and broken one. "I need to tell you—"

"I need to tell you—" her sister began at the same time.

"You first," they both said.

Clara laughed. "It has been so long since we did that. I've missed it."

"Me too." They were the most honest words Catherine had spoken in a while. She missed Clara more than she could express. "What's your news?"

"No. You tell me first. You are the oldest."

Catherine shook her head. "I don't think that always being first has served me well. Please share."

"I'm engaged." Clara's hushed tone may as well have been a euphonium blast as evidenced by the gasps that came from across the room. "Now you."

"It's twins."

"Twins?" Clara laid her hand on Catherine's bulging abdomen.

Unlike with the doctor, Catherine welcomed the touch. How she'd missed her sister. Her vision blurred. "Can you believe it? Mother always said I deserved them for all the trouble I caused."

"She told me the same."

"Why? She thought you were an angel." How often Catherine had been told to be more like her sister.

A subtle flicker of displeasure danced across Clara's features. "That's one way of saying I'm too quiet."

"What am I going to do?" The panic that had been her constant companion for the last several weeks returned full force.

Clara squeezed her hand. "We will figure it out. We always do when we work together."

"I'm so sorry about last summer. I should have—" A sob stopped Catherine's next words. Crying again. All she did was cry anymore.

Instead of slapping her like Bernard had, Clara leaned over the tray and hugged her. The hug felt like forgiveness—forgiveness she didn't deserve. "It will work out. However, I need to let you eat and rest. Dr. Palmer already gave me an earful about not upsetting you. He wasn't sure how you would take the shock of me marrying Lewis."

"Shock? More like it is about time. You have adored him since we were small. I'm jealous of that. I may have had beaus, but none that adored me or none I miss now that they are gone. If it weren't for me and my stupid trick…I should have confessed that day, not put you through all the pain."

"In some ways, I think it was better this way. I'll be back this afternoon. When you arrived, we were working to raise funds for The Rescue. I must get several letters finished so they can go out on the one o'clock train." Clara turned at the door.

Peony followed. "I should go too. Nellie needed me to pick up more baking powder. I'll come back this afternoon."

Lavender picked up a book. "You should get some more sleep when you can. Doc's office is only open to emergencies on Saturdays and Sundays. And there are enough of those to wake the dead."

"How long have you been here?"

"In this room? Two weeks since the fire. In Hiramsville?

Since last fall. I'm assuming you know about Rose's Rescue?"

"Emily wrote Clara about it all the time. I was hoping to teach there, although I didn't excel in any particular subjects, like Clara in German. Since the building burned down, is that even an option?"

"They planned on moving to a different location before the fire. The abandoned hotel project up the river would be ideal. The planners were hoping it would be a resort, but the natural hot springs farther north are more of a draw. The new place will house three times the number of women compared to the old building. Rose's Rescue saved my life. So many other women want to escape. I wish there were more rescues. You've probably thought of this, but if you didn't have a sister willing to take you in …" Lavender didn't need to complete the sentence.

Catherine finished her meal and moved her tray aside. She understood having nowhere to go. At least with Clara getting married, she could live with her. Even if she hadn't signed the agreement to stay west of the Mississippi, returning to Boston was impossible. They would never accept her back into society. If she didn't have the promise of the Fairlane's money… Catherine didn't want to contemplate her options.

Bernard's words came back to her. He'd called her many of the names people used for women like Lavender, words she'd remembered this morning. Perhaps she shouldn't be so hard on Lavender. With a child, Catherine would find few employment options. With twins impossible.

Fine dust clung to the top of Aiden's washstand. He'd been paying two women from The Rescue to come in and clean his home twice a week. One of them got married last week, and the other was too busy helping at Mrs. Reese's home. At least she still came to clean his office every day.

Aiden stirred his shaving soap into a lather. He wasn't using his house other than to change and shave. The three bedrooms and exam room off the porch were going to waste. If he moved into the office, he could house displaced women with minor inconvenience to him. Jax's injuries would keep the man to his bed for another three weeks at least. Aiden needed to be near him at night.

Avoiding his mustache, Aiden applied the shaving soap with a brush and studied the room in the mirror. He hadn't slept in his four-poster bed since the night before the fire. This room would be more comfortable for Lavender and, as it was on the main floor, she could use a wheelchair to get to the parlor and kitchen. The lack of an indoor lavatory meant the women would have to rely on chamber pots and the outhouse. He'd planned on adding a toilet but never got around to it. That couldn't be helped. Two of the three bedrooms upstairs lacked furnishings but would be no worse than the blanket pallets rolled out each night in every corner of Mrs. Reese's home. In his home exam room, there was another bed he'd rarely used since he moved into his current office. In all, six or more of the women from Rose's Rescue could live here. Why hadn't he thought of this?

Ouch.

Red mingled with a dot of the white soap. Aiden pressed the cut with a towel. Shaving cuts annoyed any man, but a doctor with cuts could endanger others. How could his patients trust him with a scalpel if he couldn't use a shaving razor? No wonder so many doctors wore neatly trimmed beards. His would come in gray, and he didn't have time to use Dr. Shirley's hair and beard dye on anything other than his mustache. For now, he left the few gray hairs at his temples as they gave him a distinguished look. There was a vast difference between looking wise and looking old. Aiden wasn't ready to look old even with his thirty-seventh birthday only weeks away.

After dressing in fresh clothing, Aiden headed to the jail, hoping to find TJ on duty. As luck would have it, he was not. Aiden returned to his office, hoping to find young Donny to send a message to TJ's wife, Emily, and Mrs. Reese about using his home for some of the women from Rose's Rescue. But Donny was nowhere to be found. In fact, the streets were emptier than normal. As he climbed the back steps to his office, Aiden remembered it was Saturday and half the town was at the local market. Which was also the reason his nurse only worked an hour this morning—an hour that had passed fifteen minutes ago.

Bonnet in hand, Mrs. Bickford waited at the door. "I finished cleaning everyone up. That ranger is grumpy as ever. He isn't going to heal right if he doesn't care."

"Thank you. Sorry I was late."

"Morning Glory is upstairs. She said she'd help Lavender when necessary. I suspect a few others will come later. I'm off to the market. I promised the children some of Nellie's jumble cakes. I hope there are some left."

"Tell her to give you the ones she set aside for me if she's out. If you see Emily or Mrs. Reese, will you send them by?"

"Should I send Donny with a message if I don't?"

Aiden nodded. "I'm turning my home into a residence for some of the women from Rose's Rescue. I'm living upstairs anyway."

"That is a fine idea. I'll be sure and send word if I don't see them." Mrs. Bickford waved as she hurried out the door.

Aiden walked up the stairs to Lavender's room, pausing outside Jax's door. The ranger's labored breathing indicated he was still in pain. Between the burns and broken bones, there was little Aiden could do to ease the pain since the ranger had started refusing laudanum a week ago. A wise choice, even if painful.

He knocked on Lavender's open door before stepping in. Miss Taylor faced away from the conversations around Lavender's bed. Morning Glory and Peony visited this morning.

"I didn't expect to see you again so soon. Is something wrong?" Lavender spoke barely above a whisper.

"Only that I am slow to come up with solutions. How would you like a change of scenery?"

"I am tired of these four walls. But I have a better window than Jax. He could benefit from a different view as well."

Lavender had a point.

"I have not stayed the night in my home since the fire. If you and others who are still homeless move in there, then Jax can have this room and I can move into his. You are well enough that you don't need my constant supervision."

"You'd give up your home for us?" asked Morning Glory.

"Why not? With Jax needing me close, it makes sense, and I get a proper bed instead of a cot."

"For how long?" asked Morning Glory.

"Jax won't be up and walking for another three to four weeks at best. I can live here indefinitely once I set up a space."

"Have you talked with Emily or Mrs. Reese?" asked Lavender.

"Not yet."

Morning Glory crossed her arms. "They aren't going to like kicking you out of your home."

"No one is kicking me out. I only go to the house to change and shave. And I have indoor plumbing here."

"Well, in that case, if they agree, I won't say no." Lavender paused. "I worry about Jax being alone."

Over the past week, Aiden had done his best not to listen in on the late-night conversations his two long-term patients held across the hall. However, he would have to be deaf and blind not to see the effect of their friendship on each other's recovery. "Maybe we can work something out so you can visit."

"I believe Clara may come back. Would you take me over to visit, then?"

"Only if you help him see this is a good idea. I don't know if he will like this change the way you do." Aiden crossed the hall, prepared for Jax's objections.

For the past hour, Catherine had stared at the bare wall, not exactly pretending to be asleep but more like finding oblivion. Why would a doctor give up his home? It didn't make sense. Father had several rental properties and always complained about how the tenants treated them. He would never allow a stranger to stay in his home. Lavender seemed cultured enough, but the other women who'd come and gone during the day … If Mother heard Morning Glory speak, she would have the girl hold a bar of Babbitt's soap in her mouth until it melted.

Someone tapped on the door. "Lunchtime."

Catherine sat up in the bed, rubbing her eyes, a wave of dizziness washing over her. Her hand flew to her stomach. Nausea had become her constant companion over the past months, and she'd lost count of the number of times she regurgitated what she'd eaten. She hoped lunch was something she could keep down. It was so embarrassing when other people knew she'd thrown up. No wonder expectant women were not out in society. Worse yet, the more nauseated she was, the more she snapped at others. No wonder Bernard left her.

A teenage girl with a disfigured face stood in the doorway, a basket in her hands. "Cold chicken to—" The girl's mouth dropped open. "My lands, you are like two peas! I thought they were exaggerating. You look a heap like your sister. If it wasn't for the bandage and the baby you are carrying, one could get you mixed up. I know I am staring, just like you're staring at me."

"Nellie"—reproof laced Lavender's voice—"meet Catherine. Catherine, this is Nellie, who is struggling to remember how we greet people."

Nellie set the basket on the table near Lavender's bed. "Now I know what people think the first time they see me. All astonishment. Only you are pretty."

Catherine blinked. "I forgot my manners as well. I shouldn't have stared at you either. Were you burned in the fire too?"

"No." Nellie set her basket down on the table next to Lavender's bed. "Thelma sent her lemon-cream calf's-foot jellies for dessert. I keep telling her to use a gelatin packet, but she insists on making it the traditional way—two whole days of work for the jellies, in the heat, no less, but Thelma insists, and Mrs. Reese keeps reminding me to mind my elders."

Apparently, the subject of Nellie's burns wasn't open to discussion. Since Catherine didn't know Thelma, she couldn't do anything other than listen and wait for her moment to talk.

"Mrs. Reese says I can learn from Thelma, but she won't show me her secret recipes."

Lavender laughed. "There is a reason they are called secrets. And, remember, Thelma has been cooking since before even the doctor was born. Getting Mrs. Reese's cook and confidant upset at you will not make learning easy."

"She doesn't want me being as good a cook as her." Nellie unpacked the basket and brought a plate to Catherine. "Cold chicken and apple salad. It's a recipe I created."

No smells tickled Catherine's nose. A white, creamy dressing coated the chicken and apple pieces, the presentation lacking color. Unable to say anything positive about the lumpy food, Catherine settled for a simple thank-you.

To each woman's plate, Nellie added a fluffy biscuit and a custard cup full of the calf's foot jelly. The fare looked no better than the dried-out bread and cheese she'd eaten on her train trip. Catherine dipped her fork into the salad. It tasted far better than it looked. Nellie took the basket across the hall.

Dr. Palmer entered the room as Catherine finished the last of her biscuit. "Good to see you eating. Any dizziness?"

Catherine shielded her mouth with her hand so she could answer. "Not now."

"Earlier?"

"When I sat up."

"That is to be expected. After lunch, let's get you walking around and see how you feel." Dr. Palmer turned to Lavender. "Mrs. Reese and Emily agreed to my plan. They are trying to figure out who else to move into the house. I'd say your change of scenery should come late this afternoon."

"Will you suggest Nellie for your house? I think she and Thelma are not sharing a kitchen well."

He chuckled. "Funny, Mrs. Reese suggested the same thing. Too many cooks in the kitchen."

"Do you know who else will be in the house?" asked Lavender.

"Not yet. It seems I have started a multi-house game of musical chairs." He turned to Catherine. "I added you to the mix. Your sister keeps lamenting that she can't marry today so she can free up one more bed. Reverend Staples won't let her until your parents arrive."

Catherine dropped the custard cup, dotting the sheet with jelly. She must have heard wrong. "My parents are coming?"

"Your father wired this morning. Didn't Clara tell you?"

"No. No." Father would insist she return to Massachusetts. She couldn't. And the lectures she would have to endure! Mother would never let her out of her sight. Catherine set her plate aside and swung her legs off the bed. "I need to leave."

Catherine stood and took a step, the room spinning as she did so. She reached for the wall to steady herself but found Dr. Palmer's chest instead. *Warm and strong*. She reeled from the wanton thought as soon as it came.

The doctor's hand cupped her elbow. "I can't let you leave if you are light-headed."

"I only stood too quickly." Twins. Her parents. It was too much. She could use her last few dollars to travel someplace and hide. But how far could she get with only twenty dollars to her name?

He guided her back to the edge of the bed, where she sat. "I meant leave town. The risk of falling and harming yourself or your babies is too great."

"I can't stay here, not if my parents are coming." Why hadn't Clara told her?

"They won't be here for days. Let's handle one problem at a time."

Catherine took a deep breath as another urgent need surfaced. "Then may I walk to the lavatory?"

She stayed in the washroom as long as she dared. Dr. Palmer must think her a lunatic wanting to leave so quickly. Why couldn't she think things through like Clara? Catherine had always been the impulsive one. But ever since she realized she was with child, she seemed to have no control. Dr. Palmer was right. Her parents wouldn't be here for days. If she had collapsed in some other town, would anyone have helped her?

Dr. Palmer waited in the hallway. "I've sent for your sister. The telegram came after her visit with you this morning. I shouldn't have told you. It was not my place."

Indeed, it wasn't the doctor's place to know more about her life than she did. Perhaps she could use that to her advantage. "Will I be well enough to return to Boston if my father demands it?"

The doctor's brow furrowed. "Possibly, but I would discourage such a long journey."

"Will you tell my father that?"

"Yes."

Relief filled her. Father would have to listen to the doctor. Wouldn't he? Nothing would be worse than going back to Brookline with her parents. Boston society would label her for life. "I'll stay for now."

⸺◆⸺

Aiden waited for Clara to arrive at his office before leaving to pack up his belongings. He needed to ask Clara her thoughts about her sister, as he had no basis for his assumptions of Catherine's mental state. He'd heard stories of expectant women losing their common sense. He'd read of women eating coal, plaster, and even rocks. Others suffered from melancholy so severe they had to be restrained for their safety. While Catherine didn't appear to suffer from extreme distress, he assumed her quick changes of mood and possible irregular behavior might have something to do with her condition.

Clara's polite answers didn't give him any insight other than the depth of devotion the twin he'd come to know had for her apparently wayward sister. After carrying Miss Lavender to Jax's room, Aiden went to the house to pack.

A wicker laundry basket and his old steamer trunk held most of his belongings. Other than various medical books, he had few items he regretted leaving in the house. The women would likely use the fine china gathering dust in the cabinet—a wedding gift for Cathleen. He had touched none of it since Cole's gang killed her, one of the many victims of the gang's tyranny. The china she never used was all he had left to remember her besides the photograph a traveling photographer had taken days after their engagement. The photographer insisted they sit with their heads braced by a metal armature. The image lacked the sparkle in Cathleen's eyes and the playfulness in her smile. Aiden tucked a few other mementos of his life before he came to Hiramsville in his trunk—not that he needed them. He didn't want anyone asking questions about his life. It was enough that they all knew of Cathleen.

Aiden tried to push the memories from his mind, but they refused to budge. Cathleen's funeral. Amputating Cole Pike's gangrene leg in an attempt to save the outlaw's life—care his Hippocratic oath demanded he provide regardless of how many people Cole had murdered.

He'd hoped for relief when Cole died at the hand of his son, but it never came.

Aiden turned away from the cupboard before older memories surfaced. One failure at a time was all he could allow himself.

TJ rapped against the back door before opening it for himself, his brother GW, and Hawke. "Emily said you needed help."

"I see she sent the cavalry. Didn't know you were in town, GW."

GW took off his hat. "Texas Rangers are not the cavalry. Hawke is here to look at what's left of Rose's and the notes my brother collected. I want to catch the arsonist."

Hawke exuded wagonfuls of the same quiet confidence the other rangers possessed. Without a word, Aiden knew this was the man who could solve the arson.

"Only a half-full trunk on my end to move. Since the women lost everything, the hardest part will be moving the patients around, especially Jax."

The rangers looked at each other. GW spoke. "I don't know if seeing us will make things better or worse."

"Better. He's lost enough without losing his friends. It may be awkward for you at first, however. His heroism in saving Lavender from the fire cost him his shooting hand, injured his shoulder, and broke his leg. I've got him strung up like a marionette, trying to save him from a limp. Don't let it take you away as well." A full lecture was likely to be ignored by the men. The longer Aiden practiced medicine, the more he became convinced that a healthy dose of optimism did more for recovery than any bottled medicine.

"We intended to go by and see him after our investigation," said Hawke.

"Miss Lavender is visiting him now. She's the only one who seems to bring a smile to his face." Aiden had even heard the injured ranger laugh a time or two when his two patients talked from their respective rooms at night.

GW and Hawke exchanged glances, confirming what Aiden suspected. If Lavender was interested in anyone, it was Jax. He once hoped in time that his and Lavender's friendship and common interest in medicine could grow into something more, but the last two weeks had moved them into a solid friendship, which Aiden had to admit was better for them. Not that Lavender wasn't pretty or nice, but he couldn't picture growing old with her.

"If you can help me take this over to the office," Aiden pointed to the trunk, "I'll see when we're moving the women in."

GW and Hawke slung the trunk between them.

TJ followed Aiden out the door with a laundry basket in his arms. "You're sure about this, Aiden? It could be months before you get your house back."

"It is only a building." One intended for a family he was likely to never have. Both widows his age, Mrs. Bickford and Donny's mother, Mrs. Owen, had already informed him they didn't intend to remarry regardless of their circumstances. Aiden was in danger of becoming as much of a laughingstock as Mr. Collins proposing to anything in a skirt that stepped off the train at the Hiramsville station. He'd briefly courted both Emily and Clara, both fifteen years younger than he was. The problem was the women who came to Hiramsville were younger and younger. Or he was getting older. Clara had been kind enough to tell him that his age, while a consideration, was not the reason she'd ended their brief courtship. It wasn't long enough to be a "ship," more like a raft or a skiff. She'd always been intended for the preacher, even if it took them both awhile to realize it. At least with the rangers in town, he didn't feel like the only old bachelor.

"You're thinking awfully hard. It's close to the anniversary, isn't it?" TJ was the only person in town who knew Aiden's history. Most people knew about Cathleen, but only TJ knew of the loss that had pushed Aiden to take a position in a no-account Texas town.

"Wednesday." Aiden sighed. "No, I am not going to hole up in a room with a bottle of whisky. I haven't touched the stuff in seven years. Not since your father locked me in that cell."

"I didn't ask."

"You thought about it." Aiden opened the back door to his office.

"No, I didn't. We all have our burdens to carry."

"Speaking of which, how is Emily? I keep telling her to slow down, but every time I go anywhere, she's working or directing something." Aiden easily switched the conversation to their mutual concern. TJ's wife had miscarried twice and was now on her third pregnancy since their marriage a year ago. By Aiden's count, she was in her fourth month—twice as long as the other two.

"Other than being annoyed at being told to rest, she's doing well. Naturally, she's concerned she'll lose this child too. She really is being careful, but she refuses to lie about all day, doing nothing."

"As long as she isn't lifting heavy things or walking distances in this heat."

"One good thing about the fire is that with the three extra houseguests, she has plenty of help."

"Has she told anyone?"

"Not this time, although I'm sure most of her friends have guessed. Emily wants to wait until she's as big as a barn. Her words. Not mine. I would never say that."

Aiden slapped TJ on the back. "Good man. I wouldn't repeat that to anyone else if I were you."

They reached the back door of the office and walked up the stairs. Laughter echoed from Jax's room. Aiden glanced in to see Lavender sitting at his bedside, where he'd left her. He would have to find a way for them to continue to talk. If nothing else, he might rig a tin-can phone they could use through the window. Aiden set his things on top of the trunk in the hall, then knocked on Jax's door before entering.

"Sorry to interrupt. Miss Lavender, are you ready to move to your new accommodations?"

"Can I wait a bit longer?"

"No rush on my part. I see Clara is still here, so I can find out where Miss Taylor is going."

"You should just call them Clara and Catherine since they're both Miss Taylor."

"I use *Miss* to keep things professional. In a few days, we won't have that problem since Clara will be Mrs. Staples."

"I hope Catherine is a candidate for your house. She is light-headed more than I think is normal, and she'd be upstairs at Mrs. Reese's."

Like most houses, there was a steep stairway at the place. Mrs. Reese complained that builders deliberately made them to cause falls, especially for a woman with hooped skirts. Mrs. Reese's stairs had wider treads than most. Still, Catherine traversing them many times a day was a concern. "I agree."

Lavender tugged at the wrap on her left hand. "May I please take this off?"

"I don't know. What is your professional opinion?"

"You're trusting me?"

"Yes. You wouldn't do anything to endanger yourself, would you?"

She picked at the edge of the linen cloth. "Perhaps I'll take it off after the move. Since I'll have to be carried."

Aiden smiled. Lavender was the solution to his need for a medical partner.

ould you stand up for me at my wedding?" Clara asked again, refusing to allow Catherine to ignore answering the question.

"Why would you want me to? I jilted Lewis, convinced you to swap places, and then tried to force him to marry me—yesterday. And unless the high-waisted dresses our grandmothers wore at our age come back into fashion in the next week, it will be impossible to disguise my scandalous condition."

"You are my sister." Clara's simple answer both pacified and alarmed Catherine.

"Mother will never allow me into the church."

"Mother isn't planning the wedding. If it were up to me, I'd have it over and done with before they arrive. But Lewis says we need to honor Father's wish to wait. If the court-house was open on Saturday, it would be done by now."

"You wouldn't get married in a church?"

"I'd marry in a barn if it meant no interference from Mother. I want to wed Friday afternoon, twenty minutes after the train arrives, but I don't know for sure if they'll be on it, so I agreed to wait until next Monday."

"Mother won't have time to change much."

"Hiramsville isn't large enough for options. Three churches, two hotels, and one doctor." Clara counted off on her fingers. "I don't understand why they're coming at all. They weren't coming to your wedding, and once they realized what happened, they wanted me to marry Lewis in haste."

"After what you said about Father hiring the Pinkertons to find me, are you surprised? Only, I can't—" A knock on the door cut Catherine's sentence short. "Enter."

Dr. Palmer stepped in. "I'm not sure where everyone is with accommodations, but I would like to ask that Miss Taylor—er, Catherine, be at my house."

"Why can't I stay with Clara?" They needed every moment they could have together.

The doctor pulled at his mustache. "Clara, do you know who is supposed to move into my house?"

Clara counted on her fingers. "Lavender, of course, then Nellie, Morning Glory, Petunia—no, I mean Peony. Petunia is staying with Mrs. Reese, and either Rae, Daffodil, or Marigold."

The doctor's brow furrowed. "Where is Catherine going?"

"Last I heard, probably Emily's."

The doctor slowly shook his head. "I think Catherine would be better off closer to town. I hate to mix things up. I was planning on giving Lavender the bedroom on the main floor as it would be the easiest to use the wheelchair. However, if she could be in the old infirmary, the two of you could have the bedroom. There is a large bed, and I assume sharing won't be a problem."

"Nellie wanted the infirmary since it's close to the kitchen."

"I'll talk with her. It's more important that Catherine not constantly walk up and down stairs."

"That would free up a room at Mrs. Reese's. I told her I could sleep on a pallet, but she wouldn't hear of it the week I am to be a bride."

The doctor turned to Catherine. "Sorry for deciding your future without your input."

"You really don't want me walking up and down stairs?"

"Fainting and stairs seldom mix. Given how you are still dizzy from time to time, I'd rather not take risks."

Clara stood. "I'd better run and tell everyone about the new arrangements."

"If Nellie is put out, have her come talk with me. I know how much she likes her privacy."

"I'll be back soon." Clara blew a kiss as she hurried out the door.

The doctor didn't leave.

Instead, he pulled the chair Clara had used back from the bed a couple of feet and sat down. "You and I need to come to a couple of understandings. I sent a message to the midwife last night, and she has refused to come, so you are stuck with my options. Fortunately, we both have Miss Lavender. Prior to the unfortunate incident that led her to Rose's Rescue, she was a student at what I consider the most prestigious women's medical college in the country. Miss Lavender has worked in a maternity hospital and undoubtedly knows more than either of us about childbearing."

An understatement, considering she's worked in a brothel. The unkind thought flashed through Catherine's mind.

"This morning you wished to dismiss Miss Lavender's opinion because you thought of her only as a fallen woman. I want to make something very clear. The years that were stolen from her life and the lives of the women at The Rescue do not define them, just as the last year of your life doesn't define you. I expect you to treat them with dignity. When it comes to Miss Lavender's medical advice, you will take it and consider her to be in every way my medical partner."

Catherine nodded. She didn't dare do otherwise. Like most men, he had all the authority, but there was something kind about his manner that made it more acceptable to follow his orders. Perhaps it was because he was defending a woman who, like her, most would ignore.

"I also expect you to be honest with us. The more we know, the better. Your sister indicated you thought you were due at the end of October."

"Or first of November."

"Any possibility it could be earlier?"

"No." Catherine felt her face heat. "They gave us a calculation page in the class we had to take about home medicine. I ran through the math several times once I realized—"

"Emily Morgan told me about those classes. So, I assume you are not naïve to the cause of your pregnancy." He didn't wait for an answer. "A more difficult question, then. Could you be due later?"

Her face felt like it was on fire.

He tipped his head. "I am not going to discuss what you say with anyone but Miss Lavender."

"What if she tells?"

"Tells who? Believe me, she is very good at keeping secrets. I wouldn't be asking these questions if it wasn't necessary." The doctor looked apologetic.

"It could be later, but I don't think so. I didn't see him for more than a month." By then, she'd known, although she didn't tell Bernard until a few weeks before graduation, sure he would promise to marry her—a promise he hadn't kept.

"Thank you. I value your honesty."

He gave her little choice in the matter. His piercing eyes could likely tell if she lied. "Clara walked you around this floor, such as it is. Were you light-headed?"

"Yes." Elaborating that it was worse than when she drank a half bottle of champagne wouldn't help.

"Did the feeling fade as you walked?"

"Yes."

"For the next few days, I want you to get up slowly and have someone nearby when you do."

"I can do that." Falling or fainting wasn't something she wanted to repeat.

"Good. I understand you kept both meals down today. Anything else I need to know?"

Catherine pinched her lips together. Telling the doctor that the cleft in his chin was rather handsome was something he didn't need to know. It was something she shouldn't even think about.

By the light of a single low-burning lamp, Aiden set his shaving cup on the narrow table. He was officially moved into his new room.

"Hey, Doc?" Jax called from the other room.

Aiden crossed the hallway, glad to see GW and Hawke still visiting their friend. They'd set up the makeshift card table to the side of Jax's bed. The hinged mattress Aiden ordered from Cincinnati allowed Jax to sit up in a reclining position. Seeing his patient smile made every penny of what Aiden once felt was an extravagant purchase worth it.

"TJ went home. Can you be our fourth in a game of cards?" asked GW.

Hawke shuffled the deck. "Answer carefully, Doc. Jax cheats."

"I do not. Dropping the ace into my sling was accidental." Laughter tinged Jax's reply—a medicine Aiden could not mix or supply and one that was sorely needed by the man.

A pile of beans sat in the middle of the table. "What are you playing for?"

"A hill of beans. Winner gets one favor from the losers. This is how TJ got us to move him and all of Emily's books into their new home. So far, Jax has won a month of caring for his horse from TJ and yet-to-be-determined labor from Hawke and me."

"Interesting way to play." Aiden sat in the vacant chair.

"Pa came up with it when TJ and I were boys. He didn't want us to get gambling fever. I think what he really wanted was for us to feel like we owed him when we mucked out the stalls. Either way, neither of us has ever lost a week's pay at a card table."

Hawke dealt the cards and changed the subject. "Doc, did they tell you about my theory that a woman started the fire?"

"This isn't back to blaming Nellie and her cooking, is it?" asked Aiden.

Jax picked up his cards with his good hand. "No. She's innocent."

"The notes TJ collected the week prior to the fire suggest that they were all written by a woman. Mr. Collins claims to have destroyed the letters he printed, so we can't look at those."

Aiden looked at his cards and placed two beans in the center of the table. "I thought TJ cleared Collins from setting the fire."

"Collins didn't set it, but he knows who wrote the letters condemning the preacher and Rose's Rescue. He slipped when I was talking to him, and instead of saying 'they,' he said 'she.' Not enough to narrow things, but it does support my deduction." Hawke laid a king face up. "The newspaperman has no love for the women from The Rescue."

"If he did, he would have married one by now." Aiden's observation slipped out.

Jax nodded. "Lavender says he's made no secret of his disdain for them. They may be the only women in town he hasn't proposed to."

Aiden picked up another card. "Still, knowing it was a woman doesn't narrow it down much."

Hawke discarded. "It may. Whoever wrote the notes also targeted the preacher. I think we are looking for someone who thinks she should be his bride. I'd say the arsonist is in Reverend Green's congregation."

"But everyone knew he was engaged."

"Was. That all changed when his bride didn't show and her twin refused his offer," said GW.

Jax's hand hovered over the cards. "As I understand it, Miss Clara accepted Reverend Staples just last night and is planning on marrying him next week."

"What?" said Hawke. "Is that general knowledge?"

Aiden shrugged. "If it isn't, it will be by the time church is over tomorrow. Reverend Staples will announce it from the pulpit."

GW laid his cards down face up, a winning hand. "I think we should stay around here a few more days. If you are right about her targeting the preacher, she won't be happy that he's getting hitched."

Jax dropped his cards on the table. "And we just gave her another target."

Aiden set his cards down as well. "What do you mean?"

"You put Miss Clara in your house, Doc, with Lavender." Jax pushed himself up with his good arm.

"Better Doc's house than Mrs. Reese's. Doc's house isn't over the caverns. The only way in is directly. The arsonist could have come from any number of buildings." GW gathered the beans, adding them to his hill. "Hawke and I will keep an eye on Doc's house. There isn't any reason for her to hurt the preacher or the church."

Jax relaxed back into the pillow. "I feel so useless."

The good humor fled faster than the winning horse at a county fair.

Aiden wished for a way to bring it back. "Anyone up for another round? I still have some beans left."

GW and Hawke stood.

"We should go," said Hawke. "We can play another round tomorrow. I still need someone to polish my boots."

Aiden looked down. Not a speck of dust clung to the ranger's black boots. "They look clean to me."

"And that's the way I intend to keep them."

Aiden helped Jax prepare for bed and adjusted his arm sling. Four of spades fell out. "Not sure how you would have cheated with this card."

"The ace would have been more useful."

Aiden watched Jax's face as he lifted Jax's arm and rotated it several ways. "I think you can do without the sling. If you were up and walking, I'd have you keep it on, but you aren't likely to move that shoulder in a way to aggravate it."

"I wish I could be out there helping." Jax stretched out his arm.

"Your leg needs to heal." Aiden didn't mention Jax's burned hand. Amputating three fingers had likely saved Jax from gangrene, but it meant Jax would never again fire a gun with his right hand. And even with the traction Aiden had used, it would take a miracle to straighten the ranger's leg. The man had given everything short of his life to save the women of Rose's Rescue.

"I don't want to wait, Doc."

"Most people don't want to. The saying "time heals all wounds" has been around since the Greeks. Bones need time."

Jax held up his bandaged hand. "Time won't heal these."

Aiden shook his head. "I tried to save them. You should know it was Lavender who convinced me to take them in the end. She said she would rather you be three fingers short than your life cut short. She knew as well as I did that if I waited too long, the gangrene would win."

Jax studied his bandages. "She wanted me to live?"

"I'd say. That third day, you were in a bad way. She insisted on being carried into your room. Then she yelled at you to not give up. Kept yelling until you opened your eyes. Well, not exactly yelling but talking loudly."

The corner of Jax's mouth lifted in a half smile. "Fine, Doc. I'll stop complaining."

"Have a good night, Jax." Aiden extinguished the lantern. The window in this room faced the busy street, his house not visible from here. Still, Aiden spent several minutes watching for any movement before going to bed. Though not as comfortable as his own, the bed was much better than the cot he'd spent the last two weeks on. Aiden quickly fell into a dreamless sleep.

Catherine rolled over as Clara climbed out of the enormous bed.

"Sorry. I didn't mean to wake you."

"You didn't." Yesterday's awkwardness remained between them.

"Do you want to come to church with me?"

Catherine sat up slowly, pleased when the world didn't tilt sideways. "I don't know if the doctor wants me to go that far."

"It is only three blocks. I'm sure Dr. Palmer would drive you in his buggy. He always takes it to church. He says if he doesn't, he'll have some emergency and need it." Clara used a cloth to wash her face and arms from a bowl of water on the washstand.

"I don't know that I'd be welcome."

"Of course you would be. Lewis understands you were not yourself Friday night when you"—Clara spun her hand in the air—"proposed to him."

The uncertainty in her sister's voice matched that in Catherine's mind. Madness. The longer she was pregnant, the madder she became. Words she couldn't say out loud. "I'm so sorry. I—"

Clara spun around and cut her off. "You've apologized already. Please don't do it again. Groveling isn't helping either of us."

Catherine's throat closed up, and her eyes watered. *No, no, no!* She wasn't going to cry again. She blinked rapidly and turned away. Bernard was right. She was a lunatic.

The bed sank as Clara sat down. "Don't cry. I didn't mean to upset you."

"You didn't. I... I..." The tears fell fast now.

Clara wrapped her arms around Catherine, the embrace feeling like home.

Catherine's tears came faster. "I'm sorry. I don't know what's wrong with me."

Clara produced a handkerchief and handed it to Catherine. When it soaked through, Clara handed her another. Catherine dried the last of her tears. Clara remained next to her, studying every move.

Catherine wanted to explain the crying, the nastiness. She'd never been the nice twin, but ever since she and Bernard first kissed, she'd become so spiteful and mean. "Maybe it is best if I don't go to church. Nellie said something about having evening services here."

"Lewis or Reverend Green conducts a devotional service for Rose's Rescue on Sunday nights. I suppose it makes sense to do it here instead of at Mrs. Reese's since, even with the wheelchair, moving Lavender isn't easy. I doubt she'll want to be hauled all over town anyway."

"It would be a bumpy ride."

Clara stood and resumed dressing. "Lewis is announcing our wedding today. If Mother and Father aren't here by next Sunday, we will announce if it needs to be put off a day or two."

"I don't understand why Mother and Father are coming at all. They were very clear for the entire last year that they would not be coming when I married Lewis."

"I do not believe they're coming for the marriage. When Mother first learned what happened, she wrote telling me to wed Lewis with all haste. If they had wished to come for my wedding, they would've said so earlier. I think they are coming because we have found you."

"More likely, they're coming so I do not cause them any embarrassment. I cannot return to Boston, so their friends will never know."

Clara buttoned her shirt. "They are worried about you. Father would not have hired the Pinkertons to find you otherwise."

"Do you really believe that? I cannot believe Father is as interested in me as he is in his reputation. Even at our last goodbye, he failed to realize which one of us was whom, giving us the money and insinuating that I was the responsible one. In our twenty years, he has never learned that we are not one person." Tears welled up in Catherine's eyes. She blinked them back.

"He knows we're not one person. But, like most fathers, he doesn't pay enough attention to his daughters to truly understand them. Father worked very hard so that we could live in our beautiful home and go to Bradford, have music lessons, and enjoy all the other advantages."

"You sound like Mother."

Clara held her hand to her cheek. "Oh my. I do, don't I? The night before the fire, Lewis took me to hear a violinist. I'm afraid I mentally criticized her as Mother would. I'm glad you're here to stop me from becoming too much like her."

"You could never become too much like her. For one, you have too much of a caring heart." A heart Catherine had taken advantage of time after time. "For another, Lewis will never have the money to hire a maid, cook, nurse, or governess. You will spend time with your children and not just at afternoon teas."

"I want to do good in the world. I just believe there are different ways than attending society, teas, and fundraising events. And it isn't because every time I sit down I hear Mother's voice saying, 'Sit straighter, like Catherine. Your sister didn't spill. Why did you?'"

"She always compared us, didn't she?" asked Catherine.

"I believe the constant comparisons we received as children were not good for either of us. How many times did we hear, 'Who's the good twin?' 'Who's the smart twin?' 'Who's the more beautiful twin?' We were always being compared. Why couldn't we both be good or smart or beautiful? I was always being told to be more outgoing and vivacious. You were always being told to be quieter and more contemplative and whatever else Mother thought I was. I have thought on this so much these past few weeks. No one here in Hiramsville, other than Lewis and Emily, could compare me to you. It was extremely freeing not being asked all the questions normally asked when we meet people."

"You mean no one asked you what it's like to be a twin?"

"Oh, they asked me that. But no one could tell me I was a hair taller than you or that I was the quiet one. As if I didn't know I don't talk as much. It must be what a non-twin feels. I think I can finally answer that question: What's it like to be a twin? Being a twin is forever being compared to your best friend, who also can be your nemesis, but you love her too much to not like her for long."

The stupid tears came again. "You still love me?"

Clara sat down on the bed. "Of course I do, you goose. I have been very upset and put out, especially these last few months, but at the same time, I have missed you so much."

"I've missed you too. When I was living in New York, trying

to reach Bernard, I wanted to talk to you so badly. I wished I'd told you the truth last year or last spring. I wished I wasn't the bad twin."

"You aren't the bad twin, although sometimes I wonder if you didn't do things just to prove you were."

A bell chimed a single tone for half past the hour. Clara looked around for a clock. There was none in the room. "Church is in a half hour. I should go. Do you need any help?"

Catherine shook her head. "No. The only thing I fit in comfortably is my wrapper. I'll put it on and go read in the parlor."

"I'll see you after church, then. I can already smell the roast Nellie put in."

"I thought it was just me." Catherine's stomach gurgled. She couldn't wait for lunch and thus went in search of food.

The morning was warm but not intolerable. Aiden drove his buggy the few blocks to church. He hated leaving the horse tied up for the hour or so of service, but he'd learned to be prepared. He climbed down just as Mrs. Forsythe, the midwife, entered the churchyard.

"Good morning, Mrs. Forsythe. I trust you received the message I sent with young Donny?"

"I did, but I chose not to respond. You were writing about one of those bruised buds, weren't you?"

Aiden struggled to keep a smile on his face. The derogatory "bruised buds" referred to the women who had gathered at Rose's Rescue to leave the life of the brothel behind. "Would it matter?"

"You know my feelings on those girls."

Narrow-minded and unforgiving. "As it happens, the woman in question is not from The Rescue."

"But she is unmarried?" This midwife was born two hundred years too late. She was better fit for a Puritan village.

"Yes." Aiden maintained his composure.

"Then, you know I will not see her. I am far too busy with the deserving members of our community. Besides, I thought you told me that when that boy was born, one of those girls had training. You did perfectly fine without me coming to that place."

Rose's Rescue was more than just a place, and little Scotty was one of the happiest babies Aiden had ever seen. "I understand your beliefs, but our primary responsibility is to the well-being of our patients. Surely the child she carries deserves your compassion."

Mrs. Forsythe's face remained stern. "I'm sorry, Doctor, but I cannot help her. My conscience will not allow it."

Unfortunately, her answer was the one he expected. Reverends Green and Staples had done much for the community and Rose's Rescue, but there were those who could not be persuaded to open their hearts and minds. Aiden took an extra moment to secure the horse so Mrs. Forsythe could enter the church.

The back pew where he preferred to sit so he could leave unobtrusively was full, Mrs. Reese having brought a number of the women from Rose's with her. Aiden hoped Mrs. Forsythe and the few who thought the way she did would not shun them.

TJ waved Aiden over to the pew where he sat with his brother. "Full house today."

"I believe that's the way the preacher likes it." Aiden sat in the end seat.

"We are being told to hush." GW nodded to where Emily played prelude. She glared at them without missing a note. If this pregnancy held, her child would never dare misbehave in church.

Reverend Staples stood and welcomed the congregation. "Last month, I disappointed everyone by canceling my wedding. However, like many disappointments, the Almighty had something else planned for me. Miss Clara Taylor has agreed to marry me."

Gasps from several congregants caused the reverend to pause. Behind Aiden, a young Eliza whined to her mother. "Ma, you said—"

"Hush!" Mrs. Carter whispered back.

The reverend cleared his throat and continued. "The wedding is tentatively set for next Monday at ten in the morning, pending the arrival of Miss Taylor's parents. Now, for our hymn today, we will sing "Onward, Christian Soldiers.""

Eliza wasn't singing the right words. "Mother dear, I must confess. The preacher's announcement brings distress. He's marrying someone else. I need some smelling salts."

To his surprise, the mother answered, keeping time with the music. "My child, I understand your pain, but your voice you must restrain."

"Her ways, they vex and trouble me—a thorn within our community."

"Now is not the time to fret. Of your place you do forget."

The daughter replied with the words in the hymnal. Aiden didn't dare look to the side, afraid that if TJ was smiling he would burst into laughter. A sobering thought stopped him. What if the women behind him were the arsonists? Likely not. Rumor had it Eliza currently courted the oldest son of Philip Tarr, the mercantile owner.

Much of the sermon was lost on Aiden as he contemplated the various women who had their eye on marrying the preacher or their daughters marrying him. The two behind him weren't the only ones shocked by the announcement. He could understand. The first days after her arrival, Clara showed little preference for Reverend Staples. Although she had been honest when Aiden asked to call on her, another man had also asked her. Aiden had several conversations and a lovely buggy ride with Clara before realizing her heart leaned in a different direction.

The sermon was nearly over when Donny appeared at Aiden's side, the boy's red face and deep breathing testifying of his run to the church. He should have been sitting with his mother and sisters. Aiden glanced at the third pew, where Donny's family normally sat. Mr. Collins and his children were there instead.

Aiden stood and followed Donny out.

"Ma told me to hurry and get you."

"Hop in my buggy." Aiden untied the horse. How many times would he make the trip to the Owen home? Mrs. Owen was dying from cancer. She knew it. Aiden knew it. There was nothing he could do to stop or slow the process. Aiden climbed in next to Donny. "How is your mother?"

"Ma is having a hard time breathing. She won't tell us, but she's in a lot of pain."

Aiden stopped at his office to grab a bottle of laudanum from his locked cabinet. Mrs. Owen had only allowed herself the use of laudanum this past week, but she didn't want to keep it in the house, afraid she would forget how much she had taken and not be aware of her children. Her late husband had taken laudanum during the last week of his life under Dr. Jones's care. In the end, he hadn't recognized his wife or children. Mrs. Owen was determined not to die with her children wondering if she still knew them.

Donny fidgeted as they drove. "Ma told Francis and Elizabeth she is dying. I think Francis already figured it out. How long does she have?"

"I'm not sure." If sheer willpower had anything to do with it, Mrs. Owen had years left. However, every medical text Aiden consulted estimated months or even weeks. The operation in June had removed some of the cancer but not all. Mrs. Owen could not survive a second surgery.

"What's going to happen when she dies? Ma doesn't have any family to take us."

Aiden pinched his lips, not sure what Donny knew. Mrs. Owen's family was buried in a Connecticut cemetery. Mr. Owen hailed from Virginia and still had a brother and sister there, but Mrs. Owen didn't want the children living with the family that had turned their backs on her husband when he married a Northerner. Mrs. Owens needed to decide her children's futures, and soon.

They arrived at the two-room home in good time, Donny hopping down before Aiden set the carriage break.

Mrs. Owen lay on her bed, dressed for church. She opened her eyes as Aiden approached. "Can one die from pain?"

"I've seen pain get so bad men have lost consciousness."

"I'm pretty sure I did, and I scared my children."

Aiden drew the laudanum from his breast pocket. "If you'll take a few drops each morning and a few more before bed, it will help keep the pain at bay."

"You know my feelings about that stuff, Doc. I don't want to put that on Donny too."

"Have you considered hiring help?" Aiden uncorked the bottle and added four drops to the tin cup of water Mrs. Owen had by her bed.

Mrs. Owen sipped from the cup. "You know we have barely enough money to feed ourselves."

"What if one of the women from The Rescue was willing to come for room and board?"

"Donny said some of them had become opium addicts. I wouldn't want to test their willpower."

"There are a few. However, they were not who I had in mind." Lavender was, of course, Aiden's first choice, but there was no way she could work here while in the wheelchair. Rae, however, had been quick to help and had no addiction he was aware of. "Let me ask the one I think would be able to help you."

"I still can't pay. I can barely afford that bottle of medicine."

Aiden would find a way to hire Donny to get the medicine money back to Mrs. Owen. "Mrs. Reese and I can worry about that. As you know, Rose's Rescue has had housing issues since the fire. A bed would go a long way."

Mrs. Owen closed her eyes and let out a deep sigh. When she opened them, her eyes glistened with unshed tears. "I am only agreeing for the children's sake. Will you send them outside?"

Aiden nodded and walked into the other room. It was empty. Donny must have already taken his sisters out of the house. Through the window he saw the girls sitting in the shade of the tree. Aiden stepped to the door and found Donny caring for his horse. He returned to the bedroom. "They are outside and occupied."

"I wrote to my husband's family. Is it terrible that I hope they don't answer? I can't imagine that even the worst of orphanages would be kinder than Mr. Owen's kin."

Aiden wished he could promise to take in the children, but with no wife to help with the girls and now no home, he didn't dare make such a promise. TJ and Emily might consider adding the Owen children to their family. It was a subject he'd avoided thus far. "Let me know when you hear from them."

"I suspect the letter will be returned unopened. I'm not sure they even know my husband passed." Mrs. Owen's breathing slowed as she spoke.

"Can you sleep for a while?"

"Have Donny wake me at three to make supper."

"I will." Aiden sat by the bedside for several more minutes. Medical advances were happening all the time. Someday they would learn how to fight cancers like Mrs. Owen's—a cure for the disease that ate away at so many bodies. If only it was now.

The Texas Ranger who had been sitting on the front porch all day opened the front door and let Reverend Green in before resuming his post. A couple of the women called him Hawke. Catherine had yet to work out the reason for the name or be formally introduced to the large man.

She squirmed in the corner chair. She'd expected Lewis to come, not the preacher she still owed an apology to for her rudeness when she'd tried to get Lewis to marry her that disastrous first night in town.

Nellie and another woman Catherine didn't recognize came from the back of the house. Lavender had already parked her chair near the window, and Morning Glory sat on the davenport.

"Good evening, ladies. I hope you don't mind that Reverend Staples and I did a divide and conquer tonight. Dr. Palmer's home won't accommodate all who wish to attend our evening devotional, and it seems Miss Lavender's fancy conveyance is difficult to take to Mrs. Reese's, where Reverend Staples is this evening. Miss Lavender, it's wonderful to see you up and around."

"It is nice to be up. I do wish we could all meet in one place."

Nellie crossed her arms and leaned against the wall. "Doesn't matter to me much. Doc doesn't have a piano either, so we don't have any music."

"The loss of your piano was a blow to us all. Perhaps we could sing without one? 'Nearer, My God, to Thee'?"

Nellie mumbled something, then nodded. She opened her mouth in a perfect O and set the pitch before launching into the first line. The rest of the women joined in, including Catherine. As the notes swelled inside her, she realized how much she missed singing. Often, she'd sit with Clara in the music room and sing until their brother pled with them to stop, claiming that every cat in Brookline was trying to join them or they could be heard in Boston. Clara had a fine voice, but the music instructor had praised Catherine more and even arranged for her to sing in a small concert, which Father had forbidden.

Somewhere in the middle of the second verse, a rich baritone joined in. Catherine turned to see Dr. Palmer, who stood in the hallway outside the parlor. His was the only voice it could be. Reverend Green had coughed once and stopped singing. The doctor's eyes closed as he sang.

Realizing she was staring, Catherine turned to face Nellie, who sang like an angel. Did the church have a choir? It should. If only music had been a subject at Bradford. She found the addition of the baritone rather alluring since she hadn't sung with a man since Christmas. What would a duet with him sound like?

Reverend Green stood in front of the cold fireplace. "I love the hymn we just sang. It was written by a woman, like you, whose life took a different course than she planned. Born in England in 1805, Sarah Flower Adams engaged in many pursuits. As a youth, she broke a record for climbing a mountain in Scotland. Supported by her husband, she followed her dream to become an actress. She appeared in several plays, including a production of Shakespeare's *Macbeth*, which won her acclaim when she was thirty-two. Shortly after, her health began to fail."

Reverend Green paused to drink from a water glass Nellie set out for him.

"Something I know all too well. After turning down a theater company in Bath, Sarah turned her focus to poetry. In 1841, her pastor asked her to write something that went with his next sermon on Jacob's ladder in Genesis 28:11–19. And so she wrote 'Nearer, My God, to Thee' in one week. You may recognize that the hymn is loosely based on this story, where Jacob goes to sleep with his head on a stone and dreams of a ladder ascending to heaven. So as to not be long-winded, I'll leave it to you to read on your own. The hymn's words, 'Nearer, my God, to Thee, nearer to Thee!' remind us that even amid tribulation, we can draw closer to God." Another round of coughing interrupted the sermon.

"No matter what challenges we face, we can turn to God for comfort and guidance. Sarah's hymn also reminds us that we can find hope even in the face of adversity. Sadly, Sarah only lived another few years, passing away at age forty-three from the tuberculosis she contracted while nursing her sister." Reverend Green paused to drink.

"Don't worry. It is not tuberculous that ails me. Our good doctor has reassured me I am not contagious. Where was I?" The reverend looked down at a paper. "While Sarah's story may seem to be a cautionary tale with such a young death, I believe it shows how we can change directions and become nearer to God. While she may have found joy on the stage and inspired others, the gift she gave the world through this hymn will live on for years. What she may have viewed as adversity and a burden has turned into a light for the entire world."

"Each of you is at a growing place in life. I suspect no one in this room, including Dr. Palmer and I, find ourselves where we thought we would be at this point in time. The question is not where have we been but where can we go, and will we become nearer to God in our journey."

The reverend shuffled back to his chair, and Nellie stood.

"I know we normally sing 'Amazing Grace,' but, if you don't mind, I'd like to sing 'Nearer, My God, to Thee' a second time."

As she sang the familiar hymn, Catherine felt a desire she'd never felt in her life. Tears filled her eyes, and she blinked them back as she sang the final verse. "'Or if, on joyful wing cleaving the sky, sun, moon, and stars forgot, upward I fly.'" The last few words she sang in her mind. *"'Nearer to Thee'!"*

As the other women conversed with each other and Reverend Green, Catherine opened her Bible to avoid conversation. Feelings more than thoughts swelled within her. She didn't have a name for what was happening in her heart. Church was a thing one did on Sundays. Wear the finest dress and sing with the finest voice. Catch someone's eye for a walk home. Everybody went. It was a great scandal not to. Unless one was ill, of course. In her Brookline church, she'd counted the little glass pieces that made up the colorful windows, the number of new bonnets, or who had made over their dress to appear new. When she was young, Father quizzed them on the sermon. Catherine had copied Clara's and Charles's answers when she could, but the "goodness of God" was an all-purpose answer that worked well most days.

This was something different. This short sermon spoke to her soul of something she wished she had. Could someone like Catherine become near to God? Reverend Green certainly implied it.

Dr. Palmer came over with two plates of strawberry cake. "Would you like one?"

"Yes, please. I've smelled it all afternoon. Nellie forbade me from touching it."

"I'm glad to see you feel like eating."

"It's eat or have Lavender dose me with peppermint tea." Four cups of it since yesterday evening had her running for the outhouse.

"Glad to know she's doing her job."

"That she is." As Catherine ate several bites of her cake, her mind wandered to her earlier thoughts of being near God. Not wanting the doctor to think there was anything wrong, she opened her mouth and uttered the first thought to form. "You sing well. Have you ever sung professionally?"

"No. Just at church and for"—Dr. Palmer paused—"for my family."

Dr. Palmer had a family? Of course, he had parents, but was there more? In a gothic novel, the handsome doctor would have to have a dark past. "Is there a choir in town?"

Aiden shook his head. "Nobody's ever thought to start one."

"With your bass and Nellie's alto, and I've been told my soprano is not half bad, we could start a group. There must be a few others. We could have quite a nice choir or glee club.

"Nellie won't sing."

"Why not?"

"Her mother sang."

"I don't understand."

"Nellie's mother told her not to be anything like her. Nellie knows she can sing well, but she only sings in front of others when she sings hymns on Sundays."

"So she could sing in a church choir?"

"Not likely. Nellie has a history."

Catherine waved her hand in front of her face. "Wasn't that the preacher's point? We sometimes have to do something new."

"I don't think he meant for you to choose someone else's new."

"I wasn't. I just thought we could sing together."

"You might get her to sing with you. As you said, your soprano is not bad. I'm sure she would sing with you."

"What about you? Would you sing with us?"

Dr. Palmer's face hardened as Catherine spoke. Even before the last word was out, she knew she'd asked the wrong question.

⬦

"I'm sorry, no." Aiden would never join another singing group.

The smile on Miss Catherine's face faded. "Why not? You have a handsome voice."

Aiden's thoughts drifted to his wife, who had died in childbirth less than a year after their marriage. The sentence was a near repeat of the question Susannah asked him only days after they met while he attended the Medical College of Ohio. Their son would be near Donny's age now. "In case you haven't noticed, I can hardly be counted on to be on time to any event or stay to the conclusion."

"What if it was a singing club but no performances?"

Susannah had started such a group in the parlor of her mother's home in Cincinnati, the gathering of four multiplying to eight, then more. At one point, Susannah's mother forbade them to sing "The Man on the Flying Trapeze" because they became so loud she was sure her chandelier would break from the noise. It had been during a practice of "Come Where My Love Lies Dreaming" that Aiden's eyes met Susannah's across the room and he knew she was destined to be his wife. "I am too unpredictable, even for practice."

Catherine's smile returned. "Well, maybe that's just what you need. A little predictability to keep things interesting. It's just for fun. There's no pressure to be perfect or even show up every time."

"I'm sorry, but no." Aiden couldn't help but feel drawn to Catherine's enthusiasm. It reminded him of Cathleen's. Or perhaps it was only the similarity in their names that brought his former fiancée to mind so often these past few days. Aiden had largely put their courtship behind him. Oddly, Catherine also reminded him of Susannah. There were weeks when he didn't think of Susannah or the son they'd lost a decade ago. No other woman had ever stirred memories of both his past loves.

Catherine finished the last strawberry on her plate. "I'm sorry. I shouldn't have pressed you. I am trying to learn to be different, but I'm not doing such a good job."

"What do you mean different?"

"I'm not a very good person." Catherine's hand covered her bulging middle. "I guess you already knew that."

"You are only twenty." Aiden quickly did the math, unsure of when the sister's birthday was.

"Twenty-one this October."

"You still have so much of life before you. It's too early to judge yourself as good or bad."

"But I've always been the bad twin." The frankness in her answer sounded as if she was resigned to such a position.

"I'm not sure there need to be opposites when referring to twins. If the two of you look alike, making you both equally attractive, there is no reason why you can't both be good, or talented, or wise. Or any number of things other siblings are."

Catherine leaned back and tilted her head, a wrinkle appearing on her forehead.

"In families of several children, it's possible for all of them to be quite good, as you put it, or all bad, often following the examples and teachings of their parents. Surely, you have heard such things as 'There isn't a bad apple in the bunch'?"

"I have." Her soft voice could barely be heard above the others speaking in the room.

Aiden leaned closer. "You are in a new place with new friends to make and a new life before you. Your sister spoke very little about you. When you arrived, your condition was a complete surprise to me. You should know I called on your sister several times, and I'm in a position where I often inadvertently hear gossip."

"She wouldn't have told of my shame."

"I think it was more of a situation where she didn't tell others of her pain."

A half smile lifted the corners of Catherine's mouth. "Which goes back to me being the bad one."

Aiden shook his head and took Catherine's hand. "As your doctor, I prescribe that you stop thinking of yourself that way. I can only imagine you are comparing your very worst with your sister's best."

Again the wrinkle appeared on her brow. "I will try."

He dropped her hand, ending the contact—something a bit more than doctorly, which he shouldn't have allowed. It couldn't be anything more than an odd mix of memories and longing that drew him to her. "Allow me to take your plate to the kitchen."

Setting the plates in the sink, Aiden escaped through the back door. Talking with Catherine stirred up too many thoughts, and he wanted to quell them before interacting with someone else. He hadn't thought of Susannah and Cathleen around other women in a very long time. He saved thoughts of either for private moments in the early-morning hours or late at night.

Instead of turning to his office, he headed for the river and crossed the bridge. Soon, he found his way to the cemetery, where he walked among the graves, letting the quiet of the place envelop him. He took time to read the headstones, occasionally reaching out to brush away dirt or leaves. He'd known so many of them, sat at their bedsides as they passed, some too young and some so old they wondered if they might be the next Methuselah.

He knelt by a stone and ran his fingers over the inscription.

Cathleen Richburg

June 2, 1850-August 9, 1876

Ever Loved

Four years ago tomorrow, he'd buried Cathleen in a wedding dress she never wore in this life. She'd moved here with her family shortly after Aiden opened his practice. Their romance had been slow to develop, Cathleen having been leery of him at first. His reputation for drinking colored the relationship long after he'd put the habit aside, and her parents insisted on a long engagement. The day before their wedding, Cole's gang kidnapped her because Aiden couldn't save Cole's son from the bullet that pierced his heart. The outlaws had dumped her in front of the mercantile a week later, hours before she took her final breath. Cathleen suffered to cause him pain. Had he realized the danger, he would have never proposed to her. Her family returned to North Carolina the summer after her death. He'd written last summer to tell them that everyone in the gang and all Cole's sons had been brought to justice one way or another. They sent a brief reply.

Twice, he'd tried to create a family of his own. Twice, he'd failed.

Aiden rolled to his feet and looked north, picturing another grave well beyond the horizon and only blocks from the home where Susannah grew up. There in Ohio, his infant son lay buried in the same coffin as his mother. Officially a stillbirth, the child had never been named. Aiden thought of the boy as James, though, the name Susannah chose. Susannah passed before their first anniversary. Ironically, he'd known Susannah less time than he had Cathleen.

He walked a few paces and leaned against a live oak. Why was Catherine stirring up these old memories? Her singing reminded him of Susannah's. They were of the same build and had sweet soprano voices. And most women who neared their confinement time reminded him of Susannah. How could they not?

Her smile reminded him of Cathleen's, as well as the similarity of their names. He found Catherine's identical twin attractive, and in an almost statistical impossibility, he found Catherine more so. Perhaps because it skirted ethics to fall for one's patient—a guideline that would be impossible to keep as the only doctor in town. If he was to find love, it would have to be with a patient. Some combination of attraction and forbidden desire had drawn him to Catherine, but whatever it was, he needed to dismiss it long enough for her to know her own mind.

n inviting breeze drifted in through the open window. Catherine focused, willing the breeze to chase away the sweltering temperatures as Sunday gave way to Monday. The darkness of the moonless night allowed the stars to twinkle at their brightest. From where she lay in bed, Catherine thought she recognized a constellation. Memories of staying at Cape Cod, listening to the waves and enjoying the coolness of Grandfather Dawes's house on the North Shore, filled her mind. Beside her, Clara slept peacefully, seemingly unaffected by the oppressive heat.

"Remember when we used to visit Grandma and Grandpa Dawes's and share a bed in their attic?" Catherine whispered, her thoughts breaking the silence of the night.

To her surprise, her sister answered. "I loved falling asleep to the sound of the waves crashing on the rocks."

"I didn't mean to wake you."

"You didn't. I was contemplating all the things I needed to do this week. I was actually thinking of Grandpa Dawes when you spoke. Missing them. Grandpa would have been so fun to have at the wedding."

"Poor Lewis. Can you imagine what a quiz he would have given him? If Grandpa had been alive—" The brass bed squeaked as Catherine rolled to her side to better see Clara in the dim light.

"Poor Mother. Grandma would sit her down and tell her not to change a single one of my plans." Clara folded her pillow to prop her head. "My favorite thing was how Grandma never made us dress alike."

"Mine was Grandpa giving me a quarter every time he mixed us up." Catherine sighed. "I loved fooling him."

"I think he knew. Grandma always did."

"Perhaps," said Catherine. "I never felt the same way I did when he gave me a quarter, no matter how often I tried to change places."

"What do you mean?"

"It's hard to describe. Love is part of it, but more like I was seen for who I was, not just as part of a pair."

Clara reached over to take Catherine's hand. "I know what you mean. It felt like we were individuals, not just twins."

Catherine squeezed her sister's hand. "Exactly. I miss them so much."

"Me too. I wonder what advice they would give me for my wedding."

"I think I know."

"How?"

"Aunt Tillie gave me a silver brush and mirror." One of the items Catherine sold during her time in New York City. "Do you remember Grandmother's story about the hairbrush?"

"Something about a woman who was like a grandmother to her but not her real one. The woman's husband brushed her hair every night, starting on their wedding night."

"Yes, that's the story. Apparently, Grandfather did the same for Grandmother. They talked out all of their problems then.

Although, as a doctor, sometimes Grandfather left in the middle of it, he always finished when he came back."

Wide awake now, Clara rested her head on her palm, elbow on the pillow. "I remember Grandmother showing me her brush once. She said it was her favorite possession. What ever happened to it, do you think?"

"Aunt Tillie has it." Thankfully, the set she'd been given was new. If she had sold the one her grandparents used, she might not be able to forgive herself. Either way, she wished she had hers to pass on to Clara.

"But she never got married."

"I don't think Mother wanted it."

"Mother wouldn't let anyone but her maid touch her hair. Can you imagine Father brushing Mother's hair?" asked Clara.

"No. Can you imagine Lewis brushing yours?"

A tiny gasp escaped Clara's lips as she fell back on the pillow. Catherine didn't need any light to know her twin blushed. "I assume your silence is a yes."

"We shouldn't talk about such things."

"Why not? You'll be married in a week, and brushing your hair is hardly scandalous."

"We used to brush each other's hair. Why did we stop?"

"Mother insisted her maid do it. I guess we got out of the habit. And at Bradford, it was easier to do my own. You were always studying or something." The past year, it was easier to avoid her sister and the pain she caused. First, by holding Lewis to an engagement when she knew he thought he'd proposed to Clara. Then she'd spent way too much time with the man who tried to court Clara while they were at school. Even if her sister wasn't very interested in Bernard, the mere fact he was interested in Clara should have kept Catherine away.

"We have a few days left. I could brush your hair in the morning."

"That would be nice. Would you mind braiding it too? Mine always falls out so fast, and lazing about all day it isn't like anyone, but the doctor will see me. Even Mother wouldn't insist it be up properly." Not that Catherine minded. The solitude wasn't as bad as she feared, as long as she didn't ponder on life too much.

"You don't want to dress up for the doctor? He is handsome."

"You said he was old."

"Not as old as Mother or Father." Clara sighed. "I just want a good man for you."

"I'm his pitiful patient. I hardly think there could be a future for us, especially since I carry another man's children. No decent man will take me."

"You shouldn't say that. There may be someone willing to be their father."

The stupid tears started again. "Hardly likely, is it?"

"You never know. Three of the women from Rose's have accepted proposals. Emily expects two of them to be quite happy in their marriages. The last she is not so sure about." Clara yawned.

Catherine opened her mouth to say she wasn't like the women who had earned their livelihood selling themselves. But that wasn't true. From the stories she'd heard, some didn't have a choice. She could have said no. "Why isn't Emily sure about the third marriage?"

"I don't know." The words mumbled together, and her sister yawned again.

"Good night." Catherine patted Clara's back.

"Sweet dreams."

One of the babies kicked just below Catherine's ribs. One of the sisters would have sweet dreams. Clara didn't have babies kicking her all night and had only her wedding to look forward to. All Catherine had was the hope that someone didn't care that her children weren't his. She'd have to be careful not to let the word about the money get around. The other women in the house were opening her eyes to a world she didn't know—a world of deception and greed, a world she was avoiding on nothing more than dumb luck. Had her family been poorer or her situation more desperate, she wouldn't be so lucky. Even now, with the promise of money, she'd only be one step from disaster.

Catherine rubbed the little bulge she imagined to be a fist or a foot. It felt as if her children were brawling like two cats in the middle of the street. How would she care for two rambunctious children? Even with money, she had no idea what to do with children.

How would the money be sent from New York anyway? Another question she should have asked Mr. Fairlane when he had her sign all those papers. The breeze fluttered the lace curtains. If she'd known how hot Texas was, she might not have agreed to all the conditions: Never see Bernard again. Easy. Never live east of the Mississippi again. At the time it hadn't seemed difficult. But location didn't change the shame she felt.

A woman on the train said that Catherine was "no better than she ought to be." And it was true. Although she hadn't solicited favors, Bernard had promised to marry her. And she succumbed to his promises, like Fantine in the ridiculously long novel she'd read in her last semester for her French class. Only she wouldn't end up like Fantine or the women whispering in the corner. She'd secured money for her future. Even with twins, she'd manage for several years or long enough to catch a husband. The first installment should be here any day. If she could be prudent, $1,000 could last for years.

If she could only learn to be prudent. How could she?

A referral to an ophthalmologist in Fort Worth, a nonvenomous snakebite that came with a panicked mother, and an infected tooth that needed extraction, all in all a rather quiet Monday morning for Aiden. Reverend Staples accompanied Reverend Green to the office for Reverend Green's appointment.

There would be no good news. He'd heard the older reverend's cough last night, the damage from the pneumonia last winter too great to overcome. Frankly, Aiden was surprised Reverend Green had lived this long. "Reverends, I'm surprised to see both of you."

"I invited Reverend Staples along so you can settle an argument from a medical point of view."

Aiden looked at the younger reverend. "This is a first for me. I thought settling arguments was more your job than mine. Would you like to come into my office or the exam room?"

Reverend Green stood. "Your office. We both know that stethoscope thing won't tell us anything new. I'm dying, and no instrument is going to tell you when my Lord will require my soul. I keep praying it won't be too soon."

Aiden ushered them into the office, which sat between two of his examination rooms. Mounted on the door was a brass number 2 instead of "Office" or his name. Aiden sat down behind the desk, leaving the other two chairs for the reverends. "How can I help you?"

Reverend Green opened his mouth, but Reverend Staples spoke first. "Reverend Green wants to move back down to de Cordova Bend, where he'll be all alone. I don't believe he should go without help, and he refuses to take any."

Aiden turned to Reverend Green and raised a brow. "Reverend Staples is getting married next week, and I can't possibly continue to reside in the manse with him and his new bride. The only help available to take to de Cordova that either of us can think of is one of the women from The Rescue, which would be entirely inappropriate as the only place for them to sleep in the little cabin is the same room as me. Which, I might point out, is why it is called a one-room cabin. I survived down there very well all spring."

Reverend Staples folded his arms. "The only reason you didn't get chased out is the church only owns two acres of land."

"So, the cabin is owned by the church?" asked Aiden.

"Yes," the reverends replied in unison.

"Then this is a church matter?"

"Not exactly. Due to the dwindling number of settlers at the bend, they have decided not to construct a building at this time." Reverend Green paused to breathe. "I was less than successful in welcoming more than two families to Sunday service, and both families left the area in June."

"The families left because they were burned out. The sheriff wouldn't want you down there alone. I don't want you to be alone either." The compassion in Reverend Staples's voice was evident.

Reverend Green shook his head. "I know the sheriff has his hands full up here, but after you're married, the notes will stop. Then we can go back to being a quiet little town."

"Have there been more notes?" The question tumbled from Aiden's mouth. "Don't answer that. We will lose focus on the subject."

"Yes. Someone left one for Reverend Green just this morning and one over at Mrs. Reese's." Reverend Green took the opportunity to change the subject.

Aiden cleared his throat. "As much as I'm interested in the letters, which I assume have been reported to TJ, we need to deal with the question at hand. If I understand correctly, the question is, 'In my professional opinion, is it safe for Reverend Green to live on his own down in the de Cordova area with no help?'"

Both men nodded.

"The simple answer is no. Reverend Green, you lost weight living down there, presumably cooking for yourself. Since returning to town, you are much stronger."

"But I can't stay with Lewis and his new bride. A newlywed couple needs privacy." Reverend Green's point was valid.

"If I hadn't just given my house to others, I would invite you to live with me. I'd ask you to join Jax and me upstairs, but I know how taxing walking up the stairs even once a day is."

"I don't want to have to go to Austin and stay with the leadership."

"Clara and I are going to Galveston for a wedding trip. That gives us another week to find a solution. And Clara told you she would be honored to have you live with us."

"But you and your bride should have the large downstairs bedroom."

Reverend Staples sighed. "Clara and I are both fine with the upstairs room."

"Neither of you has been married. You don't understand. Tell him, Doc." Reverend Green raised his chin ever so slightly.

Aiden ran a finger around his collar. In all his years, it was as close as Aiden ever witnessed the older clergyman come to breaking a trust. "There are many couples that find it necessary to live with parents or other family members. It has been my experience that this has not prevented them from living as husband and wife."

Reverend Green tapped his chin. "True, but it would be nice not to have anyone around. I counsel all my engaged couples to make sure they have time for themselves. If I am in the house, they won't have that."

"I'm sure we can find a way." Reverend Staples smiled. "You can always go clean the church if you are concerned."

Reverend Green looked heavenward.

Aiden cleared his throat. "Gentlemen, while I admire you putting each other's needs first, let us get back to the original question. Reverend Green, I strongly advise you to stay in town. While we know there is little I can do for you medically, I fear the isolation of de Cordova will be as harmful to you in spirit and mind as returning to Austin. If I heard correctly when I was over at my house checking on patients earlier today, Reverend Staples intends to leave on the one o'clock eastbound train immediately after the wedding, which gives us until his return to find a suitable situation for Reverend Green. At the rate we are playing musical rooms around this town, I anticipate there will be room for you someplace by then."

"Did you hear? I received a telegram from my mother today. She is sending funds and goods with the Taylors, who left Boston this morning—although she didn't specify the amount. We are hopeful it's enough to secure the abandoned hotel for Rose's." Reverend Staples's smile brightened the room.

"That is good news. See, there will be rooms available." Aiden wondered how much work it would take to get the place ready for occupancy.

"It wouldn't be proper for me to stay at Mrs. Reese's with us being widow and widower." The sparkle in Reverend Green's eye meant he was goading one or both of the younger men.

"I'd be more afraid of Thelma if I were you." Aiden returned the teasing. The cook was most likely to feed the older man until he needed new clothes.

"See? I can't live there." Reverend Green lifted his chin.

"Reverend, if you put that stubbornness to good use, your lungs might heal themselves in no time. You haven't coughed the entire time you've been in the office." Aiden shook his head. "I'm sure we can come up with something. Aren't you two the ones who keep saying we should leave these problems to God?"

Reverend Green and Reverend Staples looked at each other and laughed. Aiden looked heavenward. If only all medical issues solved themselves so happily.

iden closed the stall behind his horse, exited the livery, then cut through the alley to his office. A large man emerged from the shadows.

"Morning, Doc." Hawke tipped his hat.

It seemed a bit early to call it morning. If Aiden squinted at the eastern sky, he could almost pretend there was a ribbon of light blue on the horizon. "You're around early."

"I saw someone lurking under the oak tree, but they left in a hurry."

"The one in my side yard or the backyard?"

"Back. Didn't get a good look at them, but I found this."

There wasn't enough light for Aiden to discern what was written on the paper. "What does it say?"

"Nothing good. It's for Clara, warning her of disaster if she marries the preacher."

"That tree is near the bedroom where she's staying. Are you going to show it to her?"

"I don't think so. When my older sister got married, she drove my mother to distraction with every little detail. The lace was off-center on the veil. The flowers in the garden weren't blooming fast enough. I'm not going to tell a bride she's being threatened. I'll give this to TJ, and he can have Emily deliver the news if he thinks it's warranted."

"Did Reverend Staples get another note last night?"

"Don't know yet. I was going to find them. What has you up this early, or is it late?"

"A cowhand had too much to drink and shot himself in the foot."

"It's the middle of the week. I thought those cowboys normally got drunk on the weekends."

"This one is more of the everyday sort of drunk. He was too far gone to feel me patch him up. He went on and on about how much he would need to spend on a new pair of boots, a-hollerin' that he wasn't paying because I cut off the boot. Fortunately, the rancher was kind enough to pay me for coming out in the middle of the night. Men like that are enough to make me want to jump on the prohibition bandwagon next time those ladies hold a rally."

"I'll be there with you. I haven't ever known a sober outlaw. I have a theory. If you take away the alcohol, there would be less crime."

"I believe that's one of the arguments against the demon rum." Having not touched a drop in seven years, Aiden could attest to the difference in being sober. "Any chance our note-writer is a drinker?"

"Maybe not intentionally. Half of those women's cures are nothing more than alcohol and sugar syrup, or opium. Legally, they can't sell opium outright, but they call it a medicine. Even children are drinking it."

"I've had words with Phillip Tarr about the elixirs he carries at the mercantile. I don't need the cure causing more harm than good."

"That opium ring we shut down last year was the first of

many, I'm afraid." Hawke took off his hat and ran his hand through his hair.

Aiden nodded. "If you'll excuse me, I need to catch some sleep before the next crisis."

Hawke raised a hand in farewell, and Aiden slid the key into the lock. Jax's soft snore reverberated through the building. Aiden stopped at his desk to write a few notes about the night's events. As he wrote the date, his hand stilled. Ten years ago, his wife took her last breath.

Aiden collapsed back into his leather chair. The other night in the cemetery, he thought he'd dealt with the grief that usually accompanied the anniversary.

But now an avalanche of memories threatened to suffocate him. Experience told him it was better to allow them to come and melt around him than fight the emotions and memories. They were more intense this year than last, perhaps because of Catherine. He'd given up calling her Miss Taylor since Clara kept answering too. He'd had so few maternity patients over the years since most women preferred midwives over doctors.

The colors overwhelmed him: the blue, still form of the child that would never be; the red of his wife's blood as she bled; the white of her face as she drew her last breath; the green of the cemetery where Susannah was laid to rest with their child safely resting in her arms; the black armband he wore until coming to Hiramsville. Black faded into gray, leaving Aiden drained and pale as the dawn's light streamed through the window, chasing away the last of his grief.

If only grief were like the measles. You got it once, and, if you survived, you couldn't catch it again. But grief was more like a head cold. It would always come back in varying degrees of severity. For now, this wave was over. Perhaps someday he would have a wife to hold again and the grief could become no more than an errant sneeze.

Aiden mounted the stairs. Jax's snores continued. If he was lucky, he would catch an hour of dreamless sleep before someone needed him. Aiden was rarely so fortunate.

⊰•◆•⊱

Catherine opened another book. There had to be more to do than read from the doctor's robust dime-novel selection. "Lavender, may I go outside and sit?"

"As long as you stay in the shade, I don't see a problem. You are not used to our Texas heat. It takes its toll on everyone at first." The kindness in Lavender's reply softened something in Catherine. She could have just as easily pointed out that a weakened pregnant woman was especially vulnerable, but she didn't.

But being outside wouldn't keep her occupied. If only she had something meaningful to do. Nellie cooked and cleaned. Lavender studied the doctor's medical journals and texts, which must be of some value. The rest of the women spent their days at Mrs. Reese's. "Is there any sewing or knitting I could do for The Rescue?" Work, wishes, only a few weeks ago Catherine would have dismissed as below her were welcome now.

"Have you made any clothing for your babies?"

"No. I hadn't even thought of it." Mother would have hired someone or gone into Boston and bought some at Jordan and Marsh. "I guess I should. Perhaps I could go to the mercantile and purchase some cloth." Leaving the house would be a welcome distraction.

Lavender looked up from the medical journal she read, her eyes narrowed. "When Clara comes, you may ask her to go for you."

Catherine didn't have to wait long before her sister returned. "Please, I need something to do. I'm afraid I'll go out of my mind for lack of meaningful activity. If I read one more of these dime novels, I'll become an outlaw myself, simply for want of some sort of employment."

"Don't let Hawke hear you say that. He is rather tired of waiting for Lewis to get the next note about his inappropriate marriage. Guarding a house where most of the day no one is making any noise can't be easy for him."

"I imagine not. The Texas Rangers I read about are always riding or shooting or wooing some damsel they rescue from distress."

"I haven't spoken much with GW or Hawke, but from what Emily tells me, there's a lot more sitting and waiting around than one would expect."

"I suspected that was the case watching Hawke and GW on the front porch. Anyway, do you know of anything useful I can do? I suggested sewing for The Rescue, but Lavender thinks I should start sewing for my own children."

"I have some yarn left. I started a blanket while I was on the train. It looks like you could use a second one. I suppose it cools off by October." Clara fanned herself.

"You made me something after I was so nasty to you?"

"Yes, of course."

"But you were supposed to despise me."

Clara sighed. "I didn't despise you. I was angry and confused and hurt, but I still love you. After our talk the other morning, I feel I understand you a bit more. We were both hurt by all the comparisons, but we reacted to it very differently."

"You mean you handled it correctly and I made a mess of everything?"

Clara frowned. "I don't think I did everything well at all, nor did you do everything wrong. It's going to take us awhile to stop with the comparisons."

Catherine sighed. "I wish for once something could be instantaneous."

"Few things are."

"Your wedding is."

"It doesn't feel that way. If we were in Brookline, Mother would be having a fit. I am using Emily's veil and my graduation dress, so that is all done. Thelma and Nellie are making little tea cakes to hand out. Where Lewis planned a large potluck for your wedding, we decided against repeating it, especially if we have to postpone because Mother and Father arrive later than planned. You'll be standing up with me. Becky has remade my blue dress so you can wear it."

"Where did she get fabric to match?"

"She took apart the bustle."

Catherine patted her expanding front. "That seems fitting since I have a natural bustle in front now."

Clara covered her mouth and giggled. "Sorry. I shouldn't laugh."

"Why not? I'm the one who said it. Mother will say worse. She isn't going to like the idea of me standing up with you and the whole world seeing my shame."

"Mother doesn't have her Brookline friends or Boston society to impress. I doubt she'll care much after she figures that out." Clara waved her hand as if dismissing the subject. "Now, about some infant clothes for you. I'll go see what cloth I can find at Mrs. Reese's. There may even be some infant gowns that were too small for Petunia's little Scotty in the donations. If you baste some gowns together, I can take them over and use the sewing machine to finish them."

"Wise. I doubt Dr. Palmer or Lavender will allow me to go to Mrs. Reese's or use a sewing machine. The pedal will likely be too much strain." She couldn't keep the bitterness out of her voice.

Clara looked at her with concern. "I'll go to the mercantile and see if they have any soft yarn. Then you can start on a baby shawl or something."

"Thank you." Catherine watched until her sister left before opening to the last chapter of the dime novel, sure the Texas Ranger would win the day.

song floated on the breeze. Someone sang Susannah's favorite tune. Aiden followed the sound to his own backyard. How odd that someone would sing that song today at his house. Aiden walked to the back of the house, expecting to find Nellie singing as she hung the laundry. She often sang when she thought no one was about. Instead, he found Catherine knitting under the tree.

What was she doing out and singing? "Did Lavender say you could be out?"

She looked up, eyes wide. "As long as I stay in the shade. Was she wrong?"

He hadn't meant to scare her. "No, I'm just surprised to find you here."

"Are you sure? You look upset." Catherine set the needles in her lap. "I'll go back in if you think I should."

Aiden rubbed the back of his neck. "Please, stay out as long as you wish."

Catherine tilted her head. "What did I do to upset you?"

"I'm not upset."

"Then why did you come charging back here like an angry bull?"

"I didn't mean to. Do you mind?" Aiden gestured to the empty chair next to Catherine.

"No. Nellie was using it. She went inside to check on supper."

"Was she singing with you?"

"We were. I wanted to teach her the song I was singing, only I forgot some of the words to the last verse. I've been singing the first few over and over in hopes it will come to me."

"It hasn't?"

Catherine frowned. "Unfortunately not. Clara and I often make up words to fit popular songs. Neither of us liked the ending to this one since it's so sad. We made a new ending where no one dies."

Susannah didn't like the final verse either and never sang it. "Would you sing your version for me?"

Color tinged Catherine's cheeks, and she looked down at her hands. *Shy* wasn't a word he'd associated with her until that moment. "Please don't laugh," she said, and then sang, "With a sparkle in her eye, she handed me an apple pie. Eagerly I took a bite, accompanied by a lingering look. I forgot my true love couldn't cook."

Aiden's breath caught. Her words were the perfect ending, giving the song an air of joy instead of despair. Catherine waited for a response.

"That was lovely and not silly at all. My wife would have appreciated that ending."

"Your wife? I thought you were only engaged."

"I was that too. Susannah was in my life before I came to Hiramsville."

"She passed?"

Aiden nodded.

"You still miss her." There was no question in her voice.

"Today is the anniversary of her death, and it has been especially difficult."

"And the song I sang reminds you of her?"

Again, he nodded instead of speaking, afraid the emotions would resurface.

"I am so sorry. I would not have sung it if I thought it would cause you pain."

"You didn't know."

"Would you like me to sing something else to chase the tune out of your head? I can't stand it when a song tumbles over and over in my mind."

"I would. Do you know something happy?"

"What about 'Walking in the Zoo'?"

"I don't know it."

"Then you will have no memories attached to it." And Catherine launched into the song.

> *The Stilton, sir, the cheese—the okay thing to do.*
> *On Sunday afternoon—is to toddle in the Zoo.*
> *Weekdays may do for "cads," but not for me*
> *   and you.*
> *So dressed right down the road—we show them*
> *   who is who.*

Although the lighthearted song had to do with courting, the adventures of the monkey and the awful cockatoo brought a smile to Aiden's face. He joined in the final chorus.

> *The walking in the Zoo, walking in the Zoo.*
> *The okay thing on Sunday is walking in the Zoo.*
> *Walking in the Zoo, walking in the Zoo.*
> *The okay thing on Sunday is walking in the Zoo.*

"Thank you. That's what I needed today."

"I won't sing the other song in your presence again unless you ask me to."

"That isn't necessary."

"I don't want to cause you distress after how kind you've been to me. It's the least I can do at the moment."

Aiden caught himself wondering at the girl's maturity in sparing him. Perhaps she had more to her than the flighty woman he first judged her to be. "That's kind of you."

"Do many women lose their life in childbirth?"

"Far too many or with childbirth fever soon after. I'm afraid with all the medical advances we are making, we have yet to improve maternal outcomes for both mother and child."

As most expectant mothers did, Catherine laid a protective hand over her unborn children. "Is it normal, then, for a woman to think she might not live?"

"I believe most worry about themselves or the children they carry. Lavender and I are doing all we can do to make sure you all live."

"Still, you can't guarantee anything."

"Only God can do that. I do believe in Him. I've seen too many miracles not to, but, still, when it comes to our morality, I don't see any rhyme or reason to things." The admission wasn't easy, but it was the only way to explain Susannah's and Cathleen's deaths.

Catherine's gaze wandered around the yard. "I understand. If I don't survive, will you do me a favor?"

"What?"

"Don't blame yourself. Don't add my name to the sadness you carry."

"I will do my best not to." He couldn't give a better answer.

"It must be very difficult to be a doctor."

"Some days it is. Others, it's easy. It might be easier in a large hospital. Here, I know every patient and their family and lives. When I can give a family hope, it's worth it."

"I hope you find joy today, then."

"I'd settle for sleep. I've been advertising for a second doctor for months. It will help so much when we get one."

"Or when you get your bed back."

Aiden chuckled. "That will help only to a point. I need time to enjoy it. The bed at my office is very comfortable."

"Clara and I so appreciate your allowing us to use yours. Some of our best memories are being at our grandparents' home in the summer and sharing the big brass bed in the attic. It had an old-fashioned tick filled with sweet hay and lavender sprigs. It smelled so lovely. Being together this last week before she marries has been wonderful for both of us."

"I trust you're not jumping on it like you did the one in your grandparents' home."

"How did you know we jumped on the bed?"

"Just a guess. I can picture you two in all sorts of mischief."

"More than you know. And, no, I'm not jumping on your bed. I have the distinct impression that jumping is one of those activities I should not be engaging in."

"I don't recommend jumping on beds for most adults. They are more likely to go right through the ropes, slats, or springs and injure themselves." What a ridiculous topic. Yet it brought a lightness to the mood, which was exactly what he needed.

"Or they would hit their heads on the ceiling."

"Precisely."

An odd look passed over Catherine's face, and she set her knitting aside. "If you'll excuse me, Doctor."

She stood and hurried to the privy.

Aiden watched the closed door for a long moment. He hadn't expected to have Catherine brighten his day. She was much easier to talk to than her sister. Despite what she claimed about herself, she wasn't a bad person. Not at all.

Clara sat straight up in bed. "They'll be here today."

Catherine reached for her sister's hand. "Mother won't ruin your wedding. I won't let her."

"How?"

"If she's busy chastising me, she can't get too involved in your wedding." The chastisement would come from both parents. As long as she was going to receive lectures, she may as well use them to help her sister. "I'll say the most shocking things whenever she becomes too much."

"You would do that for me?" Clara slipped behind the screen to change out of her night clothes.

Catherine sat up slowly, willing the room to remain still. "I owe you so much more than what little I can do."

"I wish Lewis and I were marrying tonight or that we had followed your plan and married straightaway." Water splashed on the floorboards.

"No, you don't. You told me yourself that if you'd married him at first, you would never know for sure if he loved you."

"That is true." Clara pulled a towel off the top of the screen. "When will the train arrive?"

"About three thirty."

"Is there anything I can do to help prepare before then? It's so much harder to undo someone's plans than to make them where they don't exist." Catherine stretched.

"The only thing left to finish is your dress. Becky will be over this afternoon to do the final fitting." Splash. Thump. "Oh, fishtails."

"Are you all right?"

"I just spilled all the water down my clean corset cover and petticoat."

"In this heat, it will dry soon enough."

Clara came out from behind the screen, fanning her petticoat. "Three days. Tell me I can survive three days."

"You will. Should I come to the station?" asked Catherine. She didn't want to, knowing her parents would start in on her as soon as they saw her expanding waistline.

"Dr. Palmer will likely forbid you as it's likely to cause you undue stress. And, selfishly, I want him to agree that you can come to my wedding."

The hours passed quickly, Clara and Catherine both jumping when the courthouse clock chimed three. A moment later, a knock came at the front door. Clara let Lewis in.

He greeted everyone in the room before asking, "Are you two as nervous about your parents' arrival as I am?"

"I'm still trying to understand why they felt it necessary to come at all since they didn't plan on coming originally," said Clara.

"Father could never pass up an opportunity to lecture me. I'm afraid it's my fault. If I hadn't shown up in town on your engagement day ..." Catherine shrugged. There wasn't anything else to say. She hadn't meant to bring unpleasantness to her sister.

"On the bright side," Lewis said, "according to my mother's telegram, they will bring several crates of items for Rose's

Rescue and the funds to complete the purchase of the abandoned-hotel project. Everyone believes it can be habitable in a few weeks, November at the latest." His smile was almost as big as when he saw Clara.

"Remember, I'll be here to draw Mother's attention if she gets to be too much." Catherine drew her dress tight across her belly.

Clara took Lewis's arm. "We'll be back soon."

While she waited for Clara and Lewis to return, Catherine paced the room.

Lavender rolled her chair into Catherine's path. "If you don't sit down, I'll have Hawke come in and tie you down. Getting yourself worked up over your parents is not helpful."

"You've never met my parents."

"Let me guess. They have money but not enough to be among the social elite, so they spend most of their time trying to claw their way out of their circle, ignoring the success they do have. Each word and action is analyzed against the perfect rule. Every city has its version of Brookline, even Philadelphia."

Catherine sat and looked at Lavender. "Was your family like ours?"

"Yes. I used an inheritance to pay my tuition. My father is a successful doctor, so he indulged me."

"So you do understand."

"Better than you know. Can you imagine the kind of reception I'd get if I returned and it became known where I was the past two years?"

"But you were abducted. You had no choice."

"There's always a choice. I chose to keep living." Lavender's words hung heavy in the air, like gray-green storm clouds.

"They would be glad to know you're alive."

Lavender shook her head. "There is no place in their world for a person who has seen and done the things I have. But this is not about my future; it's about yours. I don't know how it will end with your parents, but I want you to know that you would be welcome at Rose's Rescue with us. May you never have to work as we did to put food in your children's mouths."

Catherine wasn't sure what to say. Was The Rescue meant for her too? If the promised money didn't come, she had few skills with which she could support herself and her children. "Thank you for that option."

"I hear them coming. I think I'll make myself scarce for this reunion. I'm not sure your mother is ready to be in the same room as a former lady of the night." Lavender wheeled herself through the kitchen and into her room, then shut her door just as the front door opened and Clara led their parents in.

"There she is. Do you have any idea how much you've cost me?" Father always was direct to the point.

"No. How much?" She shouldn't have answered his anger with anger even if he had skipped a greeting.

"More than you can pay me back. Pinkertons, missed work, travel to New York. Confronting the Fairlanes, which could lead to lost contracts. Now a cross-country trip to drag you back home." Mr. Taylor's face grew red as he spoke.

Her mother laid a hand on his arm. "You promised to wait until later for this." She turned to Catherine. "You appear to be further along than I expected."

"The doctor believes it's twins."

Mrs. Taylor fanned herself and swooned into the closest chair. "He must be wrong. They will be more difficult to place."

"Place?"

"You can't keep them. They will ruin your chances of marriage."

Catherine had thought of giving her children to Clara

to raise and disappearing farther west. But the more they kicked, the harder she found the idea. She'd never asked her sister if she was willing to take them. Catherine had options, but above all, she wanted this to be her choice. As for marriage, if she'd learned one thing from the last several months, she needed to be able to trust a man's word. Bernard had lied to her. So many men in their society had mistresses and such. After seeing the pain in Lavender's eyes, she never wanted to be with a man who would pay for a woman. "I am not going back to Brookline."

"Of course you are. You can't stay in this place."

"Why not? It was good enough for me when I was marrying Lewis."

Behind her parents, Lewis stiffened, his lips pinched. She was ruining things for them. Not what she intended.

"Sorry, Lewis, Clara. Mother, Father, we can discuss my misdeeds at another time. We should all be celebrating Clara's nuptials."

Mrs. Taylor turned to Clara. "Yes, we should. And just wait until you see the wedding dress I bought for you to wear. I hope you haven't gained any weight, Clara."

Clara's face paled. Catherine covered her mouth. Her mother had brought a dress. How did she even have time to get one made?

Clara stepped back into Lewis's side. "Mother, you didn't need to do that. I have my graduation dress."

"Precisely. It's your graduation dress, not a wedding dress. I found the most divine creation. You'd never know it isn't from the House of Worth. Fortuitously, a bride got cold feet and called off her wedding. It's in one of my trunks. Come to the hotel in the morning. I hope we don't need any alterations."

Catherine yawned loudly, deliberately making her mouth as large as possible.

Mrs. Taylor glared. "Where are your manners? Have you forgotten everything I taught you?"

"Pardon me. I didn't realize how tired I was. You must be exhausted after days on the train."

"Tired and hungry," said Mr. Taylor. "Is there a decent restaurant in town?"

"The hotel serves a nice dinner. Since we were unsure if you would be on today's train, we didn't plan for dinner tonight," said Lewis. "Clara and I will walk you over."

Hurrah for Lewis. He knew how to divert their parents too.

Clara returned shortly after dusk and threw herself on the bed. "Mother dragged me up to see the dress. So many bows and flounces. And the bustle! It is larger than the one on your dress."

"The dress I sold. I wonder what Mother will say when I tell her. I shall have to save that story for when you need an extra-strong diversion."

"The yawn was brilliant. And Lewis taking over like he did." Clara smiled the soft grin she always did when speaking of her fiancé.

"In my mind, I was shouting hurrah for him."

"We are leaving directly after the wedding for a honeymoon in Galveston. Lewis planned it—I think mostly to get me away from Mother and Father before Mother can pick apart the wedding."

"Considering I'm standing up with you, we know what that list will start with."

"I wonder if we should tell her before Monday."

"Not if it can be helped." Catherine didn't want her sister's wedding marred because her parents forbade her to attend.

"It's best they don't realize until they are in the church."

"Does the dress need any modification?"

"Sadly, no. It fits as if it was made for me. The bodice makes me feel very feminine as long as I don't look in the mirror." Clara covered her face. "I hardly ever say this, but I hate, detest, and loathe that dress. It's so wrong for me."

"I thought Mother was going to wait until tomorrow to get it out," Catherine said.

"As if she could. We didn't even finish the first course when she dragged me up to her room. What's worse, I can't be upset with her or Father at the moment."

"Why not?" Catherine could think of several things to be upset with, starting with the dress.

"Father gave Lewis a thick letter from his mother. It contained over $500. Lewis was so excited. It was the last of what they needed to purchase the new Rescue. Lewis was so moved he thanked Father for bringing the money out so quickly. Father became embarrassed because he hadn't contributed, then he pulled out a hundred dollars and gave it to Lewis on the spot. It will go toward the lumber we need to finish the building. Lewis's mother sent trunks and trunks of things, even curtains and furnishings. It seems half of Brookline changed parlor colors this year, so they are all the green that was so popular a few years ago."

"That is wonderful. Having them come wasn't all bad."

"No, it isn't. Like everyone else, they have their good parts mixed with the bad. We were prepared only to deal with the bad, so that's all we saw."

"So, you're saying we should try to look for the good in them?"

"I sound like one of Lewis's Sunday-night sermons on joy."

Catherine leaned over and hugged Clara. "There is nothing wrong with being happy. Today ended better than either of us thought it would."

Clara finished changing and turned out the lamp. "Yes, it did."

Someone pounded on the door to Aiden's office. Aiden threw up the window and stuck his head out. "Be down in a minute."

Mr. Taylor looked up from where he stood on the stoop. "It's a quarter past eight! You should be open."

Aiden pulled his head back in without responding. The man likely wouldn't understand the time it took to stitch up the three drunks who'd landed themself in the jail last night after using broken whiskey bottles as weapons. At least it hadn't been bullets. And he'd already been up once to help Jax. There was a reason the office wasn't open on Saturdays other than for emergencies.

Aiden pulled on a fresh shirt and vest. Shaving would have to wait. Mr. Taylor's pounding started again. Aiden hurried down the stairs and unlocked the door.

Mr. Taylor pushed his way in. "What kind of a place is this, closed on Saturday? And you not even dressed."

"As Hiramsville's only doctor, it isn't possible for me to set big-city hours. What's your emergency?"

"What's this nonsense about it not being safe for Catherine to travel?"

"When your daughter arrived here last week, she was half starved and weak as a newborn kitten. She fainted—"

"I know all that. Clara told us. I want to know why she can't return with us."

"Catherine has been improving with regard to her appetite, but she tires easily, and, knowing she is carrying twins, a four-day journey on a constantly jostling train is not recommended. Women have been known to deliver early while on trains, and they simply aren't built to deal with that sort of complication." Aiden tried to steer Mr. Taylor into the inner office.

Mr. Taylor crossed his arms and remained in the waiting area. "I can afford a Pullman car. She'll have a bed."

"That rocks back and forth like the rest of the train. While it's not as bumpy as a wooden bench, the motion can still induce early labor. If your daughter was healthy, I would have few reservations about sending her on such a trip, but she is not."

"You think I'm leaving my daughter here in this backwater town full of fallen women?"

"I am simply giving you my advice for what is medically best for Catherine."

"That's Miss Taylor to you. You have no right to be so familiar with her."

"Calling her by her given name is something both your daughters asked for to avoid confusion."

"What are the statistics on expectant women and trains?"

"I've never seen a study on it."

"Well then, we will take the risk." Mr. Taylor turned and left the office.

As Aiden watched the man walk down the street, compassion for Catherine filled him. No wonder she'd wanted to leave the moment she heard her parents were coming. Sending her back to Massachusetts would be a bigger mistake than the town council voting to allow the courthouse clock to chime on the hour, all twenty-four hours.

When Jax thumped on the floor above, Aiden rushed up the stairs to help him.

A breeze fluttered the curtains in the window.

"How would you like to stage a jailbreak?"

"What do you mean, Doc?"

"The second wheelchair arrived yesterday. And if you conspired with GW and Hawke, I bet they could sneak you out of this room in no time."

"Where would I go?"

"I have a decent-sized porch on the back of my house. Lavender has room to roll around."

Jax's interest was piqued at the mention of Lavender. Then he frowned. "Only one problem, Doc. What would I wear? I can't get trousers over this leg you've got all bound up."

"You don't happen to have Scottish ancestors, do you?"

"I don't know. Why?"

"Men in Scotland traditionally wear kilts. Even the soldiers."

"Isn't a kilt like a short skirt?" Jax shook his head. "I'm not wearing a skirt."

"But you could wear a kilt."

"The women will laugh at me."

"More likely, they will ogle your good leg." Aiden crossed his arms and pretended to be impressed by Jax's calf.

"You can't be serious."

"My grandfather was a Scot. I happen to have a green plaid kilt in one of my trunks. And calling it a skirt is fightin' words."

"I could be outside the whole day?"

"As long as Hawke and GW are able to carry you. I've been thinking of moving you down to the main floor, but there is no toilet down there."

Jax nodded at the bed pan. "It doesn't matter to me, does it? I'd like a bit of freedom."

"Well then. I'll find some rangers. If they can't plan a jail-break from this place, no one can."

Aiden left to the sound of Jax's laughter. He hoped he remembered how to fold a kilt. The day out could lighten everyone's mood.

⸻◆⸻

"I'm getting married in the morning." Clara's whisper filled the darkness of the room with joy and sadness.

Catherine squeezed her sister's hand, aware that this was likely the last time they would ever lay side by side. "And I couldn't be happier for you. I am so glad my prank didn't ruin things forever for you."

"This will sound silly, but I am glad you pulled it."

"What?" Catherine turned to try to see her sister better.

"Last year, when Lewis proposed, he wanted a wife more than he wanted me. That's why he didn't try to clarify that he had the wrong sister. He thought it was God's will he should marry you. Last week, when he proposed, he wanted me more than he wanted to fulfill the church leadership's mandate. If you hadn't interfered, I would have always wondered if he truly loved me."

Her sister was marrying for love, just like in the books. Catherine sighed. "I still shouldn't have done it. I should have confessed earlier. And, in my opinion, Lewis couldn't help but love you. I'm sure you wouldn't have wondered long."

Clara leaned over and hugged Catherine. "Please. I have forgiven you. I only wish you had confessed for yourself. You might not have—"

"Ruined myself with Bernard? We can't be sure. I believe he would have cajoled me either way. When you refused him a kiss, you didn't give in, so he turned to me. I never thought one little liberty … Sneaking around with him was so exciting, and he promised to take me away so I wouldn't have to come here. I'm sure he would have said anything to get me to agree. I suspect it was a game for him. I don't think I was the first woman he seduced."

"What gives you that idea?"

"Something his father said. I don't think I'm the first woman he paid off to leave Bernard. I feel sorry for his fiancée. I don't think he's capable of being a faithful husband."

"When did you come to this conclusion?"

"This week. I've overheard conversations about why Lavender says she will never marry. The men that would come to … um … their places of employment. The *married* ones."

Clara fanned the sheet, wafting air around both of them. "I think it's wrong how society marks these women but doesn't punish their customers the same way. Until Emily asked me to come teach at Rose's, I'd never thought about it. I mean, it was always 'those evil women' who did whatever. Only a few have shared their stories with me. Wanting to survive isn't evil. Some were just children. All were desperate. Some, like you, had been used and set aside, and they wanted to feed their children."

Catherine thought of how desperate she felt when she was kicked out of the boardinghouse for loose morals. The hotel she stayed at cost an exorbitant amount, and the hundred dollars her father had given her disappeared far sooner than it should have. She hadn't reached the point of desperation, but she could imagine it. "I'm glad I'll have the money. I hope I can find a way to support us before it runs out."

"Emily's offer to teach at The Rescue was sincere."

"It's a far better solution than returning to Brookline." Although Catherine thought of giving her children to someone to raise, being forced to part with those children was different. And she would be. Perhaps in a month or two, when she was delivered, she could give them to Clara. Clara and Lewis would be the best of parents. But that was not a topic for tonight. "We should change the subject. I'm afraid this is becoming rather melancholy."

"I still cannot believe they pulled together a celebration yesterday and brought Jax."

"And his kilt."

They both giggled. He'd been so embarrassed by it. Several of the women from Rose's complimented him on his bare leg just to make him blush. In truth, all of them were so happy to see him out of bed and well on the way to recovery. The news that the abandoned hotel had been purchased and it would only be a matter of weeks before the new Rose's Rescue could open only added to the joy.

"I think we've all been waiting for good news since the fire. Knowing Jax was recovering and seeing it are two different things," said Clara.

"I thought it funny how Dr. Palmer pretended to be upset that the rangers snuck him out of the doctor's office when we all know he arranged it."

"It's unfortunate he wouldn't allow you to come to regular services today. Lewis preached so well. Even Father was impressed."

"Dr. Palmer knew I could attend tonight's devotional here, and he's worried that three days of activity will be too much. I slept so well I didn't even hear you come in last night." Catherine had been much more tired than she'd let on.

Clara giggled.

"What?"

"I was picturing Mother's face when she realized that most of the women were from The Rescue."

"But they are dressed so normally," mimicked Catherine. "I'm not sad she decided to leave with Father soon after. It kept her from going on and on about how things should be done."

"You and I both. You should have been to lunch with us today. Mother started in, and Lewis stopped her by pointing out that the most important part of the marriage was the vows and it didn't matter how the church was decorated or what the bride wore. He even pointed out that Adam and Eve didn't have fine clothing when God put them together." Clara barely made it through the last several words without laughing.

Someone pounded on the floor above their heads. Morning Glory shouted, "Will you two go to sleep? Clara doesn't need her eyes all puffy because she was up half the night before her wedding. And I would like to get some sleep too!"

"Sorry!" the twins answered in unison. Clara and Catherine clapped their hands over their mouths to stifle their laughter.

"Good night, Catherine. I love you," whispered Clara.

"Good night, Clara. Always and forever," Catherine answered with the second part before rolling onto her right side. A few moments later, the babies began to move. Catherine rubbed the places they kicked. Would they someday tell each other good night?

13

Catherine added one last pin to Clara's coiffure. "There. Perfect."

Clara studied herself in the doctor's bedroom mirror. "Is this really happening?"

"Yes! Shall I add the veil?" Catherine held up the netting and lace.

"Please." Her twin's voice held the smallest tremor.

Should she acknowledge her sister's nerves? Better to calm them now than to wait for Mother to realize Clara's distress and add to it. "Is there anything amiss?"

"No. I'm just excited and a bit nervous. After today, I'll be a different person in so many ways. A wife."

"And you will be the most brilliant preacher's wife ever. Ready? Mother and Father are waiting in the parlor."

Clara stood. "Is my dress too much?"

"We both know the answer to that." Reminding her sister just how overdone the dress was wouldn't help. "However, you look exquisite in it. I can't wait to see Lewis's face when he sees you. He'll be struck speechless."

"Not for long, I hope. He needs to be able to speak enough to say 'I do.'"

"I'm sure he won't forget to say that. We should hurry so you can say your farewells and catch the train after the ceremony." If they missed it, they could well end up spending their wedding night in the same hotel as their parents. Catherine shuddered at the thought.

In the parlor, Mother fussed and adjusted bow after bow while Father looked at his pocket watch. Soon they were in the rented carriage, rolling down the street to the church. A few stragglers picked up their pace to find seats before Clara entered the church. A woman and what appeared to be her daughter acted as ushers, shooing everyone into the building.

Mother pointed with her fan. "Who is that woman? Doesn't she know it isn't her place to direct everyone?"

"It's all right, Mother," answered Clara. "I'm sure she's only trying to be helpful."

"If you wanted ushers, you should have had some young men dressed their best, with flowers pinned to their lapels. Honestly, I don't know how you were pulling this off without my planning."

Catherine leaned over and patted her mother's hand, hoping to calm the rising tempest. Father stopped the carriage and set the brake. He helped Mother down first, then Catherine, then Clara. They stood awkwardly, not sure what to do, as the soft tones of the harmonium spilled out of the empty doorway. Finally, Mother lifted her skirts and marched up the steps and into the church.

Clara rested her hand on the crook of her father's arm. She gave Catherine a little shove. "You're next."

As Catherine entered the one-room building, every eye in the congregation turned to her. Some jaws dropped in shock, but she lifted her chin and kept her arms at her sides.

It was a mistake to ever agree to stand up for her sister. Whatever had possessed her to say yes? The stain of Catherine's choices would affect both Clara and Lewis, but this was about what Clara wanted. So Catherine walked down the short aisle to the front, refusing to succumb to the urge to lay one hand on her belly and protect the children within.

As Catherine reached the front of the room, Clara screamed and Father yelled a string of profanities worthy of a Boston dockworker. Everyone spun to face the open doorway.

Clara stood wringing her hands. Blood dripped from her face, arms, and dress. Screams from half the women in the congregation, including Mother, mingled with Clara's. Father bounded down the stairs, yelling after somebody.

The sheriff sprung to the doorway and touched Clara's arm. "It's only paint!" Hawke and GW, who stood near the back door, exited, skirting Clara and the dripping paint. Lewis and Reverend Green rushed to the doorway, or tried to, as people exited the pews to get a better look at Clara.

Mother stood and promptly swooned. A man caught her, preventing further disaster. Catherine felt a bit light-headed herself, but the need to help her sister won out. She took a step forward before Dr. Palmer caught her by the elbow.

"Let others handle it." He guided her to a vacant seat in the closest pew. Becky, Nellie, and several women Catherine didn't recognize rushed to Clara's side and hurried the crying bride out of sight. Mrs. Reese banged on the floor with her cane, attracting the attention of those who remained. "If you'll give us a few minutes, the wedding will proceed. It's only a bit of paint."

"Yes, yes, it will." Reverend Green waved his arms, herding people back into the pews. "In the meantime, if a few of you men wouldn't mind retrieving buckets of water. I think it best if we wash the paint off the entry."

Before anyone could follow his instructions, a girl of no more than sixteen appeared in the doorway in a white dress, a veil partially obscuring her face. "Reverend Staples, I am here, so now you can marry me."

"Why, Libby Jean, what are you talking about?" asked a matronly woman near the door.

"Mama said I am to marry Reverend Staples. Mama fixed everything." Libby Jean's speech was slow and oddly accented, as if she spoke through a mouth full of marbles.

Who was this girl who thought she should marry Lewis? Catherine looked at the silent faces for clues. Some faces looked shocked; others looked at the girl with pity.

"I did everything Mama said. I am ready for a wedding. See? White, just like Queen Victoria." Libby stepped into the church, red footprints trailing behind her. Reverend Green put up a hand to stop her progress as he hurried to the girl. "Sweet child, that isn't how things are supposed to work. First, Reverend Staples would need to propose."

"Mama said he wants to, but he has been too busy with all those bruised buds from The Rescue. Mama said we just need to get his attention. She's made me write so many notes."

A hush fell over the room. Lewis joined Reverend Green and Libby Jean in the doorway. "Did you and your mother paint words on the outside of Rose's Rescue?"

The girl nodded.

"Did you leave notes for me at the manse?"

Again the girl nodded.

"Did you set The Rescue on fire?"

"We didn't mean to. Honest, preacher. Mama said it would smoke them out. We had so much smoke down in the cellar, but then there were sparks, and they caught the floor. We barely got out of there. But it will all be worth it now. I can get married just like my sisters."

Reverend Green took the girl's hand in his. "Libby Jean, I think you need to come speak with the sheriff."

"After I get married. Mama showed Reverend Staples the true color of Miss Clara. She is as red as sin. A proper woman wouldn't be helping those buds. Mama says womans like them can never reform and we need to protect the reverend and make sure he marries somebody pure like me."

Catherine was furious. How dare this girl call her sister impure? Her sister was the kindest, gentlest, purest person she knew. Clara had barely done any wrong her entire life. A hand on her shoulder prevented Catherine from standing. She turned her head to look at Dr. Palmer. "My sister isn't covered in sin. I need to tell them."

Dr. Palmer leaned closer. "It won't do any good. Can't you see that Libby Jean's a bit slow?"

Slow? Was that a new phrase for "batty as a belfry"? Catherine turned her attention back to Libby Jean.

"I got to marry him. Mama said. Mama said the whole reason I was born was to protect God's word from those who would desecrate it, and I've got to protect the reverend from sinful women."

Emily slid out of her place behind the harmonium and joined the reverends. "Libby Jean, you've gotten some red on your dress. Come with me, and we'll clean it up."

Libby Jean looked at her dress and gasped. "Oh no, let's go! Mama will be so upset she'll switch me for sure."

Emily looked around the room. "Hannah, will you give me a hand?"

Hannah agreed, and the women marched Libby Jean away.

Two men with buckets and a mop appeared and began to remove the red paint from the stairs and floor of the church. Catherine attempted to stand. Again, Dr. Palmer stopped her.

"I need to see Clara."

"It would be better if you stayed and helped your mother. I'll be back. I need to be sure no one was injured."

Catherine turned to where her mother blinked as if coming out of a deep sleep. "Is the wedding off?"

"No, Mother. Some of Clara's friends took her to clean her up."

"They'll never get the paint out of the dress. It is ruined, just ruined. They can't get married today. She needs a new dress."

"Clara has her graduation dress."

"That thing? I already forbade her to wear it."

"Mother, it's the best option. Clara isn't going to postpone her wedding for want of a dress you approve of. From what I hear, most people don't care what color a woman is married in."

"They should."

"Why? Because a queen who doesn't even rule our country made it popular?"

"Don't be absurd. Every woman wants to look her best on her wedding day."

"And she will, in the graduation dress. It is much more Clara's style."

Donny came running into the building. "Reverend Staples, I'm supposed to tell you five more minutes. And, Reverend Green, I'm supposed to say 'No long-winded speeches. The new Mr. and Mrs. Staples better be on the eastbound train.'"

Everyone laughed, the tension in the room easing. Only Reverend Green seemed upset. Though she couldn't see well from where she sat, it appeared the red paint had stained the stairs. After a test, which included Reverend Green laying his handkerchief on the floor and stepping on it, the white cloth turned red, and a man went running for some empty flour sacks. The now-covered stairs were deemed safe to walk on just as Donny returned.

"The bride is coming! Get ready!"

Emily entered first and walked over to the harmonium, where she played a Bach piece while everyone else filed back in. The women from The Rescue and the sheriff returned with Dr. Palmer. The rangers, however, did not. Reverend Green signaled for Catherine to stand, and Emily changed to Mendelssohn's "Wedding March." Clara appeared in the doorway on Father's arm. He'd changed his suit. Clara's cheeks seemed rosier than usual; otherwise, there was no indication that she'd been doused in red paint. As her sister walked down the aisle in her white graduation dress. Catherine couldn't help but glance at Mother. It was doubtful Mother understood the meaning Catherine tried to convey: *My sister is perfect without your meddling.*

When the final notes faded and Reverend Green started the ceremony, a wave of emotion engulfed Catherine, her joy for her sister colliding with her sorrow for herself. At least Clara had found her happy ending and forgiven her for her role in nearly destroying her happiness. A tear rolled down Catherine's cheek. Crying at weddings was acceptable.

⬦⬦⬦

Half the town escorted the newlyweds to the train station. Aiden pushed Lavender's wheelchair along with their group. Though the road was bumpy and jostled her, she didn't complain. Aiden was glad he was able to provide a way for her to join in.

Lavender reached back, tugged on Aiden's coat sleeve, and crooked her finger for him to bend down. "Something is off with Catherine. Her color has drained."

"As soon as the train leaves, I'll send her back to bed."

"If you can manage that without her mother following, it might be best. I heard a rumor that her parents intend to stay until Clara returns."

Aiden nodded. From what he'd witnessed of the Taylors, this complicated relationship was likely to send either girl into a defensive stance. With Clara gone, they would focus their energy on correcting Catherine. Condemnation she did not need to hear. She was doing enough of that to herself.

Aiden turned the pushing of the wheelchair over to Morning Glory and moved as close as he could to Catherine while she gave her sister a final hug. The Taylors stood not far off, watching the scene. No discernable emotions crossed their faces—a byproduct of trying to mingle with high society, he was certain.

"All aboard. That means you, preacher." Everyone laughed at the conductor's pointed announcement and made way for the new Reverend and Mrs. Staples to board.

Catherine stepped back, nearly colliding with Aiden. Instinctively, he took her elbow.

"Excuse me, Doctor. I didn't see you there."

"I was coming to talk with you."

"I can guess you wish for me to return to bed."

Aiden raised a brow. "What gave you that idea?"

"Honestly, I am exhausted, and if I look as poorly as I feel, I'd send me to bed too."

"Glad we agree. Do you mind if I also say you should have no visitors for the rest of the day?" He tilted his head toward her father.

"You'd do that for me?" Catherine's face lost a bit of the weariness around her eyes.

Aiden nodded. "I believe the added stress of visitors would put undue strain on you."

She closed her eyes and took a deep breath, something he'd seen her sister do on occasion. She opened them again. "You may not believe this, but I have every intention of following your orders."

"Good. I'll send you back with Lavender and Morning Glory, and let your parents know you are not to be disturbed."

Catherine joined Lavender and the other women as they left the train depot.

The Taylors watched the eastbound disappear in the distance, their faces still betraying little emotion. Mrs. Taylor turned to her husband. "Are you intent on looking into businesses in Dallas?"

"I am. As soon as young Staples gives up this minister rubbish, he's going to need a new career. Likely, he won't return to Boston, and he's shown no inclination to follow in his father's footsteps."

"I don't want them to stay in Texas. It is so far, and Clara is the one most likely to give me grandchildren."

"Obviously, you have forgotten your other daughter. You will accomplish your wish of becoming a grandmother twice over in just a few weeks." Mr. Taylor's voice held a tone of mockery.

"Not a real grandmother. It isn't as if she's going to keep them. It will take us months to find her a new husband. I only hope the rumors have not spread too far."

While Aiden expected adopting out the children was Catherine's parents' plan for her, it was the first he'd heard it from their mouths.

Aiden took the opportunity to step closer and interrupt their conversation. "Mr. and Mrs. Taylor, I have sent Catherine to rest for the remainder of the day. I underestimated how taxing the wedding would be for her. I'm sure the extra time in the heat didn't help."

"It was taxing on all of us. Imagine ruining a wedding dress with red paint. And why? As far as I can tell, only because my daughter took a job working with people she should not. She was forced to wear that horrid graduation dress—and for the photographer, even. What will her children say? Will they think we were poor? And having Catherine stand up with her. The shame of it, embarrassing us that way. I fully intend to have words with my daughter."

Aiden's jaw clenched. He ignored the woman's odious thoughts about Clara to focus on the bigger problem. "I must ask you to allow Catherine to rest undisturbed."

Mrs. Taylor looked around to see who might be listening. Only the stationmaster remained in the area. "Surely you wouldn't deny her mother?"

"Yes, I would."

Mr. Taylor puffed out his chest and stepped forward in a show of intimidation. "You cannot deny a mother access to her daughter."

As a soldier, Aiden had experienced his share of intimidation. This man didn't even come close to scary. Aiden relaxed his posture as much as possible to show he wasn't threatened in the least. "Perhaps with the wedding, you misunderstood how critical your daughter's condition was when she arrived in Hiramsville."

"Women faint all the time. Or perhaps they didn't teach you that in medical school?" Mr. Taylor sneered.

"What they do teach is that people who are half starved and expecting twins need to take extra care of their health." He was about to quote the latest maternal mortality-rate statistics but thought better of it.

Mrs. Taylor nodded. "Which is why Catherine is returning with us to Brookline. There is a very discreet girls' home that will take her in until she is ready to be out in society again."

"It would be better if she didn't travel."

"As I said last time we spoke, I can pay for the finest of Pullman cars." Mr. Taylor's chest puffed out farther, an action Aiden found to be almost medically impossible.

"Even the best of cars experience bumps and jolts, which in her current state could bring the twins early. Train conductors aren't midwives or doctors."

"All the sooner she can reenter society and find a husband," said Mrs. Taylor.

"But if she were to deliver on the train with no doctor or midwife, both children could die and possibly Catherine as well. She should remain here until after she is delivered."

"The only way my daughter will stay in this place is if she is married. If you are that concerned about her health"—Mr. Taylor poked Aiden in the ribs—"you should find her a husband. It shouldn't be hard. I've heard stories of a man proposing on the street when he first meets a woman here in Texas."

Mrs. Taylor gripped her husband's arm, effectively removing her husband's hand from Aiden's chest. "Clara said she received one of those proposals on her third day in town."

"There you have it, Doctor. Find the man who proposed to Clara and offer him Catherine. They look alike, so he shouldn't object." Mr. Taylor removed his wife's hand from his arm.

Aiden could think of two reasons Mr. Collins would object: one, Catherine was expecting, and, two, she was carrying twins. He was specifically looking for a woman to care for his children, not be concerned with her own. "I am not in the business of matchmaking."

"As the doctor, you know everyone in town and a great many outside of it. You are the man for the job. Since my wife has begged me to stay until Clara and Lewis return, you have a week to marry our daughter off. In her condition, a few minutes in front of the justice of the peace should work quite well."

When he set a man's bones, Aiden was aware that his skills, or lack thereof, could determine the rest of a man's life.

Choosing a husband for any woman held consequences more far-reaching than setting a bone. The man in question would raise the woman's children. The wrong choice could affect generations. "As her father, I should think you would want to interview any potential spouses."

"No. I don't. Men might think they could get some sort of monetary gain out of the situation. I will leave you to it." Mr. Taylor turned to his wife. "Come. I need to make arrangements to go to Dallas."

The couple walked off, leaving Aiden near the tracks.

The setting sun left most of the bedroom in shadow. Catherine rolled over, causing the babies to kick. Had she really slept until sunset? Dr. Palmer was right—the excitement of the day had drained her. One of the babies kicked a particularly tender place, compelling her to rise and use the chamber pot. She felt bad for using it rather than the privy, but there was no way she could cover the distance quickly enough, especially since it required her to dress.

After caring for her needs, she pulled on her wrapper and headed for the kitchen, hoping Nellie left her a plate.

In the parlor, Lavender sat reading in her wheelchair. "Did you sleep well?"

"Very."

"Your mother has been to speak to you. I turned her away."

"I assume she didn't appreciate that."

"Not in the least. I'm sure she'll come again. Nellie left you cold chicken, cornbread, and peas."

"I was about to ask."

"We have leftover wedding cake for dessert. I've been waiting for you to wake up so we can eat together."

"I'd like that."

Lavender put her book away and followed Catherine into the kitchen. The door to the old infirmary stood ajar, and she could see the bed, which didn't look as comfortable as the one in her room. Catherine remembered that she was originally meant to stay in the doctor's bedroom. "Now that Clara is gone, would you like to trade rooms so you can have the nicer bed?"

"No. It's difficult to maneuver this chair in there. The carpet next to the bed catches the wheels, and I have to back out. The infirmary is a much better room for me."

"Are you sure?"

Lavender nodded, her mouth full of cake.

They spent most of the meal discussing trivial matters as Catherine worked up the courage to ask the questions she'd been pondering. Finally, with the last bite of cake remaining on her plate, she ventured into the uncomfortable subject. "How did you find peace after leaving your last employment?"

"You mean the brothel?"

Catherine nodded.

"I'm still working on that. So much of the last few years wasn't my choice—the abduction, being sold to another master. Even my escape wasn't entirely of my own doing. Some of the things I did during that time haunt me. However, talking about them has helped me. When I arrived last fall, Reverend Green and his late wife were very helpful as I could talk with them about the anger and betrayal I felt. I miss Mrs. Green very much. She was so witty. There are others I spoke with, but Reverend Green was the one who taught me of a forgiving God and how I'm still a worthy daughter of a king. I keep praying for his health to improve."

"Do you think the reverend could help me? I wasn't forced into my situation."

"I'm sure he could. After dinner, write a note, then send it first thing in the morning. He's sure to come by midday." Lavender wheeled herself back into the parlor.

Catherine cleared the table and poured hot water from the kettle into the sink to wash them.

"What are you doing?" The horror in her mother's voice said doing housework was akin to dancing naked in the street.

Catherine glanced at the screen-covered back door where her mother stood. How long had she been there? "Washing dishes."

"The maid can do it." Mother let herself into the house.

"There is no maid. We all pitch in and do what we can."

"What of that horribly frightened child?"

"Nellie is not a maid. She is an excellent cook." Catherine wanted to defend Nellie further, but her mother spoke before she got the chance.

"If she is the cook, she can clean her own kitchen. I am surprised the doctor allows you to do such menial tasks."

Catherine rinsed the plate. "Washing a few dishes is within reason, as long as I don't strain myself."

"But we raised you to not have to do such work." Mother scrunched her nose.

"And at Bradford, they made sure we understood the running of a household. Do you think Clara and Lewis can afford a maid?"

"Of course, our minister has a cook and a maid of all work."

"And he has a very large, well-off congregation that donates enough money to support his household. You saw the congregation on Sunday. Did they look well off to you?" Goodness, she sounded like her sister defending this wild place and doing dishes. Whether because of her desire to do the opposite of whatever Mother wanted or how kind everyone had been since her arrival, Catherine wanted to clean up after herself and contribute what little she could.

"No, but still you should not be doing dishes." Mother's feather fan beat constantly.

Catherine finished the last plate and set it in the cupboard. "I'm finished now. I'd offer you a glass of something, but I would need to wash it after you finished, so I assume you don't want to cause me any more work and would decline anyway. Would you like to sit in the parlor?"

"It would be cooler on the porch, I think."

"Not by much; however, the Texas-sized mosquitoes would drive us inside after only a few minutes."

"I want to talk privately."

"Then I suggest the bedroom." Catherine couldn't imagine anything her mother could say that hadn't already been said. When they reached the bedroom, her mother closed the door.

"Your father has come to an agreement with the doctor. You may remain in Texas if you are married. The doctor is going to find you a husband."

"Dr. Palmer agreed to this?"

"After some persuading. I am here to remind you that you have no business being fussy about your mate. Few men want a woman carrying a by-blow or two. You may still have to give up the children."

A marriage to a stranger of the doctor's choosing? Try as she might, she couldn't imagine Dr. Palmer agreeing to such a thing. "Or?"

"As we've told you, you will return home with us. There is a society down in Stoughton that takes in women in your kind of trouble. They place the children. Then we pretend you've been on a grand adventure."

"And so you have explained." And not listened to Catherine's objections. She couldn't go back. She'd signed a contract. Nor did she wish to marry whatever man Father chose for her. Three days of pondering hadn't changed her opinion in the slightest.

"None of your sassiness. You should be grateful anyone is willing to help you. The doctor is insistent that if you travel, you will lose the babies, which would not be a bad thing at all in your situation. Don't you agree?"

Catherine laid a hand where the twins most often kicked. "You wish them dead?"

"It would be the simplest solution to your disgrace. If you returned to Boston no longer in the family way, it would dispel any rumors and open your pool of potential husbands."

Catherine sank onto the bed. "Married or not, I have no intention to return to Brookline or Boston society.

"You will do as your father says."

Catherine opened her mouth to argue, then closed it. Her mother wouldn't listen.

"I see you are rethinking things. It will be better this way. At least you will have a husband."

From where Catherine sat, that wasn't always a good thing.

"Your father and I are leaving for Dallas and will return Saturday evening. He wants to look at investment opportunities, and we both tire of the lack of, well everything. Two hotels and a theater that is only open on weekends. There is very little to do here."

Relief washed over Catherine. Thanks to Hiramsville's supposed paltry offerings, her parents would not be around to continue to hold her misdeeds over her head. "I hope you enjoy your time there."

Mother harrumphed. "Hardly likely. I'd much rather be on the Cape; however, it will make for diverting stories to share with my friends. I'll have to tell them something, and I can't talk about you, can I now?"

She could and would. Catherine remained quiet, hoping to end the interview.

"Of course I can't. Well, if you find a husband, I can simply say both of my daughters are married and I rarely get to see them. In time, people will forget any rumors they've heard about you. It will be easy enough to convince my friends they were confused about which twin was engaged to the preacher. Everyone knows those gossipy maids are always lying."

Had Mother always been so shallow? Critical, yes. But she'd never thought of Mother as caring only for society. If she had married Bernard, would this have been her future?

The bells in the clock tower rang for nine.

"Well, I must be going. That doctor insisted I not come, but I had to speak to you." Mother grabbed Catherine by the shoulders and air-kissed her cheeks. "Do take care."

Catherine watched her leave, the unpleasantness of the visit leaving her with the overwhelming urge to cry. She retreated to her room before any of her housemates could witness her distress. As her tears dampened her pillow, image after image came to mind: her mother dressing her and her sister to parade them down the block to the little park, confusing their names, teas she'd been required to attend, galas she'd not been invited to but watched her parents dress for, and classes on sitting properly. Why hadn't she realized that everything was about appearances? Even the hubbub about marrying a preacher was all about how Mother appeared to society. If Catherine returned to her parents' house in Massachusetts, life would be unbearable. She could only pray Dr. Palmer made a better match for her than her parents would.

⬥

Aiden sat across from TJ in the sheriff's office, while GW leaned on the wall and Hawke sat in the other chair.

TJ tapped a pencil on the paper in front of him. "Libby Jean has told us enough to keep her and her mother in jail for a very long time. I have no doubt that's where her mother belongs, but Libby Jean?"

"Are you asking me if she should be institutionalized?" asked Aiden.

"Yup."

"I've been in some of those places. Worse there than the prison in Huntsville. Although, for a woman, either place could be unsafe," said GW.

Aiden had heard of pregnancies in prison and in the asylums. There was only one way that happened, and Libby Jean would be helpless to protect herself. "The question is, where else can Libby Jean go? It's unlikely her mother will be given a sentence other than several years in jail at Huntsville for the arson."

Hawke leaned back in his chair, balancing on two legs. "We won't get to decide that. Without Libby Jean's testimony, there isn't enough evidence. The paint, paper, and ink we found at the house could belong to anyone. The notes are the only thing that can be tied to her mother. The judge will be the one to decide what's appropriate for Libby Jean."

Tap. Tap. Tap.

"Libby Jean is so easily influenced. I worry she'll be in worse trouble incarcerated," said TJ.

"I can write a letter to the judge indicating my medical opinion that Libby Jean is simple-minded and barely fifteen. I could recommend she be placed with her older sister in Dallas, where she would be far enough away she wouldn't try to pursue Reverend Staples. My worry is they put her in her grandmother's care. Mrs. Forsythe has strong views against Rose's Rescue, and Libby Jean might continue what they started."

GW pushed off the wall. "It's probably the best we can do. I'm waiting to hear if the trial will be in the county or moved. Since no one died in the arson, but a lawman was injured…"

"The judge wants the trial moved to another county. He doesn't think he can get a jury here," said TJ.

"Half the town witnessed the confession. I see his point," said Hawke.

"Our job is to make the arrest." Tap, tap. TJ laid his pencil down. "If you would write a letter, Doc, we will have done all we can do to help Libby Jean."

"Perhaps one from her school teacher could help as well." Aiden wished he could see the future. "Libby Jean could return to a normal life just as easily as she could continue down a path of destruction. Wherever she goes, she will need to be watched carefully."

"I still can't believe it was them. I'd been looking at Mrs. Carter and her daughter," said TJ.

"That's only because they ruined 'Onward Christian Soldiers' and Eliza had been so forward with the preacher," said GW. "I don't understand why all these mothers wanted their daughters to marry him. Most of those girls are not even seventeen."

"Probably trying to save them from a proposal from Mr. Collins or a cowboy," muttered TJ.

Hawke laughed. "Or from the likes of us. Don't see many mothers wanting their daughters married to lawmen."

TJ grinned. "Lucky for me, I found a woman who didn't have a mother to object."

GW leaned over and slapped the back of his brother's head. "But you had to arrest your wife to get her to notice you."

"Hey." TJ swiped at GW, who jumped out of the way.

TJ's deputy came downstairs. "I separated them. Good thing it's a Monday. Don't know what we'll do if we get a man in a jail with only three cells."

"Well, we shouldn't get anyone tonight." TJ stood. "We'll get out of here so you can get some shut-eye."

Aiden left the jail with the other men. The rangers crossed the street to the hotel.

TJ walked with him as far as the office. "Today has to go on record for the oddest wedding we've ever had around here."

Aiden agreed. "For a split second, even I thought it was blood dripping from Clara. Word around the house is that she didn't like the dress her mother brought from Boston anyway, and so she wasn't too upset to lose the gown."

"I'm happy we can all rest tonight." Hawke stopped in front of the hotel.

"Speak for yourself. I don't count on a quiet night until I see the sunrise," said Aiden.

"Doc, you're a wise man." TJ waved as he continued to his house. GW followed his brother.

Two hours later, the deputy came knocking at the door, hoping Aiden could do something to calm Libby Jean's screaming. Aiden wished it was possible to charge her mother for the crime of confusing her daughter's mind. And, once again, he prayed for a second doctor in town so they could take shifts.

Two mornings later, Aiden woke after a good night's sleep with Catherine on his mind.

A husband.

Aiden never thought he would need to find a husband for one of his patients. The most logical choice was the newspaper owner, Mr. Collins. He was the most desperate of all the men Aiden knew, but he wouldn't wish the man on Catherine. Becoming a mother of twins would be hard enough without adding three other children, even if they seemed as well-behaved as the Collins children did, which was as behaved as a pack of feral cats. Mr. Collins would want his wife to put his children first and, given his general attitude toward the women of The Rescue, it was unlikely he would accept an unwed mother as a bride. Still, Catherine was likely to not be mistreated by him, which was better than Aiden could say for a few of the other men in town. There was a rancher near de Cordova Bend who'd lost his wife and children last year to illness. Rumor had it he was looking for companionship, and Aiden knew he could afford to keep Catherine in the manner in which she'd grown up. Aiden made a note to ask Reverend Green about the man's character.

What exactly did Mr. Taylor expect from his ultimatum? Perhaps in Boston there were good and honest men just waiting around to marry a woman. In Texas, many men were hardened and jaded, barely more than compassionless outlaws. Then there were the men like Judge Granger, who'd had the entire county fooled for years. If Emily hadn't uncovered the former judge's connection to the brothel and Cole Pike's gang, he would still be sitting on the bench, corrupting the law.

Catherine would be better off taking her chances on the train than with one of them. Didn't Mr. Taylor care that Catherine's life could be in danger from the multiday train travel required to return her to Massachusetts? Apparently not. Just as her father didn't care what type of man she married. How did a father come to think this way of his own child?

There must be someone.

What about the rangers? Jax would make a good husband and should be up and walking before the twins arrived. Although he held an interest in Lavender, there were no future nuptials in that direction. No. Jax's heart and mind were already in a state of struggle. Aiden could not approach him with such a request. Hawke or GW? Neither was ready to settle down. Did active rangers marry? Aiden rubbed his jaw, unsure of the answer.

The sun rose higher. Time to start his day. Aiden finished dressing.

Looking for an excuse to talk with Collins, Aiden headed to the newspaper office to pick up the midweek edition of the Hiramsville paper. Mr. Collins's oldest son sat just inside the doorway, folding the freshly dried papers. "Is your father here?"

"Aubrey dumped ink all over herself. Pa is outback trying to wash her off."

"Do you mind if I go on through and talk to him?"

The boy shrugged. "Suit yourself. Do you want a paper?"

Aiden fished a nickel out of his pocket and took three copies, one for the office, one for himself, and one for the women living in his home. He folded the single-sheet papers again and put them in his breast pocket. He walked through the back room, around the press, and through the back door, where he found Mr. Collins scrubbing his three-year-old daughter in a large washtub. "Good morning, Collins."

"If that's what you want to call it."

"Looks like you have yourself a bit of trouble there."

"This ink doesn't come out of anything. I thought of using lye but figured it would be too harsh on her skin."

"I don't recommend using pure lye on anyone. Have you tried lemon juice?" Aiden remembered Susannah getting an ink stain out of one of his shirts by rubbing a lemon on it."

"I hadn't thought of that. Yet another reason I need a wife. They know these things."

Just the opening Aiden needed. "Have you considered Catherine Taylor?"

"Clara's twin? The one who fainted in front of Farr's store?"

"Yes."

"I won't marry her for the same reason I won't marry any of those Rescue women. I don't want a gal that's been used and discarded by another man. It's my only requirement." Mr. Collins's direct answer was along the lines of what Aiden expected. Considering he'd proposed to at least five women without even having a conversation with them, Aiden wondered just how he determined that.

"Miss Taylor was under the assumption she was engaged." Aiden stretched the truth somewhat.

"It doesn't matter. I don't want a widow either. They have too many ideas about how a husband should be." Mr. Collins lifted his daughter out of the dark-gray water and wrapped her in a stained towel. "Come Sunday, those church ladies are going to be wagging their tongues over this one. Don't know if Farr carries enough lemons to clean her up. Just turned my back for a second. Her sister was supposed to be watching her."

"I hope the lemons work, then. Do be very careful not to get the juice in her eyes."

Mr. Collins sighed. "I know that, Doc. I'm not stupid, just overworked."

"Have you thought of hiring help?"

"Libby Jean and her ma came in two days a week to clean and cook. But now that they are in jail, I need to find someone else. And don't you even recommend one of those Rescue women. I won't have those bruised buds poisoning my daughters' minds."

"Well then, good day." Aiden walked through the alley. How on earth did an educated man become so narrow-minded? Aiden didn't know much about Collins other than he hailed from Atlanta, where his father also ran a newspaper. Presumably, he had some college. The paper rarely contained any spelling errors.

One name off his list.

The only name on his list.

Maybe TJ had some ideas. Aiden changed direction and headed to the jail, where TJ sat behind the sheriff's desk. Aiden explained the problem. "Can you think of anyone she could marry?"

"If you asked me that a couple of weeks ago, I would have had a couple of names for you, but they went and married women from Rose's. Emily will have my hide if I recommend any man I thought would be a drunkard or gamble away their money."

"There has to be someone."

"There are a few cowhands I don't know well. Doubt they have enough money to afford a wife, though." A peculiar look came over TJ's face. "Doc, I think you are missing the obvious."

"Who? I already asked Collins."

"You." TJ's suggestion hung in the air, as useless as the unused gallows tower on the floor above.

Aiden shook his head. "She's my patient."

"Everyone in Hiramsville is your patient. I know you want to marry and have a family. Even if you had your eye on one of the women from Rose's, they likely wouldn't take you because you're the doctor. Almost all the single women in town are younger than the Taylor twins."

"There has to be another option. I have the means to support a wife but hardly the time."

"You don't need much time with her. For now, you can continue living in separate places. You told me you received a letter about a doctor coming down to look over the town, and you have Lavender helping. By the time the babies come, you might just have time for a family."

Aiden sat down in a wooden chair. "I've been trying to figure out how to adopt the Owen kids if it comes to it. I'll have to hire help. I don't see how Catherine could manage twins and children."

"Emily and I have room for Donny and his sisters. We've talked about it several times, and we're in agreement about taking them in. You can always be the doting uncle."

"Probably better for them to have more consistency. You still thinking of starting the ice business?"

"By next summer." TJ shook his head. "Back to finding a groom?"

"There must be someone. A ranger?" Aiden hoped TJ would have more insight into their lives.

"Jax has his eye on Lavender, if I am not mistaken."

"You are right about that. A day doesn't go by when they don't ask for news of the other. Hawke carried Lavender up to see Jax several times last week. Too bad GW and Hawke left. Either man would make a good husband."

"Honestly, I don't think my brother or Hawke are ready to settle down. Maybe you should look beyond Hiramsville." TJ shrugged.

"If you or Emily come up with anyone—"

"We will let you know. I should warn you that Emily is likely to come up with the same solution I did. She wanted to get you and Lavender together until she realized that the wind blew in another direction. I tell you, my wife is a born matchmaker."

Aiden grabbed the chance to turn the conversation away from him. "How is Emily? I didn't get a chance to speak with her this week."

"Better. She's keeping food down, and we felt the baby kick Sunday night. Most amazing thing I've ever felt." TJ smiled one of his goofy I'm-thinking-of-my-wife smiles.

"Any man who calls women the weaker sex hasn't seen one deliver a child. Believe me, most men couldn't handle the pain."

"I guess you'd know about that."

Donny ran into the office. "There you are, Doc. I've been looking everywhere. Mama says she needs you."

Finding a husband for Catherine would have to wait. He had other patients to attend to.

<hr>

Waiting for Reverend Green made it difficult to focus on anything else. Already Catherine had pulled five rows of knitting because she lost count of the pattern.

When he finally arrived, Lavender and Nellie made some excuses and vacated the parlor. Reverend Green sat down, and every question Catherine thought of flew out of her brain. She stared at him, not knowing where to start.

He sat back in the wingback chair. "How are you feeling?"

"Other than as big as a ship?"

"I'm not sure how that feels. My late wife said she felt like a whale, which, as a man, I don't understand. Is there something I might understand?"

"I am not sure you would understand this either, but Lavender said you helped her..."

"If it's your spirit that's troubled, I can help you with that. I have been dealing with my own rumpled spirit for more than seventy years."

Catherine set aside the knitting needles and yarn. "*Rumpled* is not strong enough of a word. I feel much more like I've been soiled, wadded up, and tossed in a corner. My mother says I need to give away my children to have a chance at a normal life. The man I thought would marry me sent me to a...doctor." Catherine's stomach turned at the thought of the type of doctor Bernard had sent her to. She prayed the reverend would understand the unspeakable truth without her having to utter it. "But I couldn't do it. I couldn't go through with it."

A glimmer of admiration shone in the old reverend's eyes. "You made the right decision, Catherine."

"Father says I must marry if I am to stay here. Dr. Palmer has been searching for a husband for me. It has been days, and no one...And then I think of marrying a stranger. I don't think I can do it, and who knows what will happen to the babies?"

Reverend Green leaned in, his voice gentle but firm. "Is that all?"

Catherine sighed, her shoulders slumping under the weight of her burden. "No, not even close. Two Sundays ago, when you spoke, something stirred within me, something I've never felt before. I want to be like the woman who wrote that song. Clara and I talked. I've caused her so much pain. The truth is, Reverend, I haven't always been the best sister. I nearly ruined Clara's future, and I regret that with every ounce of my being. All those foolish things I thought would bring me happiness have only led me to this point of despair. And now that I'm carrying twins with no husband, everyone who lays eyes on me will see the mark of shame that brands me as a terrible person. But I don't want to be that person. I'm always crying and sad. But I don't want to be consumed by sadness anymore."

"Catherine, it seems like you're carrying a heavy burden, a barn full of troubles, if you will."

"Enough to fill all the barns in Texas."

"I don't have all the answers. Perhaps, if we look at only one barn at a time. Know you are not alone. We all have our struggles, flaws, and moments of darkness." His voice trailed off, silence falling between them.

Catherine's eyes welled with tears as she nodded, feeling a mix of relief for finally voicing her deepest fears and a lingering ache of uncertainty. She wiped away a stray tear, her voice barely a whisper. "I don't know which one to start with. They are all so full."

"The first time I met you, the day you came to town—"

Catherine put up her hand to stop him from saying more. "Please don't remind me. I was so desperate and stupid. I wasn't thinking right. I'm so embarrassed."

"If I understand correctly, you were also half starved."

"Dr. Palmer believes that's why I fainted. I was so hungry, even though my sister had the hotel provide me with a small snack. I was about to steal an apple. Thankfully, I never got the chance, or I would have to answer for that sin too."

"Are you still upset about that day?"

"Somewhat. I apologized to Lewis and Clara for everything I said and for demanding Lewis marry me. And they have forgiven me. They even forgave me for pretending to be Clara and tricking Lewis."

"Since they asked you to be a part of their wedding, I believe their forgiveness was real."

"I know it was, but I still feel so … I don't know." Catherine waved her hands, unable to find the words to define the melancholy.

"Like you need more forgiveness?"

"Yes."

"Have you forgiven yourself?"

"What?" How could a person do that? They needed someone else's forgiveness and God's, but that God, according to the minister who preached each Sunday in Brookline, was elusive.

"I am not a doctor, but I have heard that men, and I assume women, who are deprived of food, drink, and sleep act very differently than they normally would. Some even see things that are not there. In the few times I've seen and talked with you since our first meeting, you have been much calmer. Perhaps if you realized you were not yourself that day, at least not completely, it would be easier to have compassion for yourself."

He wasn't saying anything the doctor or her sister hadn't said, but it seemed more believable. Perhaps it was the black shirt. If she hadn't been so hungry and tired, she would have waited for Clara to return. Had she known of Clara's relationship with Lewis, she never would have begged him to marry her. "I think I see what you are saying, but it feels odd to forgive myself. It's like I am making excuses."

"Recognizing that there were outside forces isn't an excuse. It's acknowledging you were weakened. You still made choices, which you have apologized to others for, which is the extent to which you can repair what happened. You have done all you can do. The rest is in God's hands."

"Then why don't I feel peace?"

"In my experience, peace takes time. Very few things in this world are instantaneous. What would you do if you wanted a piece of cake at this very moment?"

"I'd walk into the kitchen and check the pantry. Oh, my. I didn't offer you anything to eat." How could she be a better person if she didn't even remember basic manners?

Reverend Green smiled. "I wasn't asking for food. I'm trying to teach a concept. Say there is no cake. What would you do?"

"I'd go to the bakery." Was there a bakery in Hiramsville? Catherine realized she hadn't heard of one.

"Hmmm. That could work but not to the point I'm trying to make. If I want to eat cake, I need to make it. But if I don't have flour or eggs, I need to acquire those things. And if the store doesn't have flour or eggs, I need to grow the wheat and raise the chickens. Thus, the act of making a cake could take months, or even longer if I don't have a good growing year."

"And if I wanted a chocolate cake, I would have to wait even longer because cocoa doesn't grow here."

"Yes, now you see. Right now you are planting the seeds that will grow the wheat."

"So, I need time." Catherine held in a sigh. Patience was a virtue she lacked.

"And work. And even practice."

"What about this?" Catherine pointed to her womb.

"That too will take time. One thing you need to remember is that how God sees you and how others see you is not the same. We will talk more about that later. Today we have looked into just one of your barns. Watching my wife cook for almost fifty years, I learned to bake just one cake at a time. So tonight's barn is forgiving yourself, at least for those actions Lewis and Clara have forgiven you for."

"That sounds so easy."

"So does making a cake until the hen pecks at your hand for stealing an egg. Every time you start feeling guilt for tricking Lewis when he proposed or for your actions on your first day in town, remind yourself it's in the past. Then you can move on to grinding the flour."

"I see what you mean." Catherine thought for a moment. Then her stomach rumbled. "We have talked so much about cake that I would like some. May I fetch a piece for you? I believe Nellie made some. I'll need to find her and ask." Catherine pushed out of her chair in an increasingly awkward move.

"I never turn down one of Nellie's cakes."

"I'll go see if I can find her." Catherine waddled out of the parlor as fast as she could carry herself. She placed a hand under her girth to stabilize it and, looking down, walked into the kitchen and ran into the closed door. Not a door, a person.

Strong hands steadied her.

"Dr. Palmer. I didn't see you."

"Obviously not."

The unexpected contact bothered her in ways it shouldn't. "I—cake. I mean, eat Nellie. I mean, I'm looking for Nellie to ask her if—" His eyes had little brown flecks in them. She should not be noticing.

"If you may have some cake?" His smile lifted one side of his mustache.

Catherine stepped back. "And for Reverend Green."

"I'll find her and ask. Do you mind if I join you?"

Unable to answer, Catherine nodded. Something was very wrong with her. A new barn with Dr. Palmer's name painted on the side like an elixir advertisement now loomed before her. She needed to stay out of his way before she did something more stupid than she'd ever done.

Aiden waited until Catherine returned to the parlor. He'd lost himself in the conversation and listened far too long. He gathered the three slices of cake he'd already cut and nearly brought in before realizing such an action would give him away. He hadn't intended to eavesdrop. He'd come for an extra razor, assuming Catherine would be in the backyard knitting. Instead, he'd found Lavender and Nellie on the porch. They informed him that Catherine was in the parlor. Aiden retrieved the razor, and as he exited his room, a piece of the conversation caught his attention. He told himself he was only listening to help his patient. Catherine's emotions were important to her health. Aiden didn't understand it, but he saw a clear connection between a patient's mood and recovery. Or in a case like Mrs. Owen's, her survival time. She clung to life with all the tenacity of a dog guarding its master. Catherine was on a different journey. He applauded her willingness to try. He'd only started after finding himself at the bottom of a whisky bottle.

As the private conversation slowed, a twinge of guilt pricked his conscience. He'd sliced the cake as a way to busy himself.

He popped his head through the back door. "Do either of you want cake?"

Nellie held up her empty plate. She must have gotten a few slices while he eavesdropped.

Balancing the three plates, he walked into the parlor and gave Reverend Green and Catherine a plate. Aiden sat down and waited for them to start eating. Catherine hid a giggle behind her hand.

Reverend Green turned his plate clockwise in his hand. "May I bother you for a fork?"

"Of course." Aiden rummaged through the kitchen to find three forks. Someone had reorganized his cupboards and drawers. When he returned, he noticed Catherine eying him curiously. "Is there something on my face?"

Catherine shook her head, her lips curving into a smile. "No, not at all. It's just that you seem … distracted."

She wasn't wrong. "I suppose I was lost in thought for a moment."

Reverend Green cleared his throat. "Is everything all right, Dr. Palmer?"

"Just the usual worries over my patients." A truth.

"And here we are, two of them. It may interest you to know that Thelma's new honey-and-lemon drops are helping my cough. I haven't spoken this long without—" Reverend Green paused to cough into his handkerchief. "Well, I guess that's what comes from bragging."

"Or it's from me serving cake with nothing to drink. Would you like something?" asked Aiden.

"Water would be fine."

"Lavender insists I drink two glasses of milk a day. Would you mind pouring me one, please?" A faint blush appeared on her cheeks as she looked at her plate.

After handing both drinks to their respective owners, he sat back down and the three continued to chat for a while, the conversation drifting from one topic to another, none of them serious. No one brought up his search for a husband. When Reverend Green was ready to leave, Aiden walked him to the door.

The reverend motioned for Aiden to follow him outside. They walked nearly to the street, where they were out of earshot of the open windows. "Thelma's drops are helping, Doc. I'm sleeping sitting up. Is it possible I am getting stronger?"

"Would you like to come to the office so I can listen with my stethoscope?"

The reverend nodded and followed Aiden to the office.

"Do you know where you will live when the Staples return?"

"Clara insists I stay in my room. She went as far as to say either I stay or she would postpone the wedding."

Aiden laughed at the image Clara's ultimatum conjured as he held the back door for the reverend.

"Emily has asked if I'd be willing to stay out at the new Rose's. They are planning on asking Jax to be a security guard. TJ is worried that some men could get the wrong idea about the use of the hotel."

Aiden pulled out his stethoscope and listened to Reverend Green's breathing. "I don't know what Thelma put in those drops, but I am optimistic about their effect."

"One of her secrets, no doubt."

"Next time I'm at Mrs. Reese's, I'll ask. Meanwhile, I want you to come in each week for a quick listen."

In lieu of the hug he wished he could give the man, Aiden extended his hand. "Have a good afternoon."

Reverend Green straightened his shirt. "I have some advice for you too. Take care of that girl. She's trying to figure out too much at once. After meeting her parents—well, you met them too."

"If you are trying to tell me to be kind, I will be." Aiden walked back to his house. How much should he acknowledge about what he'd overheard?

Catherine remained on the couch, clutching her empty plate. "Is everything all right with Reverend Green?"

"As well as can be expected, maybe even better. And what of you?" He sat on the edge of the chair opposite her.

Catherine patted her belly. "We are all as we should be, I assume. Lavender checked on me this morning. Did she say anything was wrong?"

"No, she didn't." Aiden rubbed the back of his neck. "I overheard part of your conversation with the reverend."

Catherine reddened and looked at the hand resting protectively over her abdomen. "I want to feel…" She shook her head. "Not sad. I hoped…" A tear fell. "That everything would change and that Reverend Green could magically make me a good person."

"We talked about this. You are not a bad person. It isn't an either/or situation. I heard from Lavender how harshly your mother spoke to you." And then there was the conversation with her father. Aiden wouldn't disclose that unless he must.

"I'll never be what she wants me to be. I can't. Perhaps it's because of the twins or I have more time to think now. I realize how narrow my mother's life is. I thought I wanted her life. But listening to the women in this house talk, I don't want that life. But I don't know what I want or what I can have. Mother insists I want marriage, but I'm not so sure about that."

"Did she tell you of your father's ultimatum?"

"Yes. I return home with them unless I am married, and you are the matchmaker. I suppose no one wants me."

He paused before answering. Aiden didn't want to explain how deplorable men could be. "There are men who would marry you this very moment. However, they likely wouldn't drive you into town for church. Or worse."

"I'm not expecting much of a marriage in such a situation. I don't have many choices. A miserable life here or a miserable life there. Mother believes it's better I return to Massachusetts and lose the babies on the way. But I'm not ready to die, and I don't want them to die either. So, I only ask that you find a man who won't hate my children."

"Surely you want more than that." Most women wanted love or whatever it was the novels sold. Honestly, he'd once hoped for that too—until he realized it wasn't enough to hope for the right one to come along. He'd had to decide to work to make love come.

"In my present condition, it's the most I dare hope for. I have some money coming from Mr. Fairlane, Bernard's father. It should be enough to sweeten the deal for my husband."

"What do you mean money?"

"I signed a contract, agreeing to stay on this side of the Mississippi. I sent a telegram when I arrived. He's supposed to send me $1,000. Once my child arrives, I am to send a copy of the birth register showing the child with an unknown father, and he will send another thousand. If I am very careful, I can survive on the money for a few years. If I go east or contact the Fairlanes in any way, I forfeit the money."

"Do your parents know of this?"

"Tell my father? You must be joking. He would try to use the contracts against them. Father is a shrewd businessman, meaning he isn't very honest. I think if he matched his wits against Mr. Fairlane's, he would lose. Mr. Fairlane has more money and power."

Two thousand dollars. She could purchase a small house and live comfortably for two or three years or frugally for six or more. A man could purchase a decent spread. If word got out about her contract, Aiden's matchmaking problem would intensify. "Does anyone know about the money?"

"Clara, and maybe Lewis."

"It's best if you keep that quiet."

"I intend to. I thought you should know. I'll pay my bill when it comes."

"You've sent the first wire?"

"Exactly as instructed, to their attorney. I am surprised I've not heard back yet."

"Did they give you any money to come west?"

"Mr. Fairlane had a servant purchase me a second-class ticket and gave me ten dollars for food."

It was unlikely Catherine would see any of the money. *Dishonest* didn't begin to cover the words Aiden had for the Fairlanes. The contract likely had clauses only an attorney could unravel. A greedy husband would be disappointed to learn Catherine's money was never coming. Likely, the Fairlanes had hoped she wouldn't survive the journey. She nearly hadn't.

The back door banged shut. A moment later, Nellie came in. "Doc, you are needed at the office."

Aiden stood. "We can talk later."

Catherine nodded, and he hurried out, not having intended to spend so much time at the house. But learning more about her, he determined to find her a good husband.

⟫◆⟪

The leaves danced in the sunshine as the faintest of breezes rustled the tree. Catherine tipped her head back to watch them and breathed deeply before moving the needle in and out of the fabric in her lap. Ever since Reverend Green's visit, she'd felt happier than she had in months. Today, she was surrounded by friends helping her, something she'd never experienced, even at Bradford College.

The heat of the August day had chased all the women out of the doctor's home and onto the back porch. Catherine moved from knitting to sewing dresses for her babies. Lavender, Peony, Marigold, and Becky joined her in the finishing work. Becky and others had sewn several basic gowns from a length of soft white cotton they'd found in the barrels of goods Lewis's mother sent.

Catherine hemmed one of the little dresses in green. "Ten gowns. I can't believe you made so many."

Peony held up one of the small gowns. "It won't be nearly enough. It seemed there were days that all I did was feed Scotty, change his diaper and gown, then wash his clothes. One day he went through eight gowns."

Lavender threaded a needle with blue. "To be fair, he was ill that day."

"I suppose twins are likely to be ill at the same time. Clara and I were often sick within hours of each other."

"How did your mother manage?" asked Becky.

"She had two nurses helping her when we were little. I don't know if my mother ever changed our clothing. I'm sure she didn't feed us." Until meeting Peony, Catherine had never witnessed a mother feeding a child. Lavender told her that a woman could usually nurse twins—a thought that was rather unsettling as Catherine wondered if she would have time for anything else. At the same time, she wished to be close to her children in ways her mother had never been with Catherine and Clara.

In the distance, the train whistle blew. Saturday. Clara should be on that train with Lewis. And her parents.

Becky popped up from her chair. "Reverend Staples and Clara should be on the train. Should we go greet them?"

Lavender shook her head. "Let them arrive in peace. Clara will be around soon enough."

Less than a quarter hour later, Clara arrived on Lewis's arm, a peace about her Catherine longed to feel.

Her sister and Lewis talked about Galveston, the restaurant, the sand on the beach, and how warm the water was compared to Cape Cod. They were as happy as an ending in any novel.

Clara took Becky's seat next to Catherine. "How are you? I wasn't sure you would be here when I returned."

"Didn't you see Mother and Father? They were supposed to be on your train. They've been in Dallas all week."

Clara looked to Lewis before answering. "No, we didn't."

All her life, even when she and Clara had been at odds, usually Catherine's fault, they'd shared a closeness, knowing how the other felt. Somehow, Lewis, who constantly had a hand on Clara's back, arm, or shoulder, had usurped that closeness. Catherine's sewing slowed as she contemplated the change. There was something right about it. A woman should be closer to her spouse than her sister. It was unlikely she would feel closer to her husband, whomever Dr. Palmer found, for a very long time, if ever. "I wonder where they are."

As if summoned by the thought, her parents walked around the house. Her mother rushed to hug Clara. "There you are. No one answered the door, but we heard voices."

Her father shook Lewis's hand and said something to him Catherine couldn't hear before escorting Lewis away. Catherine exchanged worried glances with Clara. Their connection wasn't entirely gone. They both knew whatever Father had in mind wouldn't be a welcome surprise.

"Oh!" Their mother clapped her hands. "Wait until Lewis sees the new carriage we bought him. It's much more dignified and befitting a man of his position."

Catherine felt her sister shudder.

Clara stood. "Mother, we don't need a new carriage."

"Nonsense. And your father found a perfect set of matched bays."

"No." The color drained from Clara's face. She gathered her skirts and hurried around the house, Mother following.

Marigold clucked her tongue. "Not meaning any offense, Catherine, but your parents aren't thinking right. The manse's stable isn't big enough, and the preacher can't afford to board those animals. Reverend Green only took the horse they had once a week. And if I didn't come by to comb and care for it…"

"Father kept his at the livery at the end of the street. He probably has no idea." It was her only defense. Catherine didn't know a wit about caring for horses.

"That explains why Reverend Staples had so little horse knowledge when he arrived." Marigold shook her head. "I feel bad for city horses."

Lavender tapped Marigold on the knee. "It will all work out. You've taught Reverend Staples so much about horses, and he isn't one to let things go to waste."

Catherine's family didn't return, and the conversation turned to other subjects. As they finished the hemming, Catherine wondered at all the things she needed to learn. She doubted she'd need a horse. That was one more expense off her list.

According to the thermometer tacked to the post of Aiden's clinic, this Sunday was the hottest day this year, and it wasn't even noon. Reverend Green's sermon had been blessedly short. Some of his older patients would have had problems with the heat today, as would the expectant mothers and Jax.

Aiden stopped TJ on the way out of the church. "Can you help me move Jax out of his room?"

"You think you can get him in a kilt a second time?"

"In this heat, I'd gladly wear one." The thought wasn't all bad.

Jax was more than willing. "Any way you can move me down into the caves? They sound blessedly cool right now."

"I wish I could. There aren't that many that are easily accessible. You'll have to make do with my screened porch." Aiden folded the kilt.

"Is Lavender there?"

"Yes, she is."

Jax grabbed for the plaid not yet folded into a kilt. "Then, what are we waiting for?"

TJ and Aiden were sweating heavily by the time they got Jax over to Aiden's house and situated him on the back porch. All the women but Catherine were out there.

Lavender pointed inside. "Her parents were here after church. I asked them to leave. She's lying down."

There was more to that story. Aiden was happy to find his house no warmer than outside. His bedroom, or, rather, Catherine's door was open to facilitate air circulation. He knocked on the door. "It's Dr. Palmer. May I come in?"

He took the mumbled answer as confirmation and entered.

Catherine lay with her back to the door and was dressed in one of the Mother Hubbards. Sobs shook her shoulders.

Aiden rounded the bed until he could see her face. "Are you in pain?"

Catherine nodded.

"Do you mind if I sit?"

No reply.

Aiden sat down in the ladder-back chair and leaned forward, elbows on his knees. Catherine wiped her face with a soggy handkerchief and made a valiant effort to stop crying.

Aiden pulled out his own and handed it to her. She nodded and dabbed at her face.

"How much?"

She shook her head. "Not much."

Aiden waited as she brought her tears under control. Finally, her breathing settled into ragged post-cry breathing.

"Where do you hurt?"

"My back. Lavender says it's normal. I wasn't crying because I am in pain. You don-don't need to worry about me."

"Remember our conversation Wednesday, when I said I worry about your emotions?"

Catherine nodded.

"Do you want to tell me?"

"Father is upset with me." Catherine pushed herself into

a sitting position. "He received a telegram. Mr. Fairlane is suing him because of the Pinkertons. They found something they shouldn't have. I don't understand. I received a telegram too." Catherine handed him a paper.

Contract breached.
No funds.

"Good thing no one was marrying me for the money." She gave a tentative smile that made his stomach clench.

Aiden didn't have the heart to tell her he hadn't found a husband. Reverend Green had vetoed the man living in de Cordova Bend, and no other options had arisen. If her father was this upset, it didn't bode well for talking sense into him. Perhaps Reverend Staples would have an idea now that he was back. "When do your parents leave?"

"Tuesday. Father has to go back to Dallas with Lewis tomorrow to return the carriage and horses. Another reason he's upset. No one refuses one of his gifts, ever." Catherine reached behind her and rubbed her back.

"Why don't you stay down for a while? I'll have the others check on you. I have a couple of patients I want to check on in this heat." Aiden sighed.

"I feel like a nap." Catherine lay down.

Aiden stood to leave.

"Mind you, don't get overheated."

"I'll be careful."

Aiden returned to the back porch. "Lavender, will you make sure someone checks on Catherine every hour or so?"

Lavender nodded. "Did she stop crying?"

Aiden nodded.

Marigold motioned Aiden over and whispered, "Her pa called her names as bad as the ones we get called."

"Do me a favor, Marigold. If Mr. Taylor returns, tell him Catherine is not to be disturbed."

Marigold saluted. "Yes, Doc."

Aiden filled a canteen of water at the office and took his medical bag with him to check on two of his patients who lived alone. He hoped everyone else had enough sense to stay out of the sun and spend the day reading or playing cards. Most Texans knew that extremely hot days were rest days.

His last call was at the manse. Reverend Green sat in his shirt sleeves in the parlor with Reverend Staples and Clara. "Don't worry, Doc, they're keeping me cool and comfortable."

Reverend Staples still wore his vest. "Can we offer you some lemonade? Clara got a chunk of ice from Mrs. Reese."

"Yes, thank you." Aiden sat down in the chair. "I thought your parents might be here, Mrs. Staples."

"Call me Clara, and it's high time you call Lewis by his name. Father isn't happy with us at the moment since we are returning his wedding gift." Clara poured a glass of lemonade from the half-empty pitcher. Ice chips floated in the glass. "I assume they are under the fan at the hotel."

Making Hannah's life miserable. Poor woman. "Do you know anything about a lawsuit?"

Clara and Lewis looked at each other and shrugged.

"Well then, on to the next problem. I have until Tuesday morning to find Catherine a husband, or your father is going to make her get on the train. I don't know how far this heat goes, but it makes me twice as apprehensive for her well-being on a trip back to Brookland."

"Brookline. It's just west of Boston," said Lewis.

"My point is, do you know of any candidates?"

Clara shook her head. "When I first arrived, there were a few men who paid attention to me. One of them married Gardenia. Mr. Collins, of course, and—"

"The last one is a gambler." Lewis's tone made it clear the man was not an option. "I'm assuming Mr. Collins isn't an option."

"No."

Reverend Green leaned forward. "One of the preachers down Houston way lost his wife about a month ago."

Aiden shook his head. "Still a ways to travel. Is there anyone in Acton? It's the next closest town."

Reverend Green shook his head. "I'm assuming church-going is a prerequisite."

"Definitely." Clara's firm answer wouldn't get an argument from anyone.

"There are still a handful of men desperate enough to propose to any woman who comes to Texas, but the numbers are much more even than thirty years ago. There are a couple of young men in the congregation who will make fine husbands, but they need another year or two of growing up. I think Becky is stepping out with one of them," said Reverend Green.

Aiden hadn't even thought of looking at the twenty-year-olds. They seemed too young. "Whoever it is needs to be able to support a wife and children."

"That eliminates most of the cowhands. They may be saving for their own place, but if they had the money, they wouldn't be droving still," said Lewis.

"Any chance my father will leave her in my care?" asked Clara. She shook her head. "Sorry, ignorant question. He won't."

Aiden left, relieved they didn't mention him being the obvious choice. He couldn't be her doctor *and* her husband. If she died in childbirth, he would break. As it was, he'd become much too close to her as his patient.

⋘◆⋙

Pain sliced through Catherine, followed by cramping worse than any monthly. A wetness grew between her legs. Something was wrong. The babies shouldn't come for another six weeks, at the very earliest. Both Lavender and Dr. Palmer agreed on that, though they also said it wasn't uncommon for twins to be born a month early and survive. But this was far too early. They wouldn't live. She would be free. Catherine felt terrible even as the thought entered her mind. Still, her future would be very different if she didn't have to face it as an unwed mother. Another cramp took her, and she cried out as loud as she could. Nellie raced into the room.

"What's wrong?"

"I think the babies are coming."

"It's too soon!" Nellie whirled and ran back out. Catherine was thankful she didn't have to explain to Nellie that she needed help. A moment later, Nellie pushed Lavender into the room and around the bed to a point where she could best reach Catherine from her wheelchair.

Lavender placed her palm on Catherine's bulging abdomen and waited as she calmly looked at her pin watch. When another cramp seized Catherine, Lavender frowned for a moment before resuming a neutral expression. "Nellie, will you please send for the doctor and fetch the oilcloth and towels from the cupboard in the room I'm using? I'll need you to help me, as sitting ..." Lavender waved her hand.

"They are coming, aren't they?" Catherine asked, half hoping she was wrong.

"It appears so. Do you want me to send for your mother or Clara?"

"Not my mother." Catherine couldn't possibly endure another lecture. It was bad enough that all the thoughts in her head saying this was a good thing were in her mother's voice. "And I don't want Clara to see the pain I am in."

"Very well. If you change your mind, let me know."

Another pain came, and either it was not as bad or Catherine was growing used to them. If she had known on that snowy day that this awaited her, she would have told Bernard off. Slapped him if necessary. She relished the thought of causing him pain. He deserved some.

Moments later, a flurry of activity erupted as Nellie and Marigold came into the room. Under Lavender's direction, they rolled Catherine onto her side and placed the oilcloth under her. Nellie fretted about the damp sheets, but Lavender shushed her. The thought that she may have ruined Dr. Palmer's fine mattress flustered Catherine. Another item she would need to purchase with money she didn't have.

The doctor arrived soon after, his face red with exertion. "I came as soon as I could."

"Do you have my favorite stethoscope?" asked Lavender.

Both Dr. Palmer and Lavender examined Catherine, her embarrassment at such an examination evaporating before it was fully formed, pushed out by another pain.

Dr. Palmer said something meant to be reassuring as another contraction squeezed all thought out of her. Then he wheeled Lavender out of the room, leaving her to Nellie and Marigold.

Wait! Come back! The words in her mind wouldn't come out.

The hinges on the kitchen door squeaked as Aiden closed the door behind them. "I heard only one heartbeat. Did I miss something?"

Lavender frowned. "No, I heard only one as well. The baby coming first doesn't have one."

Mr. Taylor might just get his wish and be able to take his daughter home—after a week of rest. "Have you told Catherine?"

"Not my place to, Doctor."

"Any advice to prepare her?"

"From my experience, most women know. Catherine is aware a baby born so early won't survive. As for the live baby, it's not in position to be birthed. We may see yet a miracle."

Aiden tilted his head. "What kind of miracle?"

"I don't know if it has a name. I've only heard about it from some of the doctors at the maternity hospital. Sometimes a woman will deliver a child in a twin birth days or even weeks before the other. The first is almost always a stillbirth. Occasionally, the second lives."

"I've never heard of such a thing."

"I have not witnessed it myself, but several of the doctors I worked with witnessed twins born as much as six weeks apart, in which case the second child often lived."

"What did the doctors do to encourage such a miracle?"

"Complete bed rest. The conditions must be just right, though. The babies cannot be identical. Considering Clara and Catherine are, there is a possibility they will have identical twins. My teachers said there was little correlation, though, to twins birthing twins."

"Catherine said we were not to send for her mother or Clara. Do you think that's advisable?"

"In the case of their mother, definitely. I would not send for her until Catherine begs us to. Mrs. Taylor doesn't promote a calm atmosphere. As for Clara, we best wait. It can be disconcerting to see a stillbirth, especially when one is staring at one's own family."

A yell from the other room reminded Aiden where he should be. He turned Lavender's wheelchair around.

"This would be so much easier if I could stand."

"In your honest opinion, could you, without damaging the healing?"

"I might if I was on a sheepskin. The natural lanolin would protect my feet."

"I have one at the office. I'll go fetch it."

"No, send Nellie. She needs to feel useful, and I rather she not be in the room longer than necessary."

Once they were back in the room, to Aiden's relief, Lavender took charge. She directed Aiden and Marigold to help Catherine into a more comfortable position, closer to the side of the bed. Things moved quickly after that. Nellie returned with the sheepskin and was sent on another errand.

As predicted, the first baby slipped out cold and blue. After washing the baby, Lavender wrapped her in a soft cloth. "Would you like to see her?"

"Can I?" Two syllables—disbelief, uncertainty, and longing coloring the tremors in Catherine's voice.

"Yes, some mothers find it helpful to say goodbye to their little ones."

Aiden looked up from the other bowl where he cleaned his hands. He'd never heard such a thing. Would it have comforted Susannah in her last moments to hold their son? Would he have felt more at peace if he'd been able to see the child clean and cared for?

Catherine stretched out her arms.

"Doctor?" Lavender held out the child to him with all the care one would a living infant.

Aiden took the still babe. He estimated the child weighed no more than a pound and a half. The baby was about a foot long. If the child had lived, he would have written the statistics in his notebook to transfer to a file later. He placed the child in the crook of Catherine's arm.

"You said she was a girl?" Catherine ran her finger around the edge of the blanket, exposing the still, little face.

The word formed a lump below Aiden's Adam's apple. He pushed it out. "Yes."

"Sarah." The name came out as a whisper. "I would have named you Sarah."

Tears streamed down Catherine's face as she inspected a nearly translucent hand. She closed the blanket and kissed it before handing it back to Aiden, then collapsed back against the pillow.

"Lay her in the basket on the dresser, Doctor." Lavender's instructions answered the question he couldn't ask.

Aiden did as he was bidden.

"I need your help."

Once again, Aiden followed Lavender's every instruction, the woman lowering herself into the chair to rest her feet. When the afterbirth came as it should and Catherine's contractions slowed and stopped, Aiden looked at Lavender, trying to read her face. The woman would make an excellent gambler. Her face gave away none of her thoughts.

A rooster crowed. Aiden glanced out the window, surprised to see the first colors of dawn.

Lavender stood and extended her hand. "Stethoscope."

Aiden waited while Lavender listened through the device.

"Is something wrong?" asked Catherine.

Lavender removed the earpieces from her ears. "Doctor, will you confirm my count of 130?"

Aiden found the remaining twin's heartbeat. It took him several seconds to calm his heart enough to count, looking at the pin watch Lavender held for him. 128 … 132 … 136. "I'm afraid I don't agree. I got 136."

Lavender smiled wide and sat back down.

"What?" asked Catherine.

Lavender nodded to Aiden, indicating for him to answer.

"We may be experiencing a miracle." *Miracle* was the only word for it. Aiden didn't have the words to explain what he was seeing.

<hr>

Catherine clutched the sheet to her chest, pulling it tight over her still-swollen belly. "A miracle. I don't deserve one."

Lavender reached out and took Catherine's hand. "No one deserves miracles. God sends them anyway."

"What kind of miracle?" asked Catherine, her focus on the doctor.

"The other baby lives, and you have had no contractions for …" He turned to Lavender.

"Ninety-eight minutes."

"I don't understand." Catherine tried to push herself up.

Dr. Palmer placed a hand on her shoulder. "It means that with rest and care, you may carry the other twin until it is time."

Impossible. Her eye was drawn to the basket on the dresser where her daughter lay. They were telling her the other twin yet lived. How could one twin survive without the other? "Clara. I want Clara."

The doctor looked at Lavender before nodding and leaving the room.

"Not my mother or father."

Lavender let go of her hand. "Don't worry. He won't fetch them."

"How do you know?"

"We discussed what was best for you should the possibility of one twin surviving exist. We are in agreement that if you are to remain calm and restful, Clara will be the bigger help."

Catherine's hand flew to her hair. "I must look a mess."

"May I have Nellie come in and help you get presentable?" Lavender's eyes drooped, and her reassuring smile sagged.

"You must be exhausted. I'm so sorry, and you were standing. Your feet."

"My feet are fine. I haven't stood in so long I think my legs forgot how. I need to do some exercises. It felt good to be really useful."

"You should rest."

"On one condition. If you even think you are suffering the lightest of labor pains, you yell until someone fetches Dr. Palmer or me, even in the middle of the night."

"I will." Catherine glimpsed the basket. "Can we bury her?"

"Some churches allow for stillborn babies to be buried. Others don't. That's a question for the reverends."

"I think ours in Brookline did."

"Shall I have the reverend sent for as well?" Lavender laid a cloth over the top of the basket containing the still baby's body.

"Lewis should come with Clara. If he doesn't, we can send someone for him or Reverend Green."

"I'll send Nellie in." Lavender wheeled herself out of the room.

Nellie appeared with Marigold. "Lavender told us to help you change and brush your hair but under no condition let you sit up for more than a few seconds, and no standing."

She'd been reduced from a chamber pot to a bedpan. Catherine tried not to focus on the indignities of being no more than an invalid. Her eyes wandered again to little Sarah's basket. Had it hurt her baby to die? If the other one lived, what would she tell her about her sister? Still, it seemed impossible that the other could live. Dr. Palmer called it a miracle. Was it? Or was it a punishment? Maybe she wasn't meant to be a mother—a mistake for a mistake.

Clara rushed in, her long hair braided down the center of her back. "What happened? Dr. Palmer only told me to hurry. He kept Lewis over at his office and told me not to alert our parents."

Nellie folded the soiled clothes. "We'll be leaving you two alone."

A moment later, Nellie was back. She picked up the basket with little Sarah. "Lavender told me to … we are going to prepare her—" She rushed out as fast as she came in.

Catherine closed her eyes, not ready to tell her sister but needing to all at once. "One of the babies was born in the middle of the night."

"Just one?"

She nodded. All the tears came then, Catherine grieving for the little girl who would never wear pink dresses or run in the sunshine. Clara climbed onto the bed, wrapped her arms around Catherine, and held her. All doubts about Clara's acceptance of her apologies fled. Clara was here to comfort and share what of the pain she could. What little strength Catherine had drained with the tears. She closed her eyes and found oblivion in a dreamless sleep.

r. Taylor." Aiden fought to keep the exasperation out
of his voice. Sunday had been a blur. He'd gotten little
sleep after spending most of the night delivering Catherine's stillborn child. "I don't think you understand. The
situation was life-threatening; now it is grave. If you force
Catherine to endure the train ride to Boston, either she,
the remaining baby, or both will die. She is in no condition
to travel."

"So you say. But only a few days ago, you claimed that
putting her on a train could bring the children early. She
wasn't on a train yesterday, was she?" Mr. Taylor leaned
forward, the wooden chair creaking in protest. "And now you
claim that only one child is stillborn and the other may yet
live when everyone knows twins are born at the same time."

"Not all the time. There are rare instances. Miracles." Aiden
had hardly believed Lavender himself.

Mr. Taylor pointed to the framed diploma on Aiden's wall.
"I thought that school was reputable."

Aiden ignored the jab and focused on Catherine's needs.
"There are many things science has yet to explain."

"Next, you're going to tell me she saw a crow looking in her window and that's why she lost a baby. Did she see a dove that made her keep the other?" Mr. Taylor's voice rose.

"It wasn't birds."

"Speak up. I didn't hear you."

"I said, it wasn't birds. Mr. Taylor, this is a medical journal I received only a few days ago." Aiden lifted the thick magazine from his desk. "I usually peruse them as soon as they come, but I have been very busy and read it only yesterday after your daughter lost her child. On this page is an article by a British doctor, J. L. Carson, who describes a delayed birth by a mother of twins where they were born forty-four days apart. The first didn't survive; the second did. Both child and mother are doing well. Forty-four days. That is a miracle."

Mr. Taylor grabbed the medical journal. "Probably lies."

"Here in the June *Boston Medical and Surgical Journal*, is an article about Dr. H. P. C. Wilson, who delivered twins three weeks apart. The second was by surgery last May, the surgery witnessed by several other doctors. Perhaps you know one of them?" Aiden didn't add that the mother lived only another four days. "By some miracle, your daughter seems to be in position to deliver the second child safely… if she is well cared for, something that cannot occur in even the nicest of Pullman cars."

"You have an odd definition of *miracle*. Would it not have been better that she lose both children and return to Massachusetts and marry a man who could take care of her? Catherine will never survive out here."

Then why did you send Clara? Aiden pinched his lips together to keep from responding until his thoughts calmed. As far as he knew, Mr. Taylor had been perfectly happy to send both daughters off to Texas without escorts. "Why not allow her to stay until she is delivered? She has Clara and

Reverend Staples to watch over her."

Mr. Taylor sank into the chair. "You aren't a father. You don't understand the fear I felt when Clara wrote to us and we realized Catherine was lost."

"Forgive me. I know only part of the story. I thought you knew your daughter eloped."

"It was quite confusing, but having a daughter marry one of the New York Fairlanes, even if she put the cart before the horse, so to speak, was a coup for our family. It would have opened up doors for our son and I in the shipping industry. Imagine my shock when I confronted Bernard and found he'd left my daughter with a few bills and directions to a doctor. I had to save the family's reputation."

"I would think saving your daughter's life would be of more benefit."

"And what is she going to do here? Be a mother to some brat and live with a bunch of ex—"

Aiden put his hand up. "It is not for me to choose her life. I'm her doctor. Nothing more."

"I told you last week. The only way I leave Catherine here is with a wedding band on her finger. While on the train, I was assured there were plenty of men here in desperate need of wives. But none apparently desperate enough to take Catherine. I thought you could find one for her."

"It's only been a few days. There are men who would take her sight unseen, but she would be in this office with broken bones and bruises from unexplained accidents. Or her child would die under suspicious circumstances. Is that what you want for her?"

"Right now, I want her settled. Here or in Boston, it doesn't matter. I have an acquaintance in Brookline who will take her, assuming there is no evidence of her being with child. The connection isn't good, but at least she won't be my problem anymore. If daughters don't marry to help raise their father's importance, the least they can do is wed and be out of the way. Lewis, at least, did that for me."

Aiden leaned over his desk. "Sir, I have never been so confused in my life. On one hand, you profess to care for your daughters, but on the other, you would sell them off like a cattle drover would twice-branded cattle."

Mr. Taylor didn't even have the decency to sputter. "Daughters are only as good as the people they can connect your family to. What a blow to have Clara married into the clergy. I thought, surely, through Catherine, I was to be connected with New York's elite. Brookline, for all the gingerbread we put on our houses, is not the cream of Boston society."

Aiden sat in shocked silence, unable to comprehend the man's callous disregard for his daughter. How could he suggest she marry simply to prop up family connections? Aiden shook his head sadly. "Mr. Taylor, I cannot help you if you cannot see that your daughter is worth more than a connection or business transaction. There is not a man in the county I would recommend for such a marriage."

"So you have said. But the stories I hear say there are men who would marry any willing woman."

"As I explained the other night, it isn't that simple. Twenty years ago, the ratio of available women was quite different." He didn't explain about Mr. Collins rejecting Catherine due to her condition.

"In other words, they don't want to marry a woman carrying another man's child any more than a man in Boston would."

"You could leave her here, in the care of her sister." They were talking in circles at this point, Aiden helpless to turn the conversation. He poured himself a glass of water and offered another to Mr. Taylor, hoping it would cool the situation.

"Clara watching out for Catherine didn't work out in the past. If it had, we wouldn't be here." Mr. Taylor took a long drink from his glass, watching Aiden over the rim. "What about you? You are a bachelor. Why don't you marry my daughter?"

The water in Aiden's mouth erupted geyser-style all over his desk. "What?"

He smiled. "You heard me. Why don't you marry Catherine?"

"I'm her doctor."

"But you aren't married, are you?" Mr. Taylor sat back and crossed his arms.

All of Aiden's arguments with TJ ran through his mind. "No, but I am significantly older."

"A fact that didn't keep you from calling on Clara, if I remember right."

"Clara was the one who pointed out I was too old."

"You are younger than the widower in Brookline I spoke of. If my daughter's life is in as much danger as you claim, then marry her." The smile grew.

Aiden stared at the man. The thought had crossed Aiden's mind once or twice since his conversation with TJ, but there were too many reasons it was a bad idea. If he lost her, he wouldn't have the strength to not return to drinking, leaving Hiramsville without a doctor. Burying her baby girl had drained him. "It is not an advisable marriage."

"Then I'm taking her home with me, and if she dies, it will be on you."

"No. That would be your decision."

"Really? You are the one with the power to save her. You profess to care about her."

Of course he cared. She was his patient, one with whom he spoke more candidly than most. Could that translate to a harmonious marriage? A question only time could answer. "I will propose on one condition. It will be up to Catherine to accept or not. However, if she refuses me, she stays until I deem it safe for her to travel."

Mr. Taylor smiled like the Cheshire cat. The uncomfortable sense that the man planned on this very outcome filled Aiden with unease.

He waited until Mr. Taylor left to ponder his promise. Could he commit to thirty years of life with a woman he barely knew? Since Cathleen's death, he'd told others that loving a person was largely a choice. Catherine was willing to learn from her past. She possessed courage, intelligence, and wanted to meet her problems head-on, even if her solutions were misguided. And there was that spark of attraction.

Aiden closed his eyes and imagined them years from now. She'd still be pretty. He'd be grayer. Their children would be happy. He would love her.

<hr />

"You what?" Catherine pinched her arm to chase away the hallucination. There must have been something in the tea Nellie served at lunch. Her ears had to be deceiving her; there was no way Dr. Palmer had just proposed, just as it was impossible that he knelt next to her bed, holding her hand. Correction. It was his bed, in his bedroom. Was she losing her mind?

"I asked if you would marry me." Dr. Palmer looked as serious as he did whenever they spoke.

"Why? You know I have little to offer. I'm not even what one would call an upstanding citizen."

Dr. Palmer remained on his knees. "You are in need of a husband, and it seems that as a bachelor, I am the best candidate."

"I don't understand. This is the oddest dream I've ever had."

He dropped her hand and pulled the ladder-back chair closer to the bed and sat, a smile on his face. "You are not dreaming. Have you spoken to your parents?"

"Mother and Father were here this morning. They are quite insistent that I return to Boston. I told them I can't, but they won't relent." Nothing had changed with her parents since Saturday. Since then, she'd lived and died a lifetime.

"What was the condition that you could stay?"

"That I find a husband." There had been no takers as far as she knew. No one wanted an expectant bride. If Dr. Palmer wanted her, he would have asked her a week ago instead of begging who knew who to wed her.

"And I'm offering to marry you."

"So either I marry you or board the train?"

"Not much of a choice, is it? Honestly, I'm not sure what a second delivery so soon could mean for your life. With no midwife or doctor near, it could end gravely."

"So, you are proposing marriage so I don't die?" His job was to save lives. He was proposing so he wouldn't feel guilty for allowing her to go to her grave.

"Admittedly, it is a marriage of convenience."

"Who's? Not yours. Marrying me will not garner you the town's esteem. And then you will be saddled with an outcast wife and a bastard son or daughter."

"Don't use that term. I'll adopt the child and raise it as my own. It will never know it's any different than any of our children."

"Other children? You would continue the charade?"

"Until death do us part."

"I could die before we were married even a month."

"It could happen. I pray it doesn't." His eyes locked with hers.

"I can't do that to you, Doctor. You've already buried a wife and a child. You buried your last bride to be. You buried one of my children. I couldn't stand for you to have to dig another grave."

"I always hire someone." The corner of his mouth quirked up as if he were trying to make light of the situation.

"This isn't very funny. Doctors can't marry their patients to save them. I don't care what oath you took. It isn't done."

"So you'd rather risk the journey to Boston?"

"I'm not risking anything. Father is hardly likely to carry me onto the train. If I refuse to walk, they will have to leave me."

"He could hire someone to carry you."

"Do you think he would?" Even as she asked the question, she realized the answer was obvious. Her father would do what he wanted. There were men enough to hire. "Don't answer that. He would."

"I don't want you to think this proposal is only so I don't break any oaths I made as a doctor. I have wanted to remarry for quite some time; however, my schedule has made it difficult to court. I do get some benefit out of this too."

"You courted Emily and Clara."

"Yes, but I missed a number of planned evenings with both."

"Assuming I say yes, what does a marriage between us look like?"

"For the next several weeks, it will be much the same as now, adding in frequent conversations as we get to know each other. You would live here, and I would live above my office so I can care for Jax's needs. The other women would also live here."

"And after?"

"Assuming you carry the child to term and have a healthy delivery, you will need time to recover. By then, Jax will be up and the abandoned hotel well on its way to becoming the new Rescue, with the first women able to move to the new location."

"You'll have your house back."

Dr. Palmer nodded. "Yes, I can come home."

Home. A very different word than *house.* "And then?"

"We figure out where our family is going forward."

"Family ..." She whispered the word.

"Yes, Catherine, family. You, me, and the baby—a bit unconventional but still a family."

"What if you decide you don't want me?"

"Catherine, over the last two weeks, I've come to know you better than I even knew Cathleen. When you and I stand before Reverend Staples—"

"Not Lewis." He would be there, but she couldn't have him pronounce her nuptials.

"Reverend Green, and make vows, I intend to keep them." There was no mistaking the conviction in Aiden's voice.

If she said yes, it would be until death did they part, and he seemed of the mind to wrestle death to keep her here. "But what if you don't love me or I don't love you?"

"Love is often more a matter of choice than a feeling written about in dime novels. I imagine that at one time, you fancied yourself in love."

Involuntarily, her hand moved to protect the child growing within her. "I thought I could be. Obviously, what I thought was love was something else."

"Catherine, I'm choosing you. I also don't want to force you into anything. I know you are not ready. It will be weeks or months before we can consummate our union. If in those weeks you realize you don't want to be a family, we can get an annulment. With your condition and me not living here, it should be easy enough to convince the judge to invalidate our marriage."

The baby kicked. Catherine rubbed the spot. "What if the baby dies?"

"It won't."

"You can't know that any more than you can know that you won't regret this marriage."

"Not exactly true. If the baby dies, I will mourn with you,

but I won't ever regret proposing to you."

Catherine closed her eyes. The doctor was a good man—far better than she deserved. And if his interactions with Donny were any indication, he would be a good father, better than her own. If both twins had lived, Dr. Palmer would have been able to tell them apart and treat them like individuals. She slowly opened her eyes. "I will marry you."

Dr. Palmer looked at his watch. "Then I must hurry to secure a marriage license. I'm not sure how this will work since you can't be there. I'll speak with Reverend Green, and we can marry in the morning."

He stood and looked at her as an awkward silence filled the room. He cleared his throat. "I'll be back soon."

Catherine remained on her side so she didn't see him exit.

When Lewis proposed to her, they'd kissed. When Bernard told her they would marry in time, they'd kissed and more. Holding her hand while he proposed was the only intimacy Dr. Palmer offered. This certainly was a different start. The other two men were definitely wrong for her. Maybe … Catherine didn't dare complete the thought.

Securing a wedding license required more work than Aiden anticipated. The reluctant clerk agreed to come to the house to get Catherine's signature only after Mr. Taylor bellowed at him. Now they had to wait until tomorrow to be wed. Mr. Taylor grumbled about the wedding delaying his departure, but the clerk refused to budge on the law.

Aiden stopped by Mrs. Reese's home.

"Come in, Doctor. I've been hearing rumors from the girls all afternoon. Is it true? Are you getting married?"

"As you have heard, yes."

"Becky has been doing her best to make your bride a dress. I must ask—Is she not going to stand up for the ceremony?"

"Lavender is looking through my medical books, but we are of the opinion Catherine may be propped on a few pillows."

"So, you will be married in your bedroom with the bride in your bed?" Mrs. Reese laughed good-naturedly. "I'm sure it isn't funny to you, but in a few years…"

"I do see the humor, but I'm not ready to laugh yet. I want to make the day special for Catherine, and I have no idea what to do. It's a marriage of convenience, but I hope it turns into more."

"May I be blunt?"

"I expect you to be." Aiden had come specifically for that reason.

"Spend your wedding night with her."

"I can't. She—" Heat crept up his neck, though as a doctor, he shouldn't be embarrassed.

"Not in the traditional way, of course. Lie beside her. Talk. Hold her hand."

"What about Jax?"

"Have Nellie or one of the girls sleep in your room. If he needs you, she can come get you. Marigold is strong enough to help Jax in an emergency, and you leave him alone often enough."

"Will it be enough?"

"Do you have a ring?"

"I have one I purchased for Cathleen. I don't have time to get another."

"Did Cathleen ever wear it?"

"No."

"Then you purchased it for Catherine and didn't know it."

"I'm afraid she won't be able to wear it anyway. She's swelling with the heat."

"I'll be right back." Mrs. Reese stood and leaned on her cane. She'd been doing that more of late. Aiden made a mental note to watch her more closely.

Mrs. Reese returned with a small wooden box that fit in the palm of her hand. She opened it to reveal a silver-and-pearl brooch. "Mr. Reese gave this to me the night before he left for the Alamo. When our son was born weeks later, I vowed to give it to my daughter-in-law or perhaps a granddaughter one day. Of course, my son didn't live long enough to marry. I've thought of passing it on to Becky, but then Nellie would be jealous, and I have something else for both of them." She handed the box to Aiden. "I've watched you for years now. The years you drank more than you should. The year you fell in love and the day your heart broke. Of all the men in this town, I feel a kinship with, it is you. Like me, you keep your heart inside. Take this and give it to her when you have a private moment. Tell her that a man once gave it to his wife on a beautiful starry night in the face of an uncertain future." Mrs. Reese paused to dab at her eyes. "Tell her that brooch protected the wife from … from … well, from many things, and even though she was hungry, she never sold it."

"You used to wear this. I remember. Why did you stop?"

"A few months ago, I realized I needed to find a new home for it. I didn't want to be buried with it." Mrs. Reese touched the cameo at her neck. "So I purchased this to wear instead. The silhouette faces forward; it won't be that long before I meet him again. I know I'm only sixty-five and you'd say I am healthy, but I'm getting tired."

Aiden shifted in his seat.

"Don't you start doctoring me. I have no intention of going this week or even this year. But when I go, my affairs will be settled and no grave robber will dig me up because someone was featherheaded enough to bury me with my brooch."

"I don't know what to say."

"If your mother raised you with any manners, you'd say thank you."

"Thank you." He tucked the box in his breast pocket.

"Now, be off with you. Becky is in the other room, working on your bride's dress, and it's bad luck for the groom to see it. And you better plan on having that bedroom window of yours open wide so we can all cheer for you. Nellie and Thelma are working together to make a wedding lunch for you."

Aiden paused, his hand on the doorknob. "Together?"

"In my summer kitchen. See? A wedding miracle already."
Mrs. Reese smiled. "That reminds me. I heard that Lavender
stood. I keep meaning to tell you that years ago, I was given
a pair of moccasins by a lovely woman, I forget which tribe.
They were lined with fur, but I imagine sheepskin might be
better for Lavender's."

"I believe it will be some time before she can wear normal
shoes." The new skin was still red and raw.

"The bootmaker should be able to make a pair. Make sure
he uses his softest leather and full sheepskin. Mine laced up
past my ankles. Oh, I miss those."

Aiden would've asked more about the story, but time was
running short. His next stop was TJ's. He needed someone
to stand up with him.

⟞⬦⟝

Clara and Nellie washed Catherine's hair while she
remained lying down. Then, with Marigold's help and Lavender's supervision, they changed the sheets and dressed
her in the fanciest pale-pink wrapper dress she'd ever seen.
Even these simple actions tired Catherine, and she caught
herself yawning.

Clara tied the belt in a bow. "I'm sorry it isn't white. Becky
made it from the dress that had paint dumped on it."

"You mean this is the dress Mother brought you?" Catherine held the sleeve in front of her face.

"Yes. I thought the silk might feel cool on your skin." Clara
sat down on the bed behind Catherine and brushed out her
hair. "When they washed the dress, it turned pink."

"Have you told Mother I'm wearing the dress she meant
for you?"

"No." Clara leaned down so she could whisper. "The under-
things turned pink as well. Becky made you two nightgowns
from the lining. Mother gave me one of the same fabric. It

is very cooling to sleep in."

Catherine didn't have to look to know her sister blushed. Dr. Palmer had already seen Catherine in her nightgown and less. Since theirs was a marriage of convenience, any nightgown was solely for her benefit, not his.

Clara finished and moved aside. "Nellie is a genius with hair."

"I've never done a hairstyle meant to be worn while at rest," said the girl.

"It's called a braid. That's all I need. You shouldn't go through all this fuss," Catherine protested, but it felt heavenly to be clean and dressed in something a bit fancy. She closed her eyes as Nellie combed and twisted her hair, the feeling that she was in a dream having long fled. Yesterday at this time, she was mourning Sarah. Correction. She'd started mourning the loss of a daughter. A wedding was supposed to be the highlight of her life. As a child, she'd imagined what this day would look like. White dress and veil? With Lewis's proposal, she would have had that. The planned elopement with Bernard, though far from her dream of being admired, brought a measure of excitement, probably because it was so forbidden. Lying in a bed and taking her vows with a man she barely knew? There were no words for it. Should she say no when Reverend Green asked if she was willing to marry Dr. Palmer? It wasn't right to force him to wed a woman he didn't know.

She was selfish. After losing Sarah yesterday, she knew she'd never have arrived in Boston safely. Catherine didn't want to die. Was it so wrong to take his offer?

"Finished." Nellie slid off the bed and came around with a hand mirror. "What do you think?"

It was more than a braid; it was a masterpiece. Nellie even wove a few little flowers into the hairdo. "It's perfect."

The town-hall clock struck ten.

"Just in time. I told everyone ten." Clara kissed Catherine on the cheek.

The women gathered their things.

Nellie opened the window. Mrs. Reese, Emily, and several of the women stood in the yard. "We'll go outside and watch."

The window. Catherine hadn't thought there would be an audience beyond those in the room.

Lavender made her way slowly around the bed, pain marking her face with each step.

"Lavender, I'd like you to stay here. There will be room. You can sit on the bed behind me."

"Are you sure?"

"Yes." In the last several days, she'd come to trust this woman she'd initially dismissed. Lavender couldn't possibly see from the window. In a perfect world, this new friend should marry the doctor. They were perfect for each other. Instead, Dr. Palmer was doing what he couldn't with all the medicine in the world. Although Clara was officially standing up for her, Catherine wanted this new friend with her as well. Lavender had a strength Catherine wished she could borrow.

# 21

Lavender arranged herself, and Clara joined her. Reverend Green, TJ, Lewis, and her parents came in and found places around the bed. Finally, Dr. Palmer entered. There wasn't any music or a march, yet it was obvious the groom's entering last was a deliberate choice. He circled the bed and took the chair he'd sat in after proposing yesterday. Now, as he sat in it, his gaze met Catherine's. He'd shaved and trimmed his mustache. His blue silk tie had been tied to perfection. Often his ties hung limply. He lifted Catherine's hands in his.

As Reverend Green spoke, Catherine tried to focus on his words but was distracted by Dr. Palmer's eyes, which looked deeply into her own. The reverend called him Aiden. She'd heard the name before. Could she use it now? It fit him. Aiden. He was always aiding others.

He slipped a ring on her finger, then leaned over and brushed a kiss across her lips. The angle was awkward, and they barely touched, but it was enough that the people gathered outside the window cheered.

"Well, that's done." Father slapped Dr. Palmer on the back. "Welcome to the family."

Clara hugged her from behind and whispered, "Congratulations."

As TJ said his congratulations, Catherine realized Aiden had not let go of her hand. It was a kind gesture since she couldn't see those behind her. Mother was all teared up and saying something from near the foot of her bed. Catherine would have looked over her shoulder, but Lavender had a hand on her back, reminding her how important it was that she didn't move too much.

Lewis joined Clara. He patted Catherine's shoulder. "Congratulations, sister."

After a minute, Aiden cleared his throat to get everyone's attention. "If you all wouldn't mind clearing the room. It's important that Catherine not be overwhelmed. You may come visit, one at a time, later."

Father harrumphed as he passed. He hadn't actually said anything to her all morning, but Catherine didn't mind. Soon, only she, Aiden, and Lavender were left.

"Nellie is getting my chair. I'll be out of here in a moment."

Aiden bent closer and brushed a strand of hair out of Catherine's face. "How are you feeling?"

"I'm not sure." The gold band on her finger caught her eye. "Married, I guess."

He raised his eyes to Lavender, still sitting behind her on the bed.

"No contractions, and her breathing is back to normal now that the room is cleared."

Catherine should have known he was only concerned about her physical health.

She heard the chair bump into the doorjamb behind her. Lavender touched her shoulder. "Congratulations."

Then they were alone, as alone as a couple could be with

all their friends still outside their bedroom window.

Aiden glanced over his shoulder. "Looks like a regular shivaree."

"A what?"

"A shivaree is a tradition in some parts of the country where people stand outside the bride and groom's house and make noise, pull pranks, and sometimes even kidnap the bride—basically trying to interrupt the newlyweds. I haven't witnessed one for years."

"Well, this isn't exactly a normal wedding."

"No, I suppose not." Aiden smiled. "Just last week I mentioned that your sister's wedding was the oddest I've ever seen. This may have outdone it."

"One of my faults is that I try to outshine Clara." Catherine smiled so he knew she was teasing in part.

He laughed again and brought her hand to his lips. "To unusual beginnings."

"It may be a tradition. My great-great aunt … Is that right? … my grandmother's oldest sister …"

"That would be your grandaunt."

"She was asleep when she got married. Her husband held her in his arms on the front porch of the cabin while they took their vows as she'd been very ill. My grandmother said her sister moaned at the appropriate time, and the preacher accepted it as a positive answer. My grandmother was only four at the time, so the story may not be true at all."

"It sounds interesting, though. I know a groom shouldn't leave his bride; however, I would like to escort your parents to the train. I'll have them wave through the window."

"You aren't giving them a chance to speak to me?"

"I believe they've said quite enough." The corner of his mouth turned up, ducking below his mustache.

Catherine tried to convey her appreciation through her smile. "Thank you."

"Would you like Clara to come in and bring you some cake? Rumor has it Nellie and Thelma worked together on our lunch and without a single argument."

"A celebration indeed, then."

"If you feel too tired or anything, you'll let Lavender know?"

"Of course."

Aiden stood, then leaned over and brushed a kiss on her forehead. "I'll be back later."

He released her hand, and, for a moment, she was alone in the room. And for the first time in a while, she felt lonely. Could simply saying "I do" change her relationship with a man?

—◆—

Lewis also accompanied the Taylors to the train, which, considering the number of trunks they had, was helpful to the stationmaster. Aiden sighed with relief when the train's wheels started to turn.

"My feelings exactly. Growing up next to them, I didn't know Mr. Taylor that well. I saw Mrs. Taylor more often. I never realized how—" Lewis paused, searching for a word.

"Odious."

"Not the word I was looking for, but it fits. I understand now why the twins and their brother spent so much time at our home when we were young."

"Your parents aren't like them?"

"My father is to an extent. My mother was one of those mothers who spent time with us. She read books. I rarely saw our governess unless my parents were out. Clara and Catherine's parents often couldn't tell them apart if they switched hairbows. Mrs. Taylor would parade the girls out during her afternoon tea so everyone could say how darling they were, and because they'd switched bows, she'd call the girls by the wrong name. They aren't that hard to tell apart usually." Lewis shook his head. "Says the man who proposed to the wrong twin. In my defense, I was nervous, and Catherine was trying to trick me."

"I'm almost glad our wives won't have to see their parents often."

"I would like to see my mother. You can bet if we go back East, we are staying at my house."

Aiden nodded. After meeting Catherine's parents, he better understood why she had made choices she wasn't happy with. He may have made worse ones under similar circumstances. "What did you do with that buggy?"

"We returned it. Apparently, Mr. Taylor was trying to pave the way for me to have a career at a Dallas bank. He doesn't understand how I can be happy without more money. Instead, they gave Clara a set of the ugliest China I've ever seen. Two pieces are missing, and the plates are chipped."

"Sounds like they got it from one of those secondhand stores where newcomers try to sell their belongings." Lewis walked down the stairs to the street. "That's what Clara said. What did they get Catherine?"

"Nothing that I'm aware of. Mr. Taylor told me she'd cost him too much in the past few months and my gift was not being saddled with the debt."

Lewis gave a low whistle.

"Is it terrible that I want to censor all of Catherine's mail from them?"

"I've had the same thoughts about Clara's. However, I think it's better if I hold my wife while she reads it."

"I pray Catherine and I can get to that point before a letter arrives."

"You intend to make a go of this marriage?"

"I didn't lie when I made my vows. I've learned enough that I believe I can love her. Not saying it will be easy. We have an age gap. I was fighting a war when she was learning to read. She isn't ready to trust me other than as her doctor. I'm working on transitioning that to friends."

"And I thought the four years between Clara and I were an obstacle." As they reached the square, Lewis turned and motioned for Aiden to follow. "Our girls loved their maternal grandparents. There is a tradition handed down from somewhere. If I have this right, their grandmother's oldest sister's father-in-law started it on his wedding night. Clara had to draw me a chart. Anyway, he brushed out his wife's hair every night. Our girls' grandfather followed that same tradition, only, since he was a doctor, he sometimes ended up brushing out their grandmother's hair at odd times. Once, he came home at midday to brush out her hair and then returned to the hospital, where he had a critical issue. Anyway, according to Clara, her parents didn't keep the tradition, but she wanted to." Lewis entered the mercantile and went over to the display of hairbrushes. Like most items in Mr. Tarr's store, there were only two choices. Lewis picked up the better of the two brushes. "It isn't beautiful or silver handled, but it will do."

Aiden followed Lewis to the counter. "I think Emily and TJ have a similar tradition. She has a silver brush that belonged to her great-grandmother. He had it rebristled after they were married."

"Clara mentioned that she and Emily were oddly related, not exactly cousins." Lewis shook his head. "I'm not enough of a genealogist to figure it out."

Mrs. Farr came and handled Lewis's purchase. "I hear congratulations are in order, Doctor."

"Thank you."

As they left the store, Lewis handed the brush to Aiden. "It's not much of a wedding gift."

Aiden turned the brush over. "Actually, it may be just the gift I need."

They headed to Aiden's house.

"Do you think they left us any food?" asked Lewis.

"I hope so."

As they rounded the last corner, they ran into Donny, who looked as if he'd been crying. "Doc, Ma says you need to come. It's time."

"Would you like me to come too?" asked Lewis.

"No offense, Reverend, but Ma is used to Reverend Green."

"I understand. I think he's over at Doc's house."

The boy nodded. "He is. Marigold went to hitch up the buggy."

Aiden put a hand on the boy's shoulder. "Give me a moment to tell my wife where I'm going."

"It's true? You done got married?"

Aiden nodded. "I'll meet you and Reverend Green in front in just a moment."

Running up the front steps and opening the door to his house without knocking felt odd. He'd been knocking since the women moved in. Nellie and Clara were in the room with Catherine. Realizing he still held the brush Aiden had given him, he slipped it into the bureau drawer, then rounded the bed and sat on the chair he was married in.

Catherine smiled softly at him.

"I know I said I'd be back. I hoped it would be for longer, but I have a dying patient." He rubbed the back of her hand.

"I know. I heard Donny looking for you. Go. You are needed, and I have more than enough people to watch over me."

"I made a basket for the children," said Nellie. "Emily and TJ went home to make room for them. Peony and Scotty are moving back in with Mrs. Reese. Oh, and I put away some food for you."

"Take care of my wife."

"We will."

Aiden squeezed Catherine's hand and left. It seemed oddly appropriate that his wedding day included a deathbed. Perhaps it was a good omen that the marriage wouldn't.

The stars twinkled through the open window. The house was quiet. Everyone had gone to bed some time ago. Catherine couldn't sleep, a result of lying in bed all day. She ran her finger around where, for a few hours, she'd worn a wedding band. Lavender had removed it, fearing that if her fingers swelled like her ankles, it would have to be cut off.

She was married. Aiden said it would be a marriage of convenience and not much would change in their relationship for a while. Still, she hoped to talk to him more.

The back door shut, and she heard soft footfalls in the kitchen. Someone must have run to the privy. If only she could. The indignity of the bedpan was almost more than she could bear. Not that the women who helped her commented. Sometimes they even came to check on her in the middle of the night. The footfalls neared her room.

"I'm all right. I don't need the pan."

"Good to know. I'm not sure you want me helping you with that."

"Aiden?" She tried to turn over, but a firm hand on her shoulder prevented her.

"Slowly."

"It's late. What are you doing here?"

"It felt wrong to not at least talk to you tonight. Do you mind?"

"No."

Behind her, a drawer opened and closed. Instead of coming around to his chair, Aiden climbed into the bed behind her. What did this mean? He'd said they wouldn't for weeks yet.

His hand brushed over her shoulder. "Lewis gave me a wedding gift today and told me a story about a tradition. May I brush your hair?"

Catherine opened her mouth to tell him Nellie already had, then, instead, said yes.

He found the end of the braid, worked the tie off, and slowly unwound the braid. When he ran his fingers through her hair to completely release it, a shiver ran down her back.

"Are you all right?"

Catherine bit her lip. "Umm-hmm."

His touch with the brush was light. "I heard I'm supposed to count one hundred strokes, but I don't think I can count and talk. Do you mind if I estimate?"

"I'm sure it will be all right. I never count."

He brushed the length of a section twice, his fingers grazing her ear. She tried not to react to the sensations she felt. "Did Mrs. Owen pass?"

"Yes. The children didn't want to leave the house, so TJ and Emily went out to them. The funeral will be tomorrow."

"Are TJ and Emily taking the children permanently?"

His brushing slowed. "We have to figure that out. Mrs. Owen never heard from Mr. Owen's family—not that she expected to."

"You'd planned on taking them, didn't you?"

"I wanted to, but I also know that my schedule makes me a better uncle than a father. Emily says she's doing well enough, and the children are well behaved—"

"But you want to raise them."

"I always promised Donny I'd send him to college." There was longing in his voice.

"And to complicate matters, you don't have a home at the moment."

"My living conditions complicate things." His brushing stopped for a moment. "But TJ and Emily are the better choice."

She needed to see him. "I'm going to roll over slowly, like Lavender taught me."

Aiden moved back a few inches. Catherine moved onto her back and found his face in the dim light.

She reached for his cheek and found it damp with tears. She dropped her hand to his shirt and pulled him toward her until she could wrap her arms around him in an awkward hug. He was always there for everyone. He needed someone there for him. Sadness was something she understood. She released her arms. "This is awkward. Is there a better position where I can—" Hold, comfort, hug? Each word felt awkward to say.

"May I lie next to you?"

"I'll need to roll back on my side. Lavender says it's best not to be on my back for too long."

Aiden helped her turn back onto her right side and ended up behind her, where he held her, not the other way around.

"I thought I was meant to hold you."

"This works for me too. You are holding my hand."

He was still crying. Did he not want her to see? Catherine ran her thumb over his hand, wishing she could give more comfort. He rested his head behind hers. Although she'd spent several days with Bernard in Niagara Falls, the hotel room had two beds, just as Catherine's parents had separate bedrooms. He'd told her most people only shared beds when they were passionate. Once he'd finished with her, he'd gone to the smaller one alone. And she was never to come to him—a lesson she learned with a backhand to her jaw. He never just held her as Aiden did now.

Catherine whispered. "You can talk, if it will help?"

Aiden ran his fingers through her hair. "Mrs. Owen had cancer. There was never anything I could do, even if I'd known earlier. Her husband died in the posse that went after Cole Pike's gang years ago."

"The gang that killed Cathleen?"

He nodded into her back. She waited until he spoke again.

"I tried to propose to her, but she stopped me cold, told me the only reason to marry a second time was for love, not pity." Aiden took a deep breath. "She made soaps and creams. I bought them whenever I could to support her. She taught her craft to the rescued women. When Rose's burned down, two cases burned with it. I could smell the lavender."

"She sounds like a remarkable woman."

"TJ and I talked. We want her children to remember her. There is so little she had to pass on—wedding rings, a photograph…"

"Did she have nice hair?"

"Yes, why?"

"I could make some hairwork brooches or bracelets for the girls and a watch fob for Donny."

"I've heard of such things. I thought they were expensive."

"When supplemented with gold or silver, yes. Otherwise, no. When we were fifteen or so, I became quite proficient. It was all the rage among the girls in our circle."

"You would do that for them?"

"I have ample amounts of free time as a certain doctor told me I must stay in this bed for forty days and forty nights or longer."

"Sounds like a mean doctor." Aiden's voice carried a smile. He turned her hand over in his and caressed it.

"Clara should be able to help me make a braiding wheel I can use. I just need Mrs. Owen's hair."

"How much?"

"As much as you can get. The undertaker can cut it just before he shuts the casket."

"I'll ask him first thing in the morning." Aiden's voice sounded softer and more relaxed. He ran his fingers through her hair again. Then the mattress shifted as he sat up. "I should braid this before I fall asleep."

He resumed brushing. Every few strokes, his fingers made contact with her ear, neck, or back. The bed shifted again. "Do you mind if I stay here for a while?"

Catherine stared out the window at the stars, her mind racing. She couldn't deny him his request. He was her husband, yet it served no purpose for him to be here. "Stay as long as you wish."

His shoes thumped softly on the floor, and she heard the rustle of fabric. "Don't be alarmed. I'm only removing my vest and coat. I know they check on you during the night."

A dozen questions she dared not ask ran through her head, most starting with "Why?"

He yawned. "I was going to tell you…it will have to wait."

Aiden's hand caressed her shoulder. Still wanting to give him comfort, Catherine reached over to cover his hand with hers. Their fingers entwined. His breathing became deeper, Catherine matching hers to his.

⊰·◊·⊱

Aiden awoke in the room above his office before the sun crested the horizon. He threw off the sheet and stepped onto the wood floor. He felt rested despite coming to bed late last night after brushing Catherine's hair and talking late into the night, as had become their pattern since the wedding. He opened the curtains and let the golden morning light spill into the room. White, puffy clouds dotted the horizon, signaling hope for a cooler day at the end of August. He quickly shaved and dressed before crossing the hallway to Jax's room.

Jax looked up from the worn Bible he read. Having both arms free of braces provided Jax with comparably vast mobility. "What do you think, Doc? Another scorcher?"

"I hope not, but we should get you downstairs anyway, give you another chance at those crutches." Aiden had asked a carpenter to construct a pair with an alteration that provided Jax's right elbow with the support of a leather strap, making sure no force was put on his recovering hand. Last night, Jax did his best to wear out the floor of Aiden's office as he thumped back and forth.

"Mind if I go over to your house later?"

"Ready to show off your newfound freedom?"

"It's only fair. Lavender's been walking around in those moccasins since the day after you got hitched. It's about time we see eye to eye again."

"After breakfast. I don't want any of them upset because they aren't decent."

"You go over early enough."

"One, I know how to sneak in without disturbing anyone." He used the front door and went directly from the parlor to Catherine's bedroom. "Two, I am checking on my patient."

"You mean your wife."

"That too."

"Which has you smiling more each day. I think the real reason you put this new cast on and put me on crutches is so you can spend more time with her."

"I gave you a new cast because it was time, and that second break isn't healed to my satisfaction. Five weeks is the shortest amount of time I give a simple fracture." Aiden pointed to the cast that covered the lower half of Jax's left leg. "That was anything but simple."

Jax dressed in a pair of pants with a half leg Becky modified as a replacement for the kilt. Aiden helped Jax to the main floor before hurrying off to see his next patient.

He stopped to pick a daisy from his yard before entering his home. A pan clanged in the kitchen, indicating that Nellie was already up and cooking. Likely, the other women were waking too. Aiden slipped into his bedroom.

Catherine turned her head and gave him a lazy smile.

Aiden walked around so she could see him easier and handed her the flower. "How did you sleep?"

"Well, until he started kicking."

"He?" He sat down next to her.

Catherine dropped the flower on her pillow and grabbed Aiden's hand, guiding it to her abdomen, where she laid his hand flat and kept hers over it. As her doctor, Aiden had felt the baby move, but this was the first time he had at Catherine's invitation or insistence. "That better be a boy kicking that hard."

They sat like that until the kicking subsided. Aiden removed his hand. "Boy or girl, he was enjoying a stretch."

"I wonder if he was looking for his sister." Catherine bit her lip and kept her eyes lowered.

"Do you think of her often?"

"Daily. Reverend Green has been by and tells me it isn't my fault and it isn't a punishment."

"It isn't."

"But when I realized what was happening, I was almost happy for a moment. Now I feel so guilty."

If only he had the wisdom of the preacher. Aiden brushed a hair out of her face. "As often as your mother told you she wished the babies gone, it's only natural you had that thought. I don't know why you lost her. There are so many things about birth doctors still don't know. I'm sure you shouldn't feel guilt."

"It's so easy to say that. It might not be so bad if I had something else to do. The hair jewelry will go much too fast I fear."

"I'm afraid I can't give you much more than the books you've been devouring."

"I think I could write my own dime novel, I've read so many."

"Then I'll get you some paper."

"I have some. But I don't picture myself as the next Louisa May Alcott, so I don't think I'll write much anyway."

"Maybe this will distract you for a moment." Aiden pulled the little box Mrs. Reese gave him out of his pocket. "Happy anniversary."

Her nose scrunched. "Anniversary?"

"We've been married for a week."

Catherine pulled a second pillow under her head before taking the box. She removed the lid and gasped, then lightly ran her fingers over the brooch. "Aiden, it's—" She blinked rapidly. "You shouldn't have."

Aiden took out the pearl-and-silver brooch and pinned it below the collar of her nightgown. "It was Mrs. Reese's. Her husband gave it to her the night before he left for the Alamo."

Catherine grabbed the brooch and tried to unpin it. "I can't take this. It's special to her. She hardly knows me."

Aiden stilled Catherine's hands and removed them from the brooch. "She knows me. She gave it to me last week when I told her I wanted to do something special for you since our marriage was not conventional."

He bent down and lightly kissed her forehead, as he did each morning, holding the contact longer than usual this time. Unlike a week ago, she didn't stiffen or seem surprised by the action. Wanting to prolong the moment, Aiden rested his forehead on hers.

"Thank you." Her soft words fluttered between them, her breath mingling with his. She returned his kiss with one on his cheek.

He froze. It was the first time she'd kissed him. Slowly, he sat back, trying to determine if she had kissed him only out of gratitude or if she meant more by the action. The hint of pink in her cheeks provided a little clue.

Her eyes didn't meet his as she looked down at the brooch again, tracing the details with her fingertips. "This is beautiful."

"I thought you might like to wear it since you mentioned last night you didn't feel married without a ring on your finger." The gold band he gave her last week sat on the bureau. Her fingers swelled with the heat of the day, making it too uncomfortable to wear the ring. "Mrs. Reese told me to tell you that a long time ago, a man gave this brooch to his wife on a beautiful starry night when the future was uncertain. That brooch protected the wife from many things. I hope the same for you."

Catherine's eyes met Aiden's. "I like that you gave it to me at the beginning of the day instead of at the end, like Mr. Reese did with his wife."

"Me too."

A clatter in the kitchen drew their attention.

Catherine's nose scrunched. "I have to wonder if that was deliberate. Nellie drops a pan almost every morning, then Lavender gets up."

"Almost as good as a rooster."

"Do you have a busy day?"

"No more than usual. And you?"

"I'm going to eat, lie on my side, and visit with Reverend Green or whomever else is unfortunate enough to come by."

"I gave Jax a set of crutches last night. He should be around today."

Catherine pulled up her sheet. "Not now, I hope."

"You know as well as I do that he'll be dogging Lavender's heels all day."

"Doesn't give up, does he?"

"Rangers are known for not giving up until they get their man, or, in this case, their woman."

Catherine pursed her lips and shook her head. "He doesn't have a chance."

Aiden smiled back. His wife should never underestimate a determined man. Last week, he told her love was a choice, and already she was showing signs of becoming his.

The long shadows merged as dusk fell. A deep sigh escaped Catherine. Soon, Lavender would be in to add another tick mark to the slate where they tracked how many days she'd made it without going into labor. Some woman in England had completed a forty-four-day interval before birthing her second, live twin. Lavender was determined that Catherine make it just as long, especially because she was in Texas now. As Nellie and Becky demonstrated daily, there was a certain amount of pride that went into being a Texan and doing things bigger and better than everyone else in the world.

Tomorrow marked the halfway point.

Twenty-two days since Sarah had been born. The dull sadness that accompanied thinking about her child washed over Catherine. She closed her eyes, hoping not to cry. Aiden always asked about her tears if he saw them, and he would soon come to brush her hair and talk about his day. She wouldn't lie to him about her tears, so it was best that he not know they existed. Reverend Green said that time was the best thing for grief like hers.

She thought instead of what she could tell Aiden. *Three birds came to the tree outside the window today. None sang. Nellie invented a new pudding recipe. It wasn't very good.* He would have already heard about the progress on the new Rescue and the plan to hire Jax as a guard and Reverend Green as a chaperone of sorts. The building was far enough out of town that there was concern about the safety of those taking refuge there. Last Friday, Marigold had fired a warning shot at some guy skulking about. Aiden would already know about that too.

"Good evening, Catherine." Lavender walked into the room and set a lantern on the bedside table. "Dr. Palmer is going to be late tonight."

"When did you find that out?" Catherine hadn't heard anything.

"You were sleeping. He checked on you."

"Oh." She didn't remember sleeping, but then there was little else to do. Clara had to finish the hair brooches as lying on her side made it difficult to weave or sew. Knitting was impossible. Reading became tedious after a while, as lying on her side made it difficult to turn the pages.

Lavender started rubbing Catherine's feet. "They aren't as swollen today."

"I tried to move them like you told me to."

"It feels like you've been here for a hundred years, I bet."

"A hundred and one. Are you moving out to the new Rescue at the end of the week?"

"No, Nellie and I are staying here until your baby comes."

Same as what she'd heard from Clara, but she needed to hear it from Lavender. Catherine had grown to like the woman immensely. However, over the last several days, Lavender had spoken more and more of Aiden, and his nightly conversations had been peppered with Lavender's name.

"Emily said she saw you today at Dr. Palmer's office."

"Aiden is encouraging me to see patients as his nurse."

Catherine sucked in a breath when Lavender's thumb dug into the center of her foot. It wasn't as painful as the recognition that Lavender had used Aiden's Christian name.

"Sorry about that. Today was my first day, or half day. I only saw patients like Emily, and Reverend Green, who really didn't need me to listen to his lungs—the ones who won't be rude because I'm part of Rose's buds."

Catherine had heard the derogatory name for the women at The Rescue. "You shouldn't call yourself that."

Lavender started on the other foot. "We were talking after Reverend Staple's sermon last night. We know people meant to use it to shame us, but think about a bud on a tree or a flower in spring. Or on a rose bush." Lavender's face took on a soft, wistful look. "A bud promises new life, a new creation. And when they bloom, buds become something beautiful. Have you ever seen an ugly flower?"

"No." Catherine's answer came out as several notes because Lavender found a particularly painful spot.

"Me either." Lavender moved to massage Clara's hand. "We decided we liked the imagery that we were growing into something new and beautiful. Just because some anonymous old biddy came up with the term first and put it in the newspaper doesn't mean we can't change the meaning."

"So you all are taking back the name?"

"Not publicly, of course. Since most of us changed our names to flower names after coming here, we do like it."

"Why did you choose Lavender?"

"I chose Lavender because it started with *L*. Aiden pointed out my name was rather fortuitous, as lavender has all sorts of medicinal uses, just like me."

Again with the Christian name. Aiden was *her* husband, even if he had more in common with Lavender. When the two of them spoke, they understood each other in a way

Catherine didn't. All those terms. *Metacarpal. Pancreas. Artery.*

Did her husband regret marrying her so quickly? Catherine knew well the emotion she was feeling: jealousy. This time it might be warranted.

The front door opened, the sound of Aiden's shoes echoing in the hall. Lavender switched to Catherine's other hand.

"Evening, ladies."

"You're back earlier than you planned." Lavender didn't stop working on Catherine's hand and arm.

"TJ and I decided to let Donny sleep at his old home if he wants to. It's being sold in the morning to cover the mortgage."

"Is he still distraught?" asked Lavender.

"Yes. TJ is sleeping on the porch to keep an eye on him."

Catherine put the pieces together. Aiden hadn't been out on a call. She knew from others that Donny was having a difficult time accepting his mother's death, feeling like he hadn't done enough. Aiden likewise carried a burden because he couldn't do all he wanted to do to help the Owen children. "Do you need to be there?"

"No, this is my time with you, although I'm a bit early. I'll let Lavender finish while I see if there's anything to eat." He set something down and left.

Another tick in his schedule book, Mrs. Smith, at 10:00 a.m. Mr. Jones at one. Wife half hour after dusk. No appointments should last more than an hour. Catherine pinched her lips. She was being petulant, and she knew it. But Lavender started it, calling Dr. Palmer by his given name.

"Ready for your three minutes?"

Catherine nodded. The highlight of the day was being allowed to use a chamber pot and change her nightgown. She should be grateful Lavender advocated for her to do that much. She should be grateful she was alive instead of dead in some unknown town or in the girls' home in Stoughton. The clean nightgown felt soft against her skin and smelled of lavender. Of course. Probably Aiden's favorite scent.

Catherine came out from behind the screen.

"I changed your sheet. It looks like you spilled a bit of breakfast and dinner today."

Tying a napkin around her neck didn't work well for eating in bed. It could have been worse. The stains could have come from the bedpan, like last week.

Lavender helped Catherine back into bed. "I'll tell Aiden you're ready."

Just like any other appointment. What did Catherine expect? Aiden had been clear about this being a marriage of convenience, and his insistence that love was a choice didn't ring true. She'd read novel after novel. Elizabeth didn't decide to love Mr. Darcy. Louisa May Alcott could have saved readers' frustration if Jo had chosen to love Laurie. Jane Eyre certainly wouldn't have fallen for a married man. Lewis and Clara. TJ and Emily. Reverend Green and his late wife. None of them spoke of making a choice. It had just happened. Aiden came each night to make love happen. But it wasn't working. Even if he couldn't see it, Lavender was the better match for him.

What happened with Bernard wasn't love. No, lust wasn't love. Although from the looks her sister gave Lewis, it made her think that at least some of what she felt with Bernard was present in a marriage that included love.

She felt gratitude and even a close friendship with Aiden, but nothing more, even after almost three weeks of telling herself she should love him. He was handsome enough. But the daily kiss on her forehead felt more brotherly than anything. Friendship, gratitude, brotherly love. Could they build a lifetime together, or would she always be his after-dusk appointment?

Aiden came into the room and lowered the light of the lamp before picking up the hairbrush. In an hour, he'd be gone.

⟞◆⟝

Twenty-seven. He counted the strokes tonight as neither he nor Catherine spoke. "What's bothering you?"

"Nothing."

His wife wasn't telling him the truth. Lavender hadn't indicated that Catherine had contractions or difficulty. He'd brought her a new book, *The Lady of the Aroostook*, but she'd shown no interest in reading. According to Nellie, she hadn't read for several days. Lying in bed and staring out a window could lead to all sorts of melancholy.

Thirty-four.

"You should have stayed with Donny."

"Why?" *Thirty-eight.*

He brushed three strokes before she answered. "Because you're worried about him."

"I am. However, this is something Donny and TJ need to work out if he's going to live with the Morgans."

"What do you mean, if?"

"TJ and I are giving the children a choice—TJ or me."

"When was this decided?" She answered quicker this time.

"Saturday night?"

"Two days ago?" Catherine's voice carried a firmness she hadn't had of late.

"Yes."

"Oh."

Fifty-two. Aiden waited for her to amend her last thought. *Sixty-three.*

With the next stroke, he leaned forward to see more of her face. She wasn't crying. That was good. She cried easily. Clara assured him her twin hadn't been a crier previous to her current delicate condition.

When Catherine could be up, he would bring in the dressing table. Then he could see her expression, something that would be very helpful about now. All he could tell about her mood was the absence of tears. *Seventy-six.*

Eighty-eight.

"When will Donny decide?"

"I don't know. TJ and I didn't give him a deadline."

"What if his sisters decide differently?"

Ninety-one.

"They'll go with Donny. Their mother wanted them to stay together."

Ninety-five.

Ninety-six.

Ninety-seven.

Ninety-eight.

Ninety-nine.

Aiden brushed the last stroke and laid the brush on the bed.

Catherine reached back and gathered her hair out of his hands. "I can braid it."

"That's my job."

She began braiding lower than he normally did. "I don't want to keep you."

The braid grew as Aiden processed her dismissal. "I could lie down and rub your back."

"Lavender worked on my circulation already." She tied off the braid and pulled up the sheet. "Take the lamp with you when you leave."

Aiden stood, staring at her back. "Good night, then."

He was halfway to the Owen farm when he realized he hadn't given her his customary kiss. It had been obvious she'd wanted him out of there. Whatever was wrong with Catherine tonight?

TJ stirred as he approached. "What are you doing back here so soon? I thought you said it would be after midnight."

"I figured you should be home with your wife. Mine didn't want me around."

"What did you do?"

"Nothing."

TJ sat up. "You must have done something."

Aiden sat on the porch step. "She was annoyed about something when I got home. At least she wasn't crying."

"What does she have to be annoyed about?"

"Probably bored because she's stuck in bed all day. With work on The Rescue, only Nellie and Lavender are there with her, and Lavender started working at the office today."

"Did you convince Lavender to let you write to that college about her graduation certificate?"

"She still won't tell me her real name."

TJ's chair squeaked. "There can't be that many women who disappeared days before graduation."

"We promised these women their privacy. I'm just happy to have her help. It may take people awhile to warm up to her. Emily and Reverend Green made appointments just to see her."

"Emily told me. She likes Lavender better."

"Figures, but I'm not disappointed. Mrs. Forsythe has been occupied with her daughter-in-law in jail and Libby Jean's court appearance. She's already referred two women to me. I'm sure I'll endure more patients in need of obstetrics."

"Ob—what?"

"Help with delivering their children."

"Why didn't you say that?" TJ stood. "Donny was sleeping the last time I checked. Did you ask Catherine how she feels about a potential instant family?"

"I told her tonight."

The whack to the back of the head came from nowhere.

"What was that for?" Aiden rubbed the back of his head.

"Even I know better than to tell my wife something like

that. Both our wives are expecting and nervous about being moms to one child. Add three more…Emily and I had several discussions about it over the last three or four months. Catherine had how many?"

"On the night Mrs. Owen died."

"The night you got married." TJ stepped off the porch. "And here I thought you were a wise old man. You say you made a choice to love Catherine and are working on it, but how is she supposed to make the choice to love you if you don't treat her like she's your partner?"

He deserved a second smack on the head. "I talk to so many people, sometimes I forget what I've said."

"Did Lavender know about giving Donny a choice?" asked TJ.

Aiden thought over the conversations of the day. "Yes, I talked to her about him."

TJ ran a hand through his hair. "I don't go repeating gossip I hear, but you should know Catherine thinks Lavender would have been a better choice if you wanted a wife."

Of all the women at The Rescue, Lavender was the only one he'd thought of as a potential, but she wasn't ready for matrimony. And there was Jax. Even though Lavender wouldn't marry him, there was something between them. "Lavender is like a little sister or student to me."

"You do spend a lot of time talking to her."

"About medical things."

"Now she works with you. Not many men, married or not, have as much contact with a woman who isn't their wife or gal as you do Lavender."

Aiden ran a hand down his face. "Am I stupid?"

"I'm not the one making the diagnosis."

"What should I do?"

"Emily isn't expecting me back tonight. Maybe you should go see your wife."

"But I don't stay there at night."

"If it's the annulment thing, we all know you wouldn't do anything to endanger her."

In the moonlight, Aiden couldn't tell whether his friend was blushing, but he was willing to bet his favorite stethoscope he was. "An hour each evening with your wife is not enough, is it?"

"Nope."

Aiden stood and dusted off his pants. "I hadn't even thought of it with Jax—"

"He moved out Friday, I believe."

Aiden walked in a circle in front of the porch. "I thought this would be easier."

"I haven't learned much in my first year of marriage, but I have learned that's when Emily is the quietest and I need to listen the most, even if all I do is hold her hand."

"Fine. You've made your point. But if Nellie wallops me with a rolling pin because she thinks I'm breaking in ..."

"I won't arrest her."

Aiden removed his shoes as soon as he entered the house. The light of the half-moon shone across the bed. Catherine lay nearest the open window, curled into herself, her knees drawn up closer to her body than he thought should be possible. Aiden removed his tie, vest, socks, and suspenders. Knowing that Nellie or Lavender could come in during the night, he only unbuttoned the top buttons of his shirt, then slid into the empty side of the bed. Catherine's breath hitched, but she continued to sleep. Facing her back, there wasn't a hand to hold. He opted to set a hand on her shoulder and whispered, "I'm sorry" into the night.

Snore.

Catherine opened her eyes. The sound came again. Definitely a snore and close to her back. A week ago, Nellie came in to check on her and fell asleep, but she didn't snore.

Did Lavender snore?

She straightened her legs. Her foot connected with a leg—a hairy leg. Not a woman's leg. She turned her head as far as she could and caught a glimpse of a mustache.

"Aiden?"

The snoring stopped.

"What?"

The mattress moved.

"Catherine? Do you need something?"

"What are you doing here?" She rolled onto her back to see him better.

"Sleeping."

"Why?"

"Because it's the middle of the night." A chuckle rumbled from deep in his chest. "I left when you were upset, and I shouldn't have."

"You knew I was upset?" The reasons came tumbling back—Donny, Lavender, motherhood, appointment.

"It took me some time to sort it out." His hand found hers. "Do you want to talk? Or sleep?"

As always, another need surfaced. "I need to—" Catherine bit her lip. He was her doctor. He'd seen her deliver a baby. It shouldn't be that hard to tell him she needed to use the chamber pot. She'd die of mortification if he helped her with the bedpan.

Aiden rolled into a sitting position. "There's a chamber pot behind the screen, right?"

"Yes. Lavender lets me use it if someone is here to catch me and I move slowly."

"Will I do? I'll catch you."

Catherine let go of his hand and rolled over so she could get off of the bed. Aiden stood beside her and helped her up, his hand in the center of her back. She was about to tell him she didn't need that much help when she felt the warmth radiating from the spot like a protective shield.

He helped her to the screen. "I need a glass of water. Do you want one?"

She nodded, unable to find her voice.

"Don't walk back until I return."

Catherine sighed in relief. She never could have imagined a simple chamber-pot use would be so embarrassing.

He returned with a glass of water, then stood behind her as she washed her hands in the washstand bowl.

Aiden reached around her and dried her hands with a soft cloth, pulling her back into his body. Her breath caught as she felt warmth radiating from his chest. He held her close, their bodies connected by more than just his arm. He was taller and thinner than the only other man she'd been this close to.

Only Aiden wasn't asking for anything in return. He was providing comfort and support. She leaned into him, the back of her head resting on his chest. She could hear his heartbeat, steady and reassuring. She closed her eyes and let herself relax, her earlier anger dissipating. She never imagined being cared for, especially by someone like Aiden. It was more than just his medical expertise; it was his kindness, his gentle touch, and the way he seemed to genuinely care about her. Maybe this was love.

He turned her to face him. She kept her head to his chest, fearing the spell might break if she looked at him and saw only his doctor's face. Aiden's hand went to the back of her head, his fingers gently massaging her scalp. More intimate and personal than hair brushing, it soothed the last remaining bits of her anger away. She let out a sigh of contentment and leaned farther into him.

His other hand slipped down to her waist, pulling her into him until there was no space between them. His breath fanned the top of her head, and she felt her heartbeat quicken in response. They stayed like that for a moment, neither moving nor speaking.

Aiden's hand then moved from her hair to her chin, lifting it with one finger so she looked at him. "I'm sorry for not talking to you about Donny. I'm trying to get used to being married. We spend so little time together, I'm afraid of ruining things." His thumb brushed across her lower lip.

Catherine's heart now pounded so hard she could feel it in her ears, drowning out the sound of everything else. Her body trembled with a mix of anticipation and uncertainty. Did he want to kiss her? She looked up into his eyes, searching for any hint of what he felt. In that moment, she saw something she had never seen before. Desire, subtle but unmistakable. Her heart skipped a beat.

"Aiden?" she whispered. "Is this real?"

Aiden leaned down, his lips hovering above hers. "I hope so." The vulnerability in his voice only amplified her feelings. He searched her eyes before finally closing the distance between them, their lips brushing each other's in the slightest kiss and sending shivers down her spine. Catherine had barely responded before he pulled away, leaving her wanting more.

He ran a finger down her cheek, a trail of warmth in its wake. "That's as much as I can give you for now."

Give. The word reverberated through her mind. She couldn't deny the feelings awakened within her. As he helped her back into bed, she clung to every fleeting second of closeness, etching the sensation deep into her soul. Closing her eyes, she tried to steady her racing heart, but it was futile. Catherine knew that from this moment on, nothing would be the same. Aiden had stirred something profound within her. Was this the love he'd spoken of?

Aiden sat on the edge of the bed, looking down at her with a tenderness that made her chest ache. "Lavender would beat me with a rolling pin if she saw how long I had you standing."

"I'm not too sure. She was the one saying I should be up more."

"Hmm. We'll see how the rest of the night goes. I may have to agree to a walk to the parlor." He tucked her feet under the sheet.

Catherine lay back on the pillows and closed her eyes, savoring the lingering warmth of Aiden's touch. The anger and frustration she had felt earlier seemed far away now, distant and insignificant. In its place was a feeling of contentment. "Do I get to vote?"

"Maybe." Aiden lay down next to her and took her hand in his. "Now, do you want to tell me what was bothering you?"

"I'm not feeling so bothered now."

"Catherine, I didn't kiss you to make you forget you were upset with me. I wronged you by not talking about the situation with Donny and his siblings. I should have consulted you. Do you feel you could be a mother to them?"

She put a hand on his chest. "I don't know. I don't even know if I can be a mother to this one. I've made so many mistakes." The child might be better off with Clara, and Aiden would be better off if he were free, even if that kiss...

"Too much too fast?"

"Yes. But if you have promised Donny, you can't disappoint him because of me."

He traced a lazy pattern on the back of her hand. "I told you earlier that I'd be a better uncle. Perhaps Donny will see it when I explain that the choice we gave him was a bad one."

"You can't do that. Don't break his heart because of me."

"I won't. You and I will talk with TJ and Emily before we talk with Donny or his sisters again. Is that good?"

"Yes."

He continued to play with her hand. "Was there anything else upsetting you?"

Not wanting to lie, she stayed quiet.

"I'll take that as a yes. Are you ready to talk about it?"

She shook her head. "I'd rather sleep."

He brought her hand to his lips and kissed her fingertips. "Sweet dreams."

She kept her eyes on him as he moved to the other side of the bed, lying down beside her. She closed her eyes, letting the peace of the moment wash over her as she drifted off to sleep, listening to the sound of Aiden's breathing.

When Catherine woke the next morning, Aiden was gone, but the indention on the pillow remained. It hadn't been a dream.

Mrs. Bickford tapped on Aiden's door. "My daughter's here. She says my son has a bloody nose. Do you mind if I leave?"

Aiden assumed the boy had found himself in another fight. "No. Take some ice if you want. Do you want me to stop by later?"

"I'll send word if I need you to."

Aiden walked back to the kitchen area. "Lavender, Mrs. B had to leave. I don't have any patients for a while. Will you watch the office? I'm going to check on Catherine."

Lavender lifted the medical journal she reviewed. "May I read this at the desk?"

"Of course. Donny is out there too. Schoolwork." More like being sent home from school to write an essay about respect. "Send him if you need me."

At the house, he found Reverend Green visiting Catherine. A Bible lay open on the bed next to her.

He nodded greetings to both. "If this is a private conversation, I can come back."

Catherine reached for his hand. "We were just reading."

"She was reading. I was—" Reverend Green coughed into a handkerchief. It was the first cough Aiden had heard from him in a while. No blood spotted the cloth—a vast improvement.

Nellie appeared at the door with a tea tray.

Aiden stepped aside. "I didn't mean to interrupt your party."

Catherine tugged on his hand. "Join us."

"What if we take it to the parlor? I believe Catherine may recline on the davenport as well as she does here." Having conferred with Lavender earlier, Aiden was confident a few steps were unlikely to cause any undue stress.

Nellie turned around with the tray. "Moving the party."

Reverend Green followed her out of the room. By the time Aiden got Catherine situated, the reverend was well into his first cup of tea and Nellie had brought out a plate of biscuits. She was handing one to the reverend when Donny burst through the door.

"Doc, come quick! Some man is yelling—"

Aiden was out the door before Donny finished his sentence.

The boy ran along with him. "He's yelling at Miss Lavender and wants to see your wife."

Aiden stumbled. "Catherine?"

"Yup."

Why would someone Donny didn't know be looking for his wife? His mind flew back to the day Cole Pike's gang returned Cathleen to town. Not again. "Get TJ."

Donny spun and took off toward the jail. Aiden ran for his office, bursting through the backdoor.

"Called you the Darling Doctor, didn't we?" A man spoke loudly from the front. "Most said you weren't worth the money."

"Leave," Lavender answered firmly.

In four strides, Aiden reached the waiting area, where a well-dressed man cornered Lavender. She held the medical journal like a bat between them.

"Sir, what are you doing in my office?" Aiden stayed far enough that the man would have to step forward to swing at him.

"I'm looking for my wife." The man sneered. Aiden had seen the type. Soft face, soft hands, couldn't hold his own in a bar fight but would take out his anger on his wife and kids.

"Your wife?" Aiden moved back a step, drawing the man away from Lavender.

"Catherine Fairlane."

Bernard Fairlane? It had to be. "This whore says she doesn't know anyone by that name. You know she isn't a real nurse, right?"

Another step back and Lavender had a clear path to the front door. "There are no Fairlanes in Hiramsville."

"You must know the trollop. Her sainted sister married the preacher."

Apparently, Bernard hadn't heard of Catherine's marriage. "Why don't you come into my office, and we can figure out who you're looking for."

"It can't be that hard. They look the same, but my wife is carrying my child." Bernard held his hand in front of his stomach to indicate the size—a vast overestimation even if she still carried twins. "You're the only doctor in town. You must have seen her."

"We do have a midwife."

"Midwives are for the poor." Bernard took another step toward Aiden.

Lavender slid along the wall and out the front door. Once outside, she disappeared in a flash. Desperation caused her to run on her still-tender feet.

Aiden stopped next to his office door. "Would you like to have a seat?"

"I didn't sit on a train for four days to be offered a seat. I need my wife."

"I wasn't aware Mrs. Reverend Staples had a married sister. Have you spoken with her?"

"There wasn't anyone at the church or the preacher's home."

Likely, Lewis and Clara were working up at The Rescue. "This woman you are looking for is with child?"

Bernard leaned forward and hit his chest as he spoke. "My child."

"And you are?"

"Bernard Fairlane of New York and Fairlane Shipping."

"And when were you married?"

"We tried to elope…but things happened. It's a common-law thing."

The thread of anxiety that Catherine may have lied vanished. A failed elopement and an out-of-wedlock pregnancy didn't make for a common-law marriage, at least not in any state Aiden knew of.

The front door opened with a bang, ending Aiden's next question before it formed.

"Hey, Doc!" The sheriff's deputy stumbled in, clutching his shoulder.

"Mr. Fairlane, if you would give me a moment."

"Doc, it hurts!"

Bernard grunted.

Aiden hurried around his desk and partially closed the door to his office.

The deputy moaned and winked at the same time. Good thing the man was in law enforcement. He'd be laughed off the stage.

"Come to room three." Aiden chose the room closest to the back door, leaving the room door open so they would know if Bernard left the office.

"What happened?" asked Aiden in a normal voice.

"TJ sent me to check things out. Miss Lavender is shaking and not making any sense. TJ's at the house now." The deputy whispered, then said louder, "My mule kicked me. I think it's broken. Ohhh!"

A dozen profanities ran through Aiden's mind. He lowered his voice. "Tell TJ it's Bernard Fairlane from New York. Keep Reverend Green with my wife, and as long as Lavender is upset, don't let her near Catherine. No one he doesn't know goes into the house." Aiden banged on the cabinet, then said in a normal tone, "Can we get that shirt off?"

The deputy unbuttoned the top button. Aiden shook his head and pointed to the back door as he opened a drawer with his other hand. "I'll need to cut it off."

As the deputy stood, Aiden slammed the drawer.

"But it's my favorite." The deputy crossed the room to the back door as he spoke.

The moment the deputy shut the door behind himself, Aiden moaned loudly, covering any noise the deputy made. He waited a moment. "Doesn't look broken. I'll get you some ice."

Aiden exited room three, shutting the door behind him.

Bernard came out of the office. "I don't have all day. Where is she?"

"Mr. Fairlane, will you keep it down? I have a patient."

"And I'm out of patience. Someone in this one-horse town has got to know where she is." He spun on his heel and marched out the front door.

It was only a matter of time before someone explained to Bernard that he was looking for the doctor's wife and directed him to Aiden's home.

Aiden walked to the front door, switched the sign to closed, and locked the door. He took time to lock the back door behind him before sprinting to the house.

⟫◆⟪

Catherine tapped her teacup and eyed TJ, who watched her and out the window at the same time. Something was wrong. Lavender had come through the back door in hysterics. Nellie and TJ had checked on her, and then the deputy had left. The one person who wasn't lying to her was Reverend Green, who seemed as confused as she was.

When the deputy returned, TJ walked out front to meet him. Catherine watched the conversation through the window. Although the deputy gestured when he talked, TJ did not, which was incredibly unhelpful. Then the deputy left, and TJ ambled back up the walk as if spending the afternoon in someone else's home uninvited, at least by her, was normal. As he reached the porch, Aiden came into view, walking faster than normal.

Something in her belly clenched. Catherine placed her hand over it. Thankfully, it wasn't painful. She'd sat up longer in the last hour than she had in weeks. She slid the teacup onto the end table and scooted down on the couch. No longer did she have a clear view out the window.

Footsteps echoed on the front porch, and then Aiden and TJ entered. Aiden crouched down at the head of the couch, taking her hand in his. "How are you feeling?"

"What's happening?"

"I'm not completely sure, and I don't want to upset you."

"Not knowing why Lavender is closeted with Nellie and can't speak coherently or the reason the sheriff joined afternoon tea uninvited after you ran off to your office already has me in a state. Is it outlaws?"

"Not the dime-novel kind. Can you describe Bernard?"

"Bernard? Why? He wouldn't come here." Catherine leaned on her elbow to prop herself higher and get a better view out the window. Would he be there? Why would he come? Money? The lawsuit? One of those convoluted lines in the contract she signed? None of them were good enough reasons to come in person. Besides, he was supposed to get married sometime in September. Or was it August? No,

September. The announcement in the newspaper clearly said September. Last Saturday, in fact.

"Catherine, it's important." The gentle pressure of Aiden's hand on her shoulder forced her to lie back down.

"He's shorter than you and rounder, but not to the point of being fat. His hair is lighter but still brown. He puts this stuff in it that makes the hair look good but feel like dirty leather. His eyes…" The brown ones in her mind were the ones looking into hers right now, soft and caring. "They are brownish, but not like yours. More narrow and hard. He doesn't have those lovely golden flecks."

Aiden cleared his throat, his eyes twinkling. "Catherine. How old is he?"

"Twenty-five, maybe. I never asked. Older than the rest of the students. Although he never studied. School was a game for him. I'm not entirely sure he was a student."

"I wish I didn't have to tell you this, but he's in town and looking for you."

"Why?"

"He didn't say. He's angry and worked up. I don't want him near you."

Only weeks ago, she'd wished for Bernard to search for her, to be his wife, to protect his child, even after he abandoned her. All she could think about was marrying him. Characteristics like dependability never came into mind. She knew her marriage wouldn't be happy, but she'd have money and status. Last night, she'd felt a vague indication of what a more complete relationship could be. The idea was something she was still molding into a concrete form. "I don't either."

"Sadly, I don't think he'll give up until he finds you, which is only a matter of time. What should we do?" Aiden rolled forward onto his knees, keeping his face at the same level as hers.

"Do you know what he wants from me?"

"He claimed you were his wife."

"I'm not. Honest. I—" Another tightening of her abdomen, same as before.

Aiden smoothed her hair. "I know."

He covered the hand over her belly with his own. "Are you in pain?"

"No pain. It feels tight, though."

"As soon as Lavender feels better, I'll ask her to check you. However, I think what you're feeling is normal."

"What's wrong with her? She is overwrought. I've never seen anything upset her."

Aiden looked at the floor before answering. "He seemed to know her from before."

"When she went to school?"

Aiden didn't answer.

The *other* before. The reason she was here. If Bernard knew her, then he'd… The sandwich she had with her tea fought its way back up. Catherine covered her mouth and closed her eyes, willing her stomach to settle and the image of Bernard in a brothel to disappear. She was unsuccessful at both. The last vestiges of the time she'd thought special blurred into an ugliness only matched by the bile that burned her throat.

Aiden held the empty ash bucket from the fireplace for her and wiped her face with the tea towel. "Sweetheart, I'm sorry."

Reverend Green left and came back with a cool, damp towel.

Lavender came in a moment later, her red-rimmed eyes assessing Catherine. "Neither of us is doing well. Back to bed with you and some cool cloths."

"No. He's looking for me. The best way to be rid of him is to talk to him. I will not face that man lying in bed."

Lavender's eyes widened, and Catherine reached for her hand. Lavender's eyes searched Catherine's, then she looked at Aiden.

"I made a mistake by telling her that Bernard Fairlane recognized you. I thought honesty—"

"Not...a...mistake." Catherine pushed the words out, her eyes locked on Aiden's. Then she looked at Lavender. "Sorry."

There wasn't anything else to say. Lavender wasn't at fault. She knew it was what Reverend Green was saying about forgiveness—the responsibility she needed to take, the part she needed to give to God. The idea was understandable and unexplainable at the same time. "He won't leave unless I talk to him, and not in the bedroom, but here."

"Are you sure?"

"Yes. But can I change? These clothes smell."

Aiden scooped Catherine into his arms and carried her to the bedroom, Lavender following. Nellie joined them. After making sure there was water in the pitcher, Aiden left.

"I want to wear the dress I wore for Clara's wedding." It was the nicest thing she owned. "Not a wrapper."

"Under a few conditions, because that man is not worth it and you are risking your life and that of your baby." Lavender laid out her stipulations.

Catherine agreed and added one of her own. "Lavender, you leave. He can't treat you like the dirt under his shoes if you aren't here."

"Compromise. Donny went for Jax. I'll stay out back with Jax. I want to be close by."

"Fine." Catherine turned to Nellie. "Stay with her?"

The thought was for Nellie as much as Lavender. Bernard had a mean streak. He wouldn't dare hit anyone with TJ, Jax, and Aiden around, but it might not tame his mouth, and he wouldn't say a negative word to Nellie if Catherine could prevent it.

Soon, she was washed and dressed. Nellie even put her hair up quickly. Then Aiden carried her back out to the parlor. Instead of leaving Catherine alone on the davenport, he sat so she could use his lap as a pillow.

"Wait. I can't."

"This way you can lie down until he comes and I can help you sit up."

"My head in your lap? In front of the reverend? It isn't proper."

Reverend Green chuckled. "I can't think of a single thing wrong with it. My wife often would lie like that. She would read to me, and I could rub her back where it hurt."

Catherine accepted Lavender's help, then lowered her head onto Aiden's lap. At least, on her side, she couldn't see his face, only the wall opposite. "Now what?"

"We wait for the sheriff to return with him."

Waiting wasn't one of the easiest things to do when she was all too aware of Aiden's hand on her back and the silence growing until the only sound in the room was the ticking of the clock.

⟫◆⟪

In any other circumstances, sitting with his wife's head nestled in his lap would be considered romantic. Aiden looked about for anything to cut the tension. Jax arrived and went through to the kitchen, his leg having healed better than expected. After weeks of recovery, the ranger was itching for some action. If Bernard said anything derogatory to Lavender, he could well be missing his teeth before the night was over, damage Aiden would be obligated to repair. It would be worth it, he told himself, and he wished he could throw a punch or two himself. Holding Catherine would prevent that, as would TJ's presence.

The wait was short, and before long, TJ accompanied the man up the walk.

Aiden lifted Catherine into a sitting position, half holding her in his lap. There would be no way for him to hit the man. He interlaced his fingers with Catherine's and squeezed her hand. "No matter what he says, remember, I chose to be your husband."

Catherine nodded, her eyes fixed on the approaching figure. As Bernard stepped through the door, Aiden's grip on Catherine's hand tightened.

TJ ushered the man in.

"You said you didn't know where my wife was." Bernard wasted no time with greetings.

"I didn't because it is impossible for my wife to be yours." The calmness in Aiden's voice hid the fire in his chest.

"I told you she was carrying my child." Bernard stepped forward.

TJ stopped him with a hand on his shoulder. "Sit."

Aiden sighed. "My name is on the marriage license. My name will be on the birth record."

Bernard sat on the edge of the chair as if ready to spring out at any minute. "But I need them."

Catherine patted Aiden's hand, showing she wished to speak. "That isn't what you said when you left me in July."

"You stupid—"

TJ's hand on Bernard's shoulder put an end to whatever he was going to say. "Just give me the word, Doc, and I'll toss him in jail."

"You can't do that. I'm a Fairlane."

"Law says I can put anyone who's drunk or disorderly and likely to cause harm to themselves behind bars for twenty-four hours. I believe defaming the doc's wife is disorderly. And no man would say a word against another man's wife in that man's home unless he were drunker than a bull rider on the Fourth of July. Now, you were saying?"

"I was saying the brat she's carrying isn't his. It's mine. I already told him we were common-law married."

Aiden rubbed Catherine's fingers. "Are you married to this man?"

"No."

"She eloped with me."

"We never saw the judge. You kept making excuses," said Catherine.

"I would have taken you." Bernard's pleading would have been believable if his wife's back hadn't stiffened.

"Not what you said when you tossed the money on the bed, paying me off for a week of honeymooning."

"So you admit the child is mine." Bernard leaned forward in his chair.

"A child you asked me to kill." Catherine's voice was strong as she stated the fact she'd alluded to before.

Bernard made a dismissive gesture. "Things were different then."

"I believe so. According to the New York papers, you'd been engaged for the past year to an heiress. And I was too naïve, assuming your promise of marriage to me was legitimate."

Her pulse accelerated. One of the advantages of this position was that he could feel her heartbeat. "My wife is in a delicate position. It would be best if we could settle this matter calmly and civilly. Why are you in Hiramsville?"

"I came for my wife and child."

"Why?" asked TJ. "It's clear to me she isn't your wife, and her husband claims the child will have his name."

"Because my twenty-ninth birthday is in January, and I must be married and start a family or I lose it all!" When Bernard stood and stepped toward Aiden and Catherine, TJ pulled him back by his collar. Catherine leaned farther into Aiden. "I thought you were getting married this month."

"I was until your father's lousy Pinkertons questioned me about your disappearance—in front of Isabella. Do you know what Isabella's father did?" Bernard gestured wildly.

No one spoke.

"He hired those same Pinkertons to research my moral turpitude. Of course, finding out about you was easy. Somehow, they even found the maid my mother let go for immorality when I was sixteen. Father is livid. Only two of the women he paid off kept their mouths shut. And then there's you. His attorneys have advised him you didn't break the contract and he has to pay you after all, which remains to be seen. Now, I need a wife immediately. The child is a problem. However, if it came out that we eloped to Seabrook, New Hampshire, last January ..."

Catherine sat up straighter. "But we didn't."

"In your current state, you don't remember. By the time we return to New York, I'll have all the documents in order." There was an evil in Bernard's smile that rivaled that of any outlaw Aiden ever met.

Aiden felt more than heard his wife gasp. He coaxed her into a more relaxed position. "Catherine is staying here."

"How much do you want to annul your marriage? In her state, you likely haven't consummated. Not that she's worth it. Your nurse, well ..."

Catherine's body stiffened.

"Out!" Aiden couldn't move without possibly hurting her. "Get out of my home."

Bernard's smile widened.

TJ clamped his hand around Bernard's arm. "Time to go."

Bernard tried to jerk his arm away. "I'm not leaving without her."

"My wife is staying here."

TJ put his other hand on Bernard's shoulder and pushed him toward the door.

"Get your hands off me." Bernard twisted and took a swing at TJ, missing by more than a half foot.

Catherine pushed away from Aiden. "Stop!"

Both men froze.

"I'm not leaving, Bernard. Even if I wanted to, I couldn't. I nearly died traveling here! I don't ever want to see you again. When I think—" Sobs racked her body, and she collapsed back into Aiden.

Bernard broke free of TJ and stepped menacingly toward Catherine.

It was a mistake to sit behind her. Aiden couldn't defend her against this man.

TJ lunged for Bernard and yanked him back.

Jax appeared at the parlor door. "Need a hand?"

With the former ranger's help, TJ escorted Bernard out of the house.

Aiden gathered Catherine in his arms and tried to calm her. This had been a mistake. Knowing the man was upset, he should have confronted Bernard at the office and never let him near her. She needed to be calm and in bed. What had he done?

nky blackness wrapped its claws around Catherine, smothering the light and threatening to tear her away. A cacophony of voices pounded against her skull—memories from a hidden tomb, the discordant symphony of shattered dreams threatening to drive her mad. Catherine fought desperately to shield herself from the assault, her trembling hands rising to cover her ears yet finding no respite from the ceaseless onslaught.

"Stop." Her lips formed the ineffective word.

Chaos reigned. The memories crescendoed, shouting, reverberating, crisscrossing each other, fighting for dominance.

Help! Help!

Catherine reached through the darkness, desperate for something to hold on to. When her fingers brushed a solid warmth, she latched on to it with all of her strength and pushed through the darkness until that warmth fully enveloped her, a blessed silence erasing the pandemonium until nothing remained.

"How is she?" Lavender stood at the bedroom door.

Aiden lifted his head from the pillow, maintaining his hold on Catherine. "Calmer. No contractions."

"TJ wants to speak with you."

"I won't leave her."

"Five minutes. I'll sit with her."

Not knowing if she heard the world around her as one did in the void between awake and asleep, he'd kept conversations to a minimum when near her. He frowned. An irrational part of him said that if he let Catherine go, she'd never come back. In the long hours since yesterday afternoon, he'd denied his own needs for all but a few necessaries. TJ came last evening, but Aiden didn't dare leave her. Quickly, he assessed his wife. Her breathing was even, her pulse strong. He uncovered his arms, careful not to disturb her.

Catherine moaned softly but quickly resettled, a welcome change from the occasional screams that broke the silence of the night.

Lavender sat down on the bed behind Catherine and set a hand on her shoulder, understanding the need for touch. No trace of yesterday's trauma marred her face.

He should ask about Lavender's welfare, but there was no room in his mind for anyone but Catherine. Others could care for the other woman's needs.

Lavender adjusted her position and softly rubbed Catherine's shoulders. "Go."

Aiden looked back before leaving the room.

TJ sat at the kitchen table, staring into a cup of black coffee. "Lavender updated me on Catherine. I wish I could charge him for more. There isn't a law against being a jackass."

"What can you do?" Aiden poured himself a cup and sat across from him.

"Jax and I talked about it. Although Mr. Fairlane threatened any number of things, the sum total of his crimes are accosting me and Lavender at the office. Lavender doesn't want to see Bernard again, so the judge is likely to fine him a few dollars, which Mr. Fairlane won't even notice. Jax voted for escorting him to Galveston and putting him on the first ship bound for New York on a steerage ticket. Is there a way you can guarantee seasickness?"

Twice as long as a train ride. According to the Dallas paper, it was hurricane season, and, best of all, it would be days before he could get off and attempt to come back. "Is that legal?"

TJ swirled his coffee. "I read about escorting a man out of Texas in one of your dime novels. I've never heard we can't."

"But?"

"Jax isn't a ranger anymore. If a judge caught wind of the plan, he might see it as kidnapping."

"Why not just put him on the train?"

"Poetic justice, according to Jax."

"I can't say I don't like the idea, but I can't give a man something to make him sick. But any old food might work. Steerage should almost guarantee a poor trip." The more he thought about it, the better he liked the idea.

TJ stood. "I'll let you know what we decide. Expect a visit from Clara and Lewis later this morning. I felt it best to apprise them of yesterday's visit."

Aiden hadn't given Clara a thought since Catherine's collapse. The twin might bring her sister out of her state. "Thanks, TJ."

Lavender looked up as Aiden entered the bedroom. "What do you want me to do?"

"Go to the office. If people won't let you treat them, they can wait." He circled the bed to the space he'd vacated.

"Is he gone?" Lavender rubbed her arms.

"He will be." Aiden lay on the bed and gathered his wife close. As soon as he took Catherine's hand in his, she sighed.

Lavender stood by the door. "If I need you?"

Every oath he'd taken warred with the answer he wanted to give her. Instead, he said, "Only the severest of emergencies."

A kind God would not allow even a scraped knee in a ten-mile radius of Hiramsville today.

<hr>

The warmth returned.

As much as she wanted to stay cocooned in the safety of sleep, Catherine knew the time to leave had come. Cautiously, she opened her eyes.

White.

Her eyes focused on the woven threads of the cotton cloth inches from her face. Like a bull's eye, the button in the center drew her attention. Lightly, she touched it, only to have it move.

A finger traced her brow. "Are you awake?"

Aiden.

Sunlight bathed his face. What was he doing here? He'd never lain down with her during the day.

"You're here."

"Where else would I be?"

Words gathered slowly in her head. "It's day."

The corner of his mouth lifted in a smile. "You slept a long time."

"How long have you been here?"

"As long as you have."

Catherine closed her eyes. She'd been on the davenport with ... "Is he gone?"

"TJ has him at the jail. He'll leave on today's train. He won't be back. You're safe."

She brought her hand up and laid it on the button, needing to feel the solidness of him. She was in one of the light nightgowns. They'd changed her clothing. "How long was I asleep?"

"You've been unconscious since yesterday. You must be starved and thirsty. Nellie keeps checking to see when she can get you food. How do you feel?"

Safe. But he wasn't asking about her heart. Whatever she said, he would move away to feed her or whatever else. She grabbed his shirt. "Don't leave."

"I won't. I told them I wouldn't go to the office today. Lavender can see anyone who needs to be seen."

Catherine searched his eyes. How bad off was she that he felt he needed to stay? Letting go of his shirt, she moved her hand to the place it so often rested. "Is the baby all right?"

"Lavender and I have both listened. We hear a strong heartbeat, and you haven't had any signs of labor."

"Why are you staying, then?"

His eyes softened, and his fingers traced her jaw. "Because I need to brush your hair."

<hr>

The fresh shirt stuck to the damp spot behind his shoulder. Aiden tugged it down. His hasty wash hadn't included a proper towel dry. He hadn't intended to run over to the office at all today, but Clara's visit gave him time to change and shave. Unfortunately, the only shirts he found in the house that morning needed repairing. Hurriedly, he dressed and checked with Mrs. Bickford as Lavender was in with a patient. Aiden escaped the building before anyone who might need him could waylay him.

Nellie sat on the back porch, shelling peas. She looked up as he climbed the stairs. Shadows underscored her eyes.

"Did you get much sleep last night?"

"Enough, Doc."

"Taking care of yourself comes before caring for the rest of us."

"Been taking care of myself for a long time."

"I know you have. It won't hurt any of us if you spend the afternoon reading."

"Not much of a reader."

"Shame. Mrs. Bickford has a new copy of one of those ladies' magazines on the desk."

Nellie's eyes widened.

Aiden met her gaze. "I guess I won't tell you about the dress on the—"

The stool crashed as Nellie jumped up. "You reckon they have any new recipes?"

"I don't know. I never get past the illustrations of the new hair—" Aiden spoke to her back. Three years ago, he'd discovered she liked the magazine, and he'd ordered it just so Nellie could read a copy without having to share it with the working women at Belle's saloon. Thus far, Nellie had refused employment with Mrs. Reese, Rose's Rescue, and him. Given Catherine's upbringing, he needed to convince Nellie to stay on as cook, as he doubted Catherine had much experience in that area. Although Lewis hadn't complained when it came to Clara's skills.

Clara's and Catherine's voices mingled, his wife's slightly higher voice easily recognizable as he walked down the short hallway. "Comparison or not, I am the flummadiddle of the pair. How naïve and foolish could I have been?"

"You forget I was the one who first accepted his attentions. I should have sent him away after I refused his kiss. I was the one who didn't want to be left behind. I too ignored his dislikable traits because of his popularity. I wasn't used to being as noticed as I was on his arm."

"Do not try to soften this for me. I was engaged. He showered you with his attention. I never should have even spoken to him about anything more important than—"

It was past time to make his presence known. Aiden tapped on the doorjamb.

The twins lay face-to-face on the bed. Clara sat up, simultaneously patting her hair and smoothing her dress. "Dr. Palmer...Aiden...I..."

"Please don't get up on my account. I suspect Lewis and I will often find you cloistered in conversation. If you have no need of me, I'll retire to the parlor."

The women exchanged glances. He hadn't seen them together for some days. Even if Catherine didn't have the new pink scar on her forehead and hadn't been in a delicate condition, there were dozens of other differences. Clara's face was more round, her eyes a fraction narrower. Catherine had a freckle where Clara did not. He failed to see how Lewis, nervous or not, had ever confused the two enough to propose to the wrong one. Then he remembered he had been nervous enough when he proposed to Susannah that he'd looked at her nose most of the time, afraid that if he focused on her eyes, he'd see rejection in them. And the sisters' noses were almost perfectly identical. Of course, Lewis would not have had hours to study either face as closely as Aiden had Catherine's.

Clara answered for both of them. "I can stay another hour. I'll call if you're needed."

"I won't be far. Lavender has set aside a rather extensive pile of articles she believes I need to read." Aiden sat in his favorite chair and opened the journal on top of the stack. The black and white on the page merged, his mind refusing to process the words. He leaned his head back and closed his eyes. Catherine was safe. He didn't need to be by her side every minute, but he wanted to be.

Shut the door," whispered Catherine.

Clara rolled off the bed and shut it completely. "Are you afraid of being heard?"

"Aiden has eavesdropped before."

Clara climbed back on the bed. "He was there yesterday. You aren't going to say something he doesn't know."

"I don't want to talk about yesterday. I don't want to talk about my stupidity in allowing Bernard to convince me he would sweep me away. I want to talk about the child."

Clara laid her hand on top of Catherine's, where it protected her baby. "What about it?"

"If something happens to me, I want you to raise it."

"Does Aiden know?"

"No. Why?"

"He's your husband."

"In name only. He married me only to make sure I didn't get on the train with Father. Aiden saves lives. He even told me I could get an annulment after the baby is born."

"He defended you against Ber—"

"Don't say his name. Aiden wasn't defending me. He was making sure I didn't exhaust myself. He is more terrified I'll have this baby and that it or I will die than I am. He can't raise a child alone. He wanted to raise Mrs. Owen's children so badly but knew he couldn't. He knows I can't. Aiden isn't stupid. I offer nothing to his world. I can barely cook. I don't know a thing about caring for a child, not to mention this isn't even his child."

"But you kissed. You said—"

"I shouldn't have told you. It was late at night. I'm sure it was a mistake. According to Nellie, he's the type of man who is good—really, truly good."

"I sensed that in the times he called on me."

"I'm not good."

Clara raised up on her elbows. "I'm going to be extremely exasperated if you continue to say that, because it isn't true."

"Fine. When compared to Aiden. He needs someone who is so much more than me."

"Officially exasperated. Anything you say along these lines is now dismissed based on Lavender's sometimes-expectant-women-do-odd-things counsel. I may ask Nellie to feed you coal for lunch."

"Clara." Catherine drew the word out in exasperation.

"I know you better than anyone. I've spent my entire life loving you and competing against you at the same time. There were days I thought I hated you or you hated me. These past few weeks, I've started understanding you. You've always wanted to be loved for being you, just like I have, only you chose a different way." Clara pointed to the door. "Out there is a man who is trying his hardest to love and care for you. Why don't you let him?"

"I can't."

"Why not?"

Catherine fidgeted with the sheet, avoiding Clara's gaze. "I don't know how to be in love with someone. I don't know how to be the wife he needs. He claims love is a choice. Last time I thought I was in love, I made a choice and look where it got me. I didn't choose to love you. You didn't choose to love Lewis. I don't know how I can choose to love him. I'm going to fail him. He's kind to me, and he makes me feel safe, but he deserves someone better, someone who can give him the life he deserves, the love he deserves."

Clara rolled onto her back. "You're scared."

Outside the window, a meadowlark trilled. Another answered. A breeze rustled the leaves of the tree. They had yet to change colors, Texas Septembers were still as warm as Massachusetts summers. Fall may not come at all so far south. Catherine tried to focus on those things and not on her sister's declaration. She wasn't scared. She was terrified. Failing Aiden would be far worse than having Bernard drag her off to New York to live a loveless life.

⸺⬦⸺

"She's sleeping." Clara plopped into the chair opposite Aiden.

"You spoke for a long time."

Clara shrugged. "We are twins."

"Without breaking that bond, is there anything you can tell me?"

Clara leaned her head back against the upholstered chair and studied the ceiling. "Don't give up on her. In the—what has it been—a month, six weeks?"

"Nearly six."

"In the last six weeks, she's been introspective. A year ago, I would have never thought she could be. I'm the silent one." Clara shook her head. "And there I go, comparing us. I don't know what she's discussing with Reverend Green. Until today, she seemed…I don't know, more peaceful?"

He'd seen the same thing. Of course, not knowing Catherine before, he had no basis for comparison, only Catherine's judgment of herself. "Anything else?"

"If you mean about Bernard's visit, she didn't say much. I think she hates herself for ever being involved with him."

"Understandable." He'd heard enough to realize that Catherine didn't know at the time she wasn't the only woman in his life or that the man was the type that visited brothels.

"I need to leave. I'll come back tomorrow."

"I'm counting on it." Aiden showed his sister-in-law out. Being married to a twin was going to be challenging in ways he hadn't expected. A husband wanted to be first in his wife's life—well, with children mixed in—but a husband of a twin could well end up being second. Not that he expected instant devotion from Catherine. She'd married him out of desperation, obligation, self-preservation, or a mix of the three. He removed his shoes and walked to the bedroom door.

Catherine lay with her back to him. He counted her respirations.

She wasn't sleeping.

He walked around the bed and waited. In less than a minute, she opened her eyes.

"Did I wake you?"

"No."

"Do you want me to stay?"

"Do you want me to talk?"

"Only if you want to."

"What if I want you to talk?"

Aiden sat on the edge of the bed. "What about?"

"You."

"Like what?"

"Where you grew up."

"I was born in Indiana." Aiden then proceeded to tell of his life growing up as a Quaker in Indiana, focusing on the happier moments. During the time he spoke of going to school, her eyes closed. By the time he reached learning to fish, her breathing evened out. Apparently, his life story was dull enough to put someone to sleep. Of course, he never got to how a boy with antislavery leanings ended up working in a hospital for the Confederates. That story would have kept her awake.

ctober 1. You are almost there," Lavender said as she felt Catherine's abdomen. "I will be very proud if you go five more days and beat the British woman—although Aiden is not likely to write a paper about it for publication, so no one will ever know."

"So, it's safe to have the baby?"

"Still a mite early, and he'll be on the small side, but he should be big enough to live. Every day you can carry him from here is a bonus."

"Why do you keep calling it a boy? I don't want a boy. What if the child looks like—"

"I've never seen a woman get to choose what she gives birth to. And it doesn't matter, girl or boy, the child is as likely to come looking as much like the mother as the father after a week or so."

"Why a week?"

Lavender surged. "A lot of babies favor the father at first. According to old wives' tales, it's so the father will claim the child."

Catherine started shaking her head, gaining speed with each shake. "I can't have a child that looks like him. I can't."

Lavender pulled Catherine's nightgown back into place and sat down next to her. "If you want my opinion, babies look mostly the same. They almost always have blue eyes. Some have hair. Most don't. The ones who are bruised have their bruises fade. If you look only for the father's features, you will see them. If you look only for yours, you will see those. I bet you'll even find similarities to Aiden if you look hard enough."

"He isn't the father."

"Yes, but he has two eyes, two ears, a nose, and a mouth. Something is likely to look similar. And if the baby has a mustache…"

Catherine laughed.

Lavender patted her hand. "No matter what your baby is, there's one thing it will never be, and that is Bernard. You will raise him or her to be better. And Aiden will too. I've seen him with Donny. Aiden will be the best of fathers. Being a father takes more than a fifteen-minute tryst with a woman, and no matter if that child has ten eyes and two noses, you will love him."

"Ew, ten eyes? I'd rather it have a mustache."

"Not me. I can't stand the feel of a mustache or a beard, especially if it has tobacco juice or food in it." Lavender shuddered.

Catherine locked eyes with Lavender for a long moment before Lavender looked away. She waited until the moment passed, then said, "Thank you for trying to prepare me for this child."

Lavender's smile didn't touch her eyes. "I see how much joy little Scotty brings to Peony. I want you to have that joy too."

"She doesn't know who the father is, does she?"

Lavender shook her head. "Peony worked in Fort Worth at one of those places where the women had ten or more clients an hour when it was busy. She's fortunate to have survived. Scotty may not have a father, but he has at least twenty aunts."

"How soon are you moving out to The Rescue?"

"I told Aiden I would stay here until your baby is born. I'll stay for the first couple of days so you have help."

"Aiden hired Nellie for the first three months."

"Nellie told me. She's still not sure about being paid for what she's always done for room and board."

"They never paid her?"

"The Rescue tried to pay her, but she put most of the money in the donation box. Mrs. Reese has always slipped her a bit of spending money. When she worked for Belle, the girls would give her a bit here and there. But enough gossiping. I need to get over to the office, where I have a patient coming in."

Catherine read another book until Nellie came in with lunch.

"Will you stay and eat with me today?"

"I don't know if I should."

"Why not?"

"'Cause I'm getting paid now, like a proper cook."

"You've always been a proper cook. Dr. Palmer just didn't think of paying you earlier."

"Oh, he thunk, I mean thought, about it plenty, but I wouldn't let him because he gave up his house for us. He got all het up about it and went and ordered two lengths of dress cloth. Of course, I gave one to Becky, and she made me a right pretty new dress out of the other."

"The green one you wore Sunday?"

Nellie smiled wide. "It's my first one with a bustle. Mrs. Reese says I should be dressin' more fancy now. I don't see the point since I'll never be more than a domestic. That's a fancy term for a housemaid. Although your sister thought I might work in a ladies' hair shop."

"Right now, I think you should eat, either with me or on your own. It's your choice."

Nellie hurried to get her own plate.

"Would you like to work styling hair?"

"I don't know that there are enough women around heres who be willing to pay for a hairdresser, and I am not moving to a big city." Nellie shuddered.

"Why not?'

"Too many people staring."

"At what?"

Nellie pointed to her face.

"Oh, I forgot about those."

"How can you forget? They be right there. Do I need to tell Doc to check yours eyes?"

"No. I can see them, but other than when you are grouchy, I don't notice them anymore."

"That must be one of those unusual expectant-mother things Lavender talks about."

"I don't think so. I think I've just gotten to know you and see you differently than when I first arrived in Hiramsville."

Nellie ate several bites of her sandwich, her brow furrowed. "Emily says she doesn't see them either. Maybe it's just you women from Massachusetts, see."

"I bet you most of the women at The Rescue don't think of you as scarred. How did you get them, anyway?"

"My mother did it. Said it was to save me. There was a man who'd taken too much interest, and I was much too young. Everyone thinks I should be angry with her. But I'm not. She didn't mean to hurt me. She even gave me laudanum to make me sleep when she did it because she didn't want to get my eyes and was afraid I'd fight her. My mother wasn't bad. She just didn't want me to live the life she lived. She thought if I was ugly, no one would want me. She said she was younger than me the first time they gave her to a man and knew how terrible it be."

"Do you mean younger than fifteen?"

"No, ma'am. Younger than nine."

Catherine forced her mouth closed. She knew that some girls or women from Rose's had been forced into the brothels at a young age but never that young.

"Don't look so shocked. Mom said it happened all the time. She wanted to protect me, and she did. I'm so ugly now that no man's gonna touch me my whole life." Nellie raised her hand to keep Catherine from saying anything else. "I know Doc, Emily, your sister, Reverend Green, and a heap of other folks tell me that the right man could love me. Y'all forget how many men I've been around in my life. I've seen them. I know how they look at me. There isn't a man in the world gonna love me enough to want to marry this. Don't you go feeling bad for me. My mama wanted to protect me, and she did, and having lived at Rose's and Belle's, I think I'm better off the way I am."

Catherine finished her lunch. "Do you know Dr. Palmer claims that love is a choice? He even says he loves me, and look at how I came to him, carrying another man's baby. I don't think you should say never."

"Do you think he really loves you?"

Catherine stared at the ceiling for a long moment. "He's never said he loves me, but then, Bernard said he loved me, and that was a lie, but Doc treats me well and not just because I'm his patient. I think he's decided to love me and is just waiting to feel it."

"Do you love him?"

If one of her mother's maids or cooks had dared ask such a question, she would've been let go on the spot, but this was Nellie. She was more than just a cook. She'd become a friend. "I'm not sure. I think I want to."

"I guess that's a start. I know little about love. I know people who love me. My mama did even though she did this, and Becky does, although she gets angry with me sometimes, and Mrs. Reese must as she keeps me around. And I think Dr. Palmer likes me in his way too. Did you know he orders a magazine each month just so I can read it, and when it disappears from his office, he never asks me where it goes? He's a real good man. The only times he ever stepped foot in Belle's place was when we needed a doctor. He didn't go to the other brothel either. He treated all of us like we were real people. Old Doc Jones never did that."

Only Aiden would have ever married a patient so she didn't die on a four-day train trip. Nellie was right. He was a good man and far too good for Catherine.

Aiden raised the window sash a couple of inches. After the long summer, the cool nights of October didn't require as much air circulation. "Is that better?"

The mattress creaked under Catherine. "It's fine for now. You know that in ten minutes I'll just pull up the blanket anyway. I can never quite decide if I'm hot or cold."

"That's autumn for you. One minute you think it's summer, the next you think winter might come."

"Does winter ever come to Texas?"

Aiden chuckled. "When it comes, it comes with a vengeance, but it's only here for a couple of weeks." He settled into the bed behind her and started brushing her hair, an easier task with her sitting up.

"Clara and I always had fresh-pressed cider for our birthday. I'll miss it this year."

The brush in Aiden's hand caught on a snarl. His mind raced. He'd been so focused on the baby's birth he'd forgotten about Catherine's birthday. "There are several orchards to the northeast of here. I'm sure we could get a crate of apples

255

here by the sixteenth. Or maybe fresh cider. I don't know anyone with a press here."

"You could?" She sat a little taller. "I wonder if Nellie knows how to make apple-cider donuts."

"I will not wake her to find out." Aiden chuckled and tried to remember how many strokes he'd brushed. Ten?

"What would you like for your birthday, other than for the new doctor to arrive?"

"I've mentioned that a time or two?"

"Daily. If Dr. Brian Clark doesn't arrive soon, I'm going to take him to task."

"All I want is for you and this baby to be with me and for one of Nellie's jumble cakes." That was as close to the real wish as he dared say. He wanted Catherine to want to be with him, to reciprocate the feelings he had for her.

"I was able to cross off another day today. We're up to forty-four. This baby will probably be born before your birthday. I couldn't go another fifteen days in bed. Plus, that would put us at fifty-nine days. Either way, the baby will not be eating any cake."

"Yes, I noted you reached the forty-fourth day in my charts."

"Are you going to write about me in one of those medical journals?"

Twenty. Aiden stopped brushing for a moment. "I wasn't planning on it. Unless there's something significantly different from what I read, I don't know that it would be very helpful to other doctors. All we've done is keep you down and as calm as possible."

Catherine sat silent for a minute. "Thank you. I don't want doctors to come to Hiramsville looking at me as if I were some oddity."

"I wouldn't allow that. Besides, few would want to travel as far as Hiramsville just to see that you and your baby exist."

"Clara came by today. She had a letter from Mother. Mr.

Fairlane is no longer suing Father. Mama asked when you were going to send me back."

Fifty-six. Aiden set the brush down and adjusted Catherine so he could see her face. "I told you when I said 'I do,' I meant it until death do we part. I won't be sending you back, and I do hope you would like to stay."

Catherine bit her lip. "I know you say that, but …"

He searched her eyes, pleading for her to understand. "There are no buts, Catherine. There isn't anyone else in my life but you and this child, who is going to be called mine. I hope I've made that clear enough to everyone by now."

"You've said it often enough, and I know I'm supposed to believe it. I'm really trying, Aiden, I am." She reached out and took his hand.

He could see it, but she was still so unsure. He didn't know how to prove he was going to stay other than leaning over and kissing her forehead. He thought of kissing her lips, but they hadn't since the one night. For weeks, he'd thought it an accident not to be repeated as he hadn't wanted to press her. Catherine needed to choose whatever their relationship was going to be. He would press her no further. Aiden returned to brushing her hair. "It isn't so terrible, is it?"

She turned her head slightly and met his gaze. "No, it's not terrible at all. It's quite nice. Talking, having you brush my hair … there's something very special about this."

A sense of relief filled him, knowing she enjoyed their nightly ritual. "Well, it's the least I can do to make you comfortable."

Catherine leaned back into him, her head resting against his chest. Aiden could feel the steady rise and fall of her breathing. He set down the brush and enjoyed the peacefulness of the moment.

Her eyes opened, and she turned her head to face him, her eyes meeting his. "Aiden, I want to try."

"Try what?" Dare he hope?

"Try to have a real marriage. I want to give us a chance."

Aiden's heart tapped out a little jig. Was Catherine finally ready to let him into her heart? He looked at her, his eyes pleading with her to mean what she said. "Are you sure, Catherine?"

She smiled at him, a soft, gentle smile that lit up her face. "Yes, I'm sure. I want to be with you, Aiden. I want to have a genuine marriage and genuine family with you."

Joy and relief washed over him. He turned to face her better, contemplating how much he dared kiss her. Further intimacies would have to wait for weeks. He did the math in his head. Catherine might complain about the forty days they had forced her to lie in bed. It would be almost as long before… Aiden pushed the thought out of his mind.

He kissed her, softly at first, savoring the touch of her lips against his, the passion he'd dammed up for the past weeks threatening to spill over the banks like the Brazos in a spring flood. He fought to keep it back as his lips pressed more hungrily against hers and his arms surrounded her protectively. The kiss intensified, full of longing and hope. Catherine relaxed into him, her body melting into his. She responded eagerly, her lips caressing his, so familiar yet so new. He lifted her gently. For the first time since they got married, Aiden felt like they were connected, two halves of a whole united.

"Catherine," Aiden murmured softly against her hair, "I love you."

Catherine lifted her head, her lips curved in a smile. She ran a finger down the side of his mustache before leaning in to gently press another kiss against his lips.

Aiden tucked her head under his chin. She hadn't returned his declaration. Could it be enough that she wanted to stay? Perhaps he'd hear the words someday.

After several minutes, she said, "I should probably get some sleep."

"Your doctor would agree. He'd probably chastise me for—"

She pressed a finger over his mouth. "You can tell him it's my fault. He's always after me for wanting to do too much."

"Noted, Mrs. Palmer. I shall tell the doctor his opinion isn't wanted."

Catherine smiled and buried her head in his shoulder. "Not at the moment."

Aiden helped her into a better position and adjusted the pillows. After extinguishing the lamp on the nightstand next to them, he cast aside his shirt and pants and opted for his old nightshirt. He wanted to feel close to his wife tonight, and he couldn't do that wearing his doctor's clothes.

The crickets had long since quieted, and no moon lit the bedroom. Catherine's stomach tightened, and the pain in her lower back intensified. She took a deep breath, trying to relax as Lavender taught her. Minutes later, the tightness and pain increased.

This pain differed from that of weeks ago—deeper, as if it needed to grow in force with the remaining child.

Aiden still slept beside her. He'd done that more in recent weeks. Tonight was the first time he'd shed his day clothes. They hadn't talked after he turned out the light, nor had they kissed. But he'd held her as she drifted off to sleep.

Another contraction. An urge to get up and walk around pulled Catherine to the edge of the bed. Was it safe? Lavender told her they would use a birthing stool this time and she could walk if she felt like it.

Another contraction. Catherine patiently waited for it to pass, then rolled over and nudged her husband. "Aiden, Aiden, wake up. It's time."

Aiden's eyes flew open, and he sat up. "It's time? The baby's coming?"

"Yes."

Aiden rolled over to get out of the bed and fell to the floor, the clatter he made trying to get up and pull on his pants sure to wake both Lavender and Nellie. Aiden righted himself and grabbed for the shirt he'd hung on the bedpost. He pulled it over his head—backward. Catherine covered her mouth to keep from laughing. Light spilled in from the hallway.

"Is anything wrong?" asked Lavender.

Behind her, Nellie held the kitchen lantern high.

"She's having a baby." Aiden's shirt now faced the front, albeit inside out. One suspender hung loosely down by his trousers. His nightshirt, still on, was tangled with the other suspender.

Catherine giggled. "Yes. I am having a baby, and the doctor seems to have suddenly become useless."

Lavender stepped into the room. "Dr. Palmer, it's time for you to leave."

"But I'm the doctor."

"Not tonight. We've discussed this. I will help deliver Catherine's child. You will take care of the rest of the town."

"What if—"

"I'll find you at the office if you are needed." Lavender gave him a little push.

Aiden stumbled out the bedroom door, then returned a moment later. "I didn't tell Catherine goodbye."

Lavender threw up her hands. "Nellie, let's get dressed and gather the kit I assembled. The baby isn't coming in the next few minutes."

Nellie left the lantern on the bureau.

Aiden looked at the retreating women as if he was losing his lifeline. Catherine reached her hand out to him. "You've been telling me for weeks that everything will come out fine. Should I believe you?"

"Yes, sorry. I was only startled." His voice was much calmer.

"Then take off your nightshirt and put your shirt on correctly. I'd hate for anyone to think you were less than calm."

Aiden looked down, frowned, and pulled his shirt off again. "Not my finest moment."

Catherine opened her mouth to answer, but a contraction stopped the words. "Ooooooh."

When it ended, Aiden leaned over and kissed her forehead. "Lavender is back. I need to go."

Catherine released his hand.

Lavender entered with Nellie. "Let's get you comfortable."

Was that even possible?

⊰◆⊱

Mrs. Bickford slammed her book on the desk. "Dr. Palmer, if you don't stop pacing, I'm going to send Donny to get TJ to haul you out of here."

"Sorry." Aiden stopped near the front door and rubbed the back of his neck. "It's been hours."

"Often is."

"I know, but—" Aiden took a step.

Mrs. Bickford stood. "You trusted Lavender enough to hire her, didn't you?"

"Yes."

"Her doctor's training had a focus on maternity, correct?"

"Yes."

"Do you trust her?"

"Yes."

"Then either go upstairs, read something, or take a walk. I'm putting up the Doctor Is Out sign because you aren't fit to treat a skinned knee." Mrs. Bickford went to the door and hung the sign. "Go on with you, now. In fact, go upstairs and change. Don't shave, though. I'm not in the mood to plaster your face."

Aiden retreated to his room upstairs. How much longer would this be his room? Until now, there had been no chance of their marriage becoming a real one. But now, for the first time, he felt confident she wouldn't ask for an annulment, which would be possible for only a few more weeks. A woman needed to heal. He didn't need Lavender to lecture him about that. He could read the medical journal as well as she could. Yet, there was no reason they couldn't go on sleeping as they had last night. He could offer his help at night. He'd diapered children before.

He washed and changed, keeping one ear open for any arrival downstairs. Against his nurse's advice, he shaved—a feat he accomplished without a nick. Once in fresh clothing, he felt calmer. He went to the window in the room Jax recently vacated, where he could see the roof of his home. A wisp of smoke came from the kitchen chimney. Nellie must be cooking or boiling more water. If only he knew.

Below, the front door opened. Aiden was halfway down the stairs before it shut.

"Is Dr. Palmer in?"

"I'm here, Lewis." Aiden hurtled the last few feet.

"Come spend the afternoon at the manse. Reverend Green is visiting and waiting to hear the news as well. Clara reassures me they will find you as soon as the baby is here."

What was taking so long? He tried to calm his worry. Eight hours wasn't that long. He'd told a nervous husband that very thing last spring. "I want to be close by."

"Mrs. Bickford needs to leave soon, and you don't want to be here alone. Donny can run the distance between our homes in less than two minutes. The baby won't finish its first cry before he's on the doorstep."

"Someday we need to time that kid." Aiden locked the door to his personal office. "Mrs. Bickford, it seems I'm being removed from my office as well."

His nurse laughed. "Just as well, Doc. See you in the morning." Mrs. Bickford waved him out of the office.

Reverend Green sat in his favorite chair, contemplating a tray of sandwiches and tea cakes. "Mrs. Reese sent these over. We may have enough to last us through the night."

"I hope we don't need all of them." Aiden took a sandwich and sat on the davenport.

Lewis did the same. "There is enough variety here that we shan't grow bored with the fare. I haven't seen cakes like this since my mother's teas."

"Between painting and papering rooms, they've been testing the kitchen at the new Rose's. I am not an expert, but even Thelma's gushing over the new ovens. They've given me the job of official taste tester since no one allows me to do anything other than play chaperone for Jax. Which, frankly, isn't needed," said Reverend Green.

"I thought Jax was interested in Lavender," said Aiden.

Reverend Green chuckled. "He is interested, all right, but he knows better than to do anything but admire from a distance. As for Miss Lavender, she's much like your wife."

Aiden jumped when the reverend pointed a finger at him. "What about my wife?"

"Your wife loves you."

"But she doesn't." At least not yet.

Reverend Green smiled and looked at Lewis. "I find most people have a problem clearly seeing their own hearts. Doc, you're going to need to be patient with her for a while yet. I suggest using Job as a model."

The words cut Aiden, and he felt the need to defend himself. "I haven't given up on her. I've been trying—"

Reverend Green held up a hand. "I know you have. I'm merely telling you not to give up. One of these days, she'll be able to see herself as you do."

The front door banged open, and Donny rushed in. "Doc, I heard the baby. Miss Clara told me to come get you the second I heard a cry."

"Go." Reverend Green waved him out of the room.

Aiden ran across town, possibly breaking Donny's record. He had to wait a few minutes before Lavender allowed him into the bedroom.

Catherine was radiant, sitting up in bed in a fresh nightgown, holding the squirming bundle. "Are you well?"

Catherine nodded.

"Mother and child are both in perfect health. You can read my notes later." Lavender answered from behind him. She then shut the door, leaving them alone.

⟫⟨

"Would you like to see him?" asked Catherine as she pulled back the blanket.

"It's a boy?" Aiden's face softened. He reached out not to the baby but to her, cupping the side of her face and brushing her cheek with his thumb. "And you are well?"

"I am." She returned his searching gaze. She wasn't Susannah or Cathleen. She was alive. Hopefully, that would bring her husband some peace.

Aiden dropped his hand and finally looked at her son. As far as she could tell, the baldheaded child didn't favor either parent—although Clara announced the baby had Catherine's nose and, by extension, her own.

"Would you like to hold him?"

Aiden's smile grew as wide as his mustache as he reached for the child, then cradled him against his chest. "Hello. I'm Aiden Palmer. May I be your father?"

The baby yawned.

Catherine tried to swallow past the lump that formed in her throat, and tears pooled in her eyes. He'd asked permission of the baby. She never expected him to … In that moment, she understood. Even if the baby had been born with a mustache, he couldn't be more Aiden's child than he was now.

"May I?" Aiden looked up at her.

She nodded until the word came out. "Yes."

"Did you hear that? I get to be your papa." He smiled at their child, then leaned against the headboard so they could both watch their sleeping son. A warm contentment washed over Catherine, and the lump in her throat faded.

Aiden set the child back in her arms. "What do you want to name him?"

"I thought of Timison, after my grandfather on my mother's side, since I named his sister Sarah after his wife, my grandmother. I also thought of naming him after Reverend Green, but I don't know his name."

"Isaac."

"Timison Isaac. Do you like it?" Catherine whispered.

"His initials will spell Tip."

"Tim, Timmy, Tip. I don't think it's too bad compared to the other names he's likely to be called." She snuggled into Aiden's side.

"I like the names you've chosen."

"Reverend Green's helped me so much. Even Clara didn't know his name, though they'd lived in the same house and she works with him daily." She'd thought of naming the boy after Aiden, but thought he might prefer naming his own son that one day, if…

"You can live in the same house for a long time and still not know someone." He wasn't talking about the reverend. He was talking about her, although it applied equally to him.

There was so much he had yet to share of his life.

Would she ever know him? He knew her worst side—or most of it. Only Clara and Reverend Green knew of the mean things she'd done as a child. Lewis probably knew most of them too. If this child was anything like her…

Aiden brushed a kiss across her temple. "I should let you rest. You just yawned."

"I did?"

He reached for the baby. "I'll put him in the cradle."

There was a cradle? Catherine yawned. Of course there was. Aiden would have made sure of that detail. She yawned again and sunk into the bed. Aiden kissed her forehead again. Always so kind.

iden lifted his ten-day-old son from Catherine's arms and handed him to Clara before assisting his wife down.

"I hadn't expected there to be so many people. There must be close to five hundred." Clara snuggled the baby before giving him back to her sister. "I need to see if they need my help in the kitchen. I hope we made enough cake."

The October day had yet to warm to its fullest. Catherine adjusted the knitted shawl over Tip. "I didn't realize there were so many people in town. But then, the only time I've been outside was Clara's wedding day."

Aiden laid a protective hand on his wife's back and guided her around the throng to the place reserved for members of the board. "Our little church holds only a small part of the population. There are about 750 people in the area if you count Acton and the Springs."

After short speeches from Mrs. Reese and Emily, Reverend Green dedicated the building. As promised, the formal portion of the celebration was kept to under twenty minutes.

While most people went inside for a tour, several women from Rose's surrounded Catherine, all vying for a chance to see Tip. Catherine turned him in her arms so they could get a better look.

"May we hold him while you tour the building?" asked Peony.

Catherine settled her little one into Peony's arms.

Aiden tucked his wife's hand in his arm as they entered the building. He'd been inside several times, but this was the first time he could show Catherine. With more than four times the square footage of the old building, the new Rose's Rescue could help so many more women.

They entered the large ballroom, where folding dividers divided the room into three separate spaces. One held various refreshments, the center area was empty, and the back portion was a classroom. Like the original Rose's Rescue, the classroom area was set up with round tables. Windows lined the north wall, giving plenty of light without overwhelming the room.

Catherine examined one of the curtains. "I think these were ours. Here is the mended tear from when we played hide-and-seek. Green was all the rage. Lewis's mother did well to gather all the old parlor curtains now that our neighborhood has switched to gold."

"Did all your neighbors keep their houses the same?"

"I suppose. If one man had his house painted, it wouldn't be long until painters could be seen up and down the street."

They moved on to the next room. What should have been the dining room contained seven sewing machines and the same number of cutting tables. A well-dressed man inspected one of the machines. Aiden paused. "Mr. Call, correct?"

"Yes. You're the doctor. I'm sorry. I forgot your name."

"Dr. Palmer, and this is my wife, Mrs. Palmer." It was the first time he'd introduced Catherine as such. He couldn't help but stand a bit taller as he did. "Mr. Call owns ladies' dress shops in Fort Worth and Dallas."

"Mrs. Palmer. If I am not mistaken, you are wearing a dress fashioned by Rose's women. My customers will be so pleased to know they're back in business."

Catherine smoothed her skirt. "How can you tell?"

"I have an eye for these things." Mr. Call smiled broadly.

"We so appreciate the donation of the sewing machines," said Aiden.

"Purely selfish on my part. Since the fire, the orders have piled up. And now that we have cooler weather, the city's society women must have new frocks." He laughed good-naturedly.

Mrs. Reese entered the room, and Mr. Call excused himself to speak with her.

Catherine leaned in close. "Does he pay them a fair price?"

"I believe he does. You can imagine what Emily and Mrs. Reese would do if he did not."

"I'd be more worried about Marigold."

Aiden suppressed a laugh. He suspected Marigold had a bit of outlaw in her history. She'd bested TJ at target practice.

They continued into the kitchen, which was separated from the main building by a dog trot.

Nellie stood in the middle of the enormous room. "Three stoves. I'm glad I'm working for you, Doc. I wouldn't want to be in charge here. Even with all the windows, in summer, this room will be a preview to Hades. Miss Emily says I shouldn't say the other place."

Catherine laughed. "Anyplace with fire and brimstone is accurate."

"Just wait until we start your cooking lessons." Nellie's eyes twinkled.

As others came into the kitchen, commenting on the large space, Aiden and Catherine exited through the back door. A vegetable-and-herb garden abutted the kitchen. A half-fin-ished barn stood at the back of the yard. Since it housed only Jax's horse, there was no rush to finish it. Eventually, Mrs. Reese had plans for draft horses and a wagon.

A smaller house stood not far from it. Aiden nodded to the small building. "That's where Reverend Green and Jax live."

"From what Reverend Green said, I didn't picture it as a separate building."

"Probably because he spends most of his day sitting on the porch of the main building. I believe his health is improving by being up here."

The midwife came around the corner. Aiden was surprised to see her there, considering her stance on Rose's and its students. "Mrs. Forsythe, how do you do?"

"I hoped I would find you here, Doc. I needed to tell you I'm moving to Dallas to live with my granddaughters. I don't know if you heard. My daughter-in-law is to be incarcerated for arson. The court has ruled that my sweet Libby Jean may live with her sister, but she is not allowed to come to the county again."

"When will you be leaving?"

"Two, maybe three weeks. I need to clean out the house and sell it."

"And your patients?"

"I'll bring over my notebooks. I don't know how many will allow that woman you have working with you to see them, but as near as I can tell, she knows what she is doing, and I told them so."

"Thank you for your endorsement."

"Not an endorsement, just the truth." Mrs. Forsythe studied the hotel for a moment. "I think this place is a fine thing. Just don't tell anyone I said so."

Aiden stared in astonishment as she hurried off.

"Was that the midwife?" asked Catherine.

"Yes, I'm sorry. I forgot you haven't had a chance to meet everyone. Her granddaughter was the one who threw paint on Clara."

"I gathered. She seems rather sad."

Hands in pockets, Donny walked up to them.

"Something wrong?" asked Aiden

"I need some advice, Doc." He motioned to Catherine. "Private, like."

"I need to find Tip anyway." Catherine nodded and walked off in search of their son, who was likely hungry by now.

"What's the problem?"

"Ma's recipes. Miss Emily told me Mom showed these women how to make some of her salves and balms. She asked us if we wanted to share them with The Rescue. My sisters didn't care, but they are Ma's secrets."

Aiden looked for somewhere they could talk privately and led Donny to a bench under a large pecan tree. "So you are of the mind that the recipes shouldn't be shared."

"I dunno. I mean, Ma already shared them, but they are hers. And she didn't have much to pass on."

"Is it that The Rescue would be making them or that you wouldn't have the papers?"

Donny thought for a moment. "Ma had such pretty handwriting."

"What if you gave The Rescue a copy of the recipe and you kept the originals for you and your sisters?"

Donny sat a bit straighter. "Would it be okay not to give them the bluebonnet one?"

"Of course, if it is special to you."

"Ma said she made it when she was expecting me." Donny's eyes clouded.

Aiden laid a hand on the boy's back. "Think about it for a day or even a week. Most decisions don't need to be made in haste."

"Thanks, Doc." Donny ran off. Did that boy ever slow down?

Aiden had an image of Tip running as fast one day. He only hoped he could keep up.

Nestled in the corner of the second floor of Rose's was a private parlor. Two rocking chairs, still smelling of newly oiled wood, took up most of the space. Petunia nursed Scotty in one, rocking him gently. She held one of his hands to keep him from sticking it in her mouth as he had tried to for the last few minutes.

"Does he always play like that?" Catherine looked down at the small, contented figure she held. Tip's eyes blinked sleepily as he ate.

"Only when he's not falling asleep. I learned to keep my hair out of range by the time he was three months old." Petunia shared other advice on motherhood as they rocked their babies.

Catherine listened intently. Petunia's help had been invaluable over the past week. Feeding a child wasn't as easy as one would assume. If not for her new friend's help, Catherine would have dissolved into a puddle of tears before Tip was four days old.

From the window, Catherine watched people leaving. "It looks like the party is over."

"I'm not sad to see them gone. I'm not fond of crowds." Petunia shifted her son to her shoulder, where he burped and promptly fell asleep.

Tip had long since finished and slept in Catherine's arms.

"I'll put this one in his crib. You can put Tip in the basket in the corner."

Catherine stood. "I think we should be leaving soon."

"Not just yet. The board has a meeting, and your husband needs to stay."

Catherine placed Tip in the basket and followed Petunia back downstairs. No one milled around the entranceway as they had only a half hour ago.

Catherine stood on the bottom step, getting a better look at the room that would have been the hotel lobby but now was a large parlor. "It seems bigger without half the town here."

"Mrs. Reese thinks next to the theater, Rose's has the largest spaces in town. Have you seen the ballroom?" Petunia stepped toward the large double doors.

"Yes."

"You should see it again." Petunia motioned Catherine near.

Catherine pointed to the back hall. "I was going to see if there was anything left to eat."

"Please?" Petunia reached for Catherine's elbow.

Catherine hesitated for a moment, but not willing to offend her new friend, allowed Petunia to take her to the ballroom.

Petunia opened the door and propelled Catherine in first. Everyone she knew, and a few people she didn't recognize, stood in a large semicircle. Nellie started the first note, and everyone joined in. "For she's a jolly good fellow..."

Catherine searched Aiden's and Clara's faces, unsure of what was happening. At the end of the song, aware the babies were sleeping, everyone quiet-yelled, "Happy birthday!"

Catherine looked at her twin. "It's yours too."

Clara came to Catherine's side. "Yes, but since everyone missed out on your wedding and we didn't get to do much to prepare for little Timison, or Tip, as Aiden says, this is for you and Aiden. Although he thought he was only planning a party for you."

Catherine looked around, wide-eyed. "You shouldn't have."

"And give up the opportunity to make apple-cider donuts?" asked Nellie. "That's been the best part. You nearly found them when you came to inspect the kitchen."

"I was so worried Doc would see the cake." Becky stepped to the side, revealing a white, frosted layer cake. "Congratulations!"

Aiden stepped to Catherine's side. "But we already had cake on our wedding day."

Mrs. Reese used her fan to scold Aiden. "We didn't have a proper party with you insisting your bride stay in bed and she was so tired. Lavender sent most of us away."

Catherine clutched Aiden's arm. "This is all too much. Thank you."

Donny held up a blanket. "Most of the presents are for the baby. The best thing is the donuts. Nellie's made me taste them all week to be sure she had the right recipe. Wednesday's were awful." He put a hand on his stomach.

Nellie stuck out her tongue.

Everyone laughed.

The last streaks of pink lined the western sky as they rode home, Catherine feeling as tired as Tip. She leaned into Aiden's shoulder, not bothering to hide her yawn.

"I shouldn't have kept you out so long." Aiden patted her leg with his free hand.

"Don't say that. It was perfect. I can't believe they went to all that trouble. And the new quilt for our bed…I can't believe you didn't know." She yawned again. "Or you didn't get called out to help someone."

"I did. That's why Lavender and Jax left about an hour ago."

Catherine sat up. "Has she gone on a house call?"

"This will be her first time, other than delivering Tip."

"Do you think she'll ever let Jax court her?"

"I hope she can someday."

"Did you want to court her?" She hadn't seen any evidence of partiality on either part. Still, she needed to know once and for all if her jealousy was founded or simply a product of the boredom of being in bed so long.

"The thought crossed my mind once or twice, but I knew she didn't want a man in her life. Besides, she is much like a younger sister to me now. And, as you have noticed, there is Jax."

"Is she going to keep working for you?"

"I don't know. She wants to wait for the new doctor to arrive to decide. But with Mrs. Forsythe moving to Dallas, Hiramsville needs Lavender."

"That elusive doctor is making me feel very put out." Catherine thought of the telegram Aiden received two days ago, moving Dr. Clark's arrival day well into November. "I'm beginning to think he'll never arrive."

"He'd better. I'd like to have a night where I can finish brushing your hair without interruption."

The past three nights had been rather inconvenient, although Tip had provided the interruption to one of them. Catherine leaned deeper into his side. "That would be nice."

Aiden chuckled, his laugh vibrating through her. Catherine closed her eyes, savoring the moment and the peace she felt. Today was perhaps the first birthday she wasn't interested in what she might receive. She hadn't expected anything, although she hoped Aiden would remember her desire for fresh cider. She and Clara had planned a dinner celebration for Sunday. A ruse on her sister's part, which Catherine would insist happen if, for no other reason, she could give Clara her gift. It had arrived from the catalog the same day as Aiden's birthday gift.

Aiden had already extracted a promise from her to not plan any type of celebration for his birthday, claiming if she did, fate would prevent him from attending. He couldn't stop her from baking a cake all by herself.

iden paced the floor. As long as he kept moving, Tip stayed asleep. Colic—a fancy term for "The doctor has no idea why the baby cries all night." Every night for two weeks, they'd been up with him. For half of his little life, Tip had not been able to sleep, and neither had anyone else in the house. Nellie had moved to Mrs. Reese's and only came over in the daytime so Catherine could sleep.

None of his medical journals had the answers. The few women he asked gave him ideas after laughing about the fact that he didn't know the solution. He ignored the advice to administer Tip a popular infant sleeping aid, knowing it contained opium. There had to be a better solution. Although part of him didn't mind that, his son needed him for comfort, as Aiden felt he did so little as a father otherwise.

Catherine padded out of the bedroom, reaching her arms out not for Aiden but for Tip. "You need sleep."

"So do you," he answered in a soft voice so as not to wake Tip.

"I can catch naps during the day. The town's doctor can't."

Dr. Clark should have been here a week ago. The man

may have caught wind that his duties would include being on call several nights a week.

"We could try to lay him down again." Aiden adjusted his hold, bringing Tip from his shoulder into his arms. Tip stirred but didn't wake.

"If he cries, I'll walk with him."

Tip stirred, and his mouth puckered.

Aiden tried something that worked last night. "Swing low, sweet chariot, coming for to carry me home."

Catherine's eyes widened, and she laid her hand on her chest. Aiden hadn't sung much around her because he didn't want to give her any more ideas about the singing group.

When Tip's breathing deepened, Aiden sang the next verse as he walked to their room and laid his son down in the cradle. He sang softer as he climbed into bed, where Catherine joined him. When she opened her mouth to say something, Aiden set his finger on her lips and shook his head as he started another verse. When it ended, the room was silent.

Catherine pressed her lips to his cheek, a silent thank-you, the only kind she'd given him since the night she agreed to stay. A platonic marriage. He'd hoped they wouldn't revert, hardly touching during her month-and-half-long recovery period. Lavender had shown him several articles extolling the practice of a six-week convalescence.

Maybe once Tip slept through the night and they could move him from his cradle to another room ... Maybe then Aiden could convince Catherine to love him. He knew she was trying. The lopsided cake she'd made last week for his birthday was proof. Aiden wasn't sure if the new nightshirts contained some hidden meaning or if she'd grown tired of mending his old threadbare one. Some silent agreement kept them from discussing matters between them, the same agreement that kept their relationship platonic—unless

Catherine shared his concerns that if they did start kissing, all the things they'd been feeling and suppressing would carry them away like a Texas tornado.

⟞◆⟝

Six weeks old. Just as Petunia predicted, Tip slept through the night. Following the advice of her friend, Catherine played with him as much as she could during the day. Tip would stick out his tongue and try to make faces, his smiles coming most often when he played with the rattle Donny had carved.

Lavender finished checking the baby over. "He is growing like he should be. And you seem to be back to full health. My work here is done."

"I hope you'll still come to visit." Catherine took Tip back.

"Of course I will." Lavender stretched and put her feet on the ottoman. "I need to put my feet up. Every time I try to at work, Aiden looks at me like he's going to give me a lecture. He knows as well as I do that it will take months for my burns to fully heal. And since Dr. Clark decided small-town life isn't for him, I've been on my feet more than I'd like."

Three days. The man had barely been in town long enough to see it before he left. Catherine bit her lip. She'd hoped Dr. Clark would stay and she wouldn't have to ask the next question. "I need your help."

"How?"

"Can you convince Aiden to let you take the night calls for one of these next few days?" Her cheeks started to burn. "I want to—"

Lavender smiled and leaned forward. "Make it so an annulment isn't so easy?"

"Yes, that."

"Can I tell you a secret?"

Catherine nodded.

"Aiden already asked me to take Wednesday night since it's the quietest. And he blushed almost as much as you are."

"He did?"

Lavender sat back, a smile on her lips. "Now you just have to convince Tip to give you the night off."

atherine picked up a spool of blue thread from the display in the mercantile. She wanted to do something special to mark their three-month anniversary and the promised night alone. The thought of making something for Aiden flew from her head when a man entered, looking at her with a malevolence Catherine couldn't name. She moved to the fabrics. The man's eyes followed her. He'd been near the church earlier. "Nellie, do you know how long that man has been watching us?"

"I thought he was just looking at me."

"I think he followed us from Clara's." He was as tall as Jax and looked to be as strong. He wasn't one of the rangers that accompanied TJ's brother to town.

"Hmm." Nellie stepped closer as the man continued to look at them.

Catherine set the spool down and took Tip from Nellie. "If he follows us out, I'm going to pay TJ a visit at the sheriff's office. Get what you need. I'll wait."

While Nellie went to the counter and purchased a sugar cone, Catherine wandered to the display of new books, the man's eyes continuing to follow her. Who was he?

She kept her steps deliberately slow as they exited. The man followed.

"Should we visit Hannah?" Catherine asked loudly enough for the man to hear as she neared the door of the hotel. She didn't care what Nellie answered.

They found Hannah in the hotel dining room, cleaning up after lunch. "Mrs. Palmer, did you bring Tip just to see me?"

"Of course."

The man watched them through the window. Catherine turned her back to him and offered Hannah the baby. When Hannah was close enough, Catherine whispered, "There's a man with a brown leather vest watching us through the window. Do you know him?"

"He and his friends came in last night. They have two rooms. Is he bothering you?" Hannah rested Tip on her ample shoulder.

"I think he's following me."

"You can leave through the kitchen. Likely, you can be in the sheriff's office before he figures out what happened." Hannah handed the baby back. "Nellie, show her the way."

TJ wasn't there. The deputy stood as they entered. "May I help you?"

"This is going to sound silly, but I think a man is following me. Hannah said he came into town last night with his friends."

"Four of them?"

Catherine looked at Nellie, who shrugged. "Hannah couldn't say, but they took two rooms."

The deputy's lips thinned. "TJ went out to meet them. They smell like trouble. You should hurry home."

"Not if he's following me. We'll be alone."

The deputy rubbed the back of his neck. "Oh, maybe the doctor's office, then. The sheriff told me not to leave."

Not helpful. However, they would be on busy streets most of the way. If the man was following, he wouldn't accost them in front of people. "Come on, Nellie."

"No." Nellie set her basket on the sheriff's desk.

"What?"

"I don't know him, but I know men like him." Nellie looked around the room. "Deputy, do you mind if we borrow that pillow?"

Nellie walked over to the worn sofa and picked up an equally threadbare pillow.

"No, why?"

"Blanket, please." Nellie held out her hand to Catherine.

Catherine took the blanket off Tip's back.

Nellie wrapped Tip's blanket around the pillow. "I'll keep Tip here. That way if that man and his friends try anything, they won't hurt him. School is almost out. Donny can come get me if it's safe."

Catherine hesitated. Next to Aiden, she trusted Nellie most. "Won't he notice you aren't with me?"

"Likely not. If he does, I'll be in the safest place in town." Nellie pointed to the kitchen. The main level of the jail was a residence where the deputy now lived.

"The kitchen is pretty dirty, ma'am." The deputy's face reddened.

"Of course it is. Well I ain't cleanin' it. Don't you dare 'ma'am' me. What do you think I'm going to do while I'm here? Twiddle my thumbs? No, I'm going to hold a baby. And this room is too cold, so your cookstove better have some wood."

If she wasn't scared of the man lurking outside, Catherine would have laughed at the deputy being cowed by a fifteen-year-old half his size. She handed her son to Nellie. "Keep him safe."

"I will."

Although similar in size, the pillow was lighter than Tip. Catherine added the sugar cone to the fake baby-in-a-blanket and left. She crossed the street at the corner. By the time she reached the first shop, the man was following her again. This was not how today was supposed to go. Nellie was going to help her make Aiden a cake to celebrate Tip's sleeping through the night again and that they could move him out of their bedroom. Lavender was staying at the office tonight with Marigold to handle any emergencies. Alone in their room, she would tell Aiden the three words that had been tumbling inside her for weeks. Whether it was choice or fate, she loved him.

When the man drew closer, Catherine quickened her step. She shouldn't have been daydreaming about Aiden.

She turned the corner and hurried down to the second building, where Aiden's office was. Mrs. Bickford came out of the small kitchen in the back. "Mrs. Palmer, the doctor is in room one with a patient if you want to wait in his office. If you are here for Miss Lavender, she was called out a few minutes ago."

"Emily?" Her friend had complained about being as big as a barn on Sunday.

"You know I can't say. But I sent Donny to look for TJ."

Catherine tried to calm her nerves. If there was trouble, only the deputy was nearby. Catherine went into Aiden's office to not be in the way. She set the pillow on the chair and waited. No one came into the building. Perhaps it was nothing. Another one of her emotions being weird, like crying most of Tip's second week of life.

The door to room one opened, and she heard Aiden tell someone goodbye. A moment later, he entered his office and closed the door. "To what do I owe this vis—" His eyes fell to the pillow. "Catherine?"

"There was a man following us. Hannah advised us to go to the jail, but TJ wasn't there. The deputy said four men ...

anyway. Nellie has Tip safe at the jail. She'll stay there until we know it's safe. I left with the blanket wrapped like a baby, and the man followed me."

"Have you—" A scream from the lobby cut off his words.

<hr>

Aiden threw open the door. A man held Mrs. Bickford with his hand over her mouth. Two other men stood near her.

Aiden looked back at his wife. "Lock it!"

The door closed behind him, and he heard the click.

"How can I help you?"

"The woman and baby that just came in here. Are they yours?" asked the tallest man.

"Which woman?" Aiden's best tactic was to stall.

"I thought you said there were no more patients here." The man turned on the short one next to him.

"There aren't. Ask her." The short one pointed to Mrs. Bickford.

Aiden's poor nurse was shaking in the third man's arms.

"Besides yourself and the doc, who else is here?" The man holding Mrs. Bickford pulled out a knife and held it in front of her face.

Mrs. Bickford's eyes pled with Aiden. The truth would come out anyway. Aiden gave a slight nod.

"Just the doctor's wife and baby."

Aiden stepped forward. "What do you want?"

"It's pretty simple, Doc. No one will get hurt if you do what we say. All I need you to do is sign these papers." The tall man pulled a sheaf of papers from his vest.

"What are they?"

"Annulment papers."

"I don't want an annulment."

"Then we'll have to do this the hard way."

The front door opened, and Donny ran in.

Aiden yelled at him, "Get out!"

The short man lunged at Donny, but Donny was faster. The man started after him but was stopped by one who appeared to be a boss. "Leave the boy. We need to finish our business here."

Aiden stepped forward. "What's the hard way?"

"See, we're gonna make this woman scream until we find your wife. Then, if you don't sign these papers, we'll just have to make her a widow."

"Let Mrs. Bickford go, and I'll read your papers."

"Sign the papers and we'll let her go."

Aiden's head spun. There had to be a way to get Mrs. Bickford out of here. "You claim if I sign the papers, you'll let me live. How do I know you're not lying? Hand me the papers and let her go."

The three men looked at each other. The tall one patted the gun still in his belt. "How about this? Mrs. Bickford can go into that room there." He pointed to room number one. "She can even lock herself in. If you don't sign, we'll break down the door and kill her before we break down the door of that other room and drag your wife out. Remember, we only have to deliver her to our employer. We don't have to treat her like a lady. Don't do anything stupid, or Catherine will pay."

They knew her name. There was only one man who would orchestrate this. Bernard. "And my son?"

"The brat will come with us. You'd be surprised what a woman will do to protect her child."

Worse and worse. Hopefully, Donny had raised the alarm. Aiden stepped forward and took the papers. "Mrs. Bickford goes into room one."

The man holding her shoved her away from him. "You're a lucky woman. The doc cares about you."

Aiden read the papers. The annulment was based on the

fact that Catherine was married to another man and had married Aiden under false pretenses. Some lawyer had gone to an awful lot of trouble. The men fidgeted. How much more time could he buy? TJ was home by now, and Jax was likely up at The Rescue. He hoped the deputy would obey TJ's last order and stay at the jail with his baby. Aiden stepped behind Mrs. Bickford's desk.

"What ya doing?"

Aiden didn't look up to see who spoke. "I need a pen if I'm going to sign these."

As he hoped, there was a jar of ink with the dip pen in the top drawer. Mrs. Bickford didn't like the newfangled ink-filled pens. Aiden set the papers down, keeping the men's attention all on him. Unlike room two, room one had a window. He hoped Mrs. Bickford had enough wits about her to use it as an exit.

As slowly as he dared, Aiden unscrewed the cap to the ink jar, then made a show of dipping the pen into it. He lifted the pen out, and with his left hand, picked up the ink, throwing an arc of the stuff across the three men's faces.

They roared, the two smaller men wiping at their eyes, the third lunging at Aiden. Aiden drove the sharpened pen into the man's arm and pushed Mrs. Bickford's desk forward, ramming the three. He then leaped to the entrance of the hallway, standing between the three men and the second room, which served as his office and where Catherine was trapped. They were on him in seconds.

"Woh-who-ey! Who-ey! Who-ey! Woh-who-ey! who-ey!" The rebel yell that came out of Aiden's mouth was an automatic reaction to the assault. Like it had sixteen years ago, it gave him an extra dose of strength, and he drove his fists into his attackers, this time not to save himself but the lives of the two most precious things in his life. He should have told Catherine he loved her again and again. He should have peppered her with kisses and cherished her while Tip slept, even if there was a chance they'd be interrupted.

If he survived, he would never kiss her on the forehead again. His wife would never question if he'd only married her to save her life. How ironic that he finally had something to live for but was going to die.

He lashed out again and again, yelling as he did. Someone pinned him by the arms, and something crashed to the floor. Then a fist plowed into his diaphragm, robbing him of air as another knocked his head back. A gun fired. And another. The last thing he heard as he hit the floor was Catherine screaming his name.

iden!”

A third shot was fired. More yelling and then silence.

Was he alive? Catherine scrambled for the key. She had to know.

“Mrs. Palmer?” She didn't recognize the man's voice. Was it one of the men who'd come for her?

“Catherine? Are you in there? It's Marigold.”

“Yes.” Her voice shook like her hands. She slipped the key in the lock only to have it fall to the floor.

“Don't come out yet,” said someone.

“Is he dead? Please tell me Aiden isn't dead.”

“He's alive.” Again Marigold's voice came through the door.

Catherine found the key and opened the door. No one was going to keep her from Aiden. Blood covered the floor and Aiden's face. He wasn't moving. Catherine clutched the doorframe.

She.

Would.

Not.

Swoon.

Mrs. Bickford knelt near Aiden's head, holding a cloth to it. "He's bleeding, but I don't think he was shot."

Men filled the room, men Catherine recognized from church and her walks around town. The bootmaker and Mr. Tarr held a bleeding man between them. A man from the bank and Mr. Collins stood near the back door with guns trained on the third man, who held his hands over his head. The postmaster bent over the man who'd followed her as he lay on the floor. A growing pool of blood surrounded him.

"Dead."

TJ pushed his way into the room. "What happened?"

Everyone started talking at once.

Marigold whistled a sharp note.

Silence filled the room.

Mrs. Bickford stood, her face pale. "First things first. Help me get Doc into room one. Sheriff, I need Lavender. I can't do this alone. I know your wife needs her too, but—"

"Lavender is coming. Mrs. Reese and Thelma are with Emily. They tell me it's too soon for the baby to come and things are likely to calm down. If not, they'll send word when the baby is born." TJ handcuffed the man who'd surrendered to Mr. Collins.

Catherine followed Marigold, the postmaster, Mr. Collins, and the man from the bank as they carried Aiden into the examination room. "What can I do?"

"Where is your baby?" asked TJ.

"With Nellie at the jail." Catherine pointed to the dead man. "That man was following me. I didn't think he'd hurt—"

The room spun, and she reached for the doorjamb.

Marigold forced Catherine to sit in a chair. "Everyone, out of this room. TJ, get those men in jail. And if you need to know, I shot the dead man. Can I be a deputy now?"

Catherine didn't hear the answer. Marigold stayed with her after the men left. Donny slipped in and helped

Mrs. Bickford with Aiden by holding a towel to his head wound.

Lavender arrived and took over, her movements quick and precise. She started a monologue. "Nose is broken. Donny, will you move that towel? Cut to the head with some swelling. Signs of a concussion. I need ice. Donny, there should be some in the icebox. Mrs. Bickford, will you get the sutures ready? I can't find any broken bones. Lots of bruising."

Whispered conversations continued. Catherine wanted to help. She could get ice. Oh, Donny already had it. Aiden couldn't die.

Lavender came and knelt in front of Catherine. "I can't see anything from the outside. Aiden took quite a beating, but he's alive. He isn't awake because the blow to the head gave him a concussion. You need to concentrate on that. I'm not going to leave him. Mrs. Reese is with Emily and knows what to do, so no worrying that I'm leaving Emily alone. As for me, Jax will be here with me, and he'll stand guard over both of us. I want you home, taking care of that baby."

Catherine searched Lavender's face. Her friend's eyes didn't meet hers. "What aren't you telling me?"

"There is a lot of bruising. He may be injured where I can't see. Only time will tell."

"Could he die?"

Lavender looked away. It was answer enough.

"May I speak with him before I go?"

Lavender nodded.

Catherine walked on unsteady feet over to the bed. Blood clotted in Aiden's hair and mustache. His left eye was swollen shut, his nose was crooked, and a bruise darkened his jawline. His lip was split and puffy, a stark contrast to the paleness of his skin. The only sound in the room was his shallow breathing. He might not be awake, but he was in pain. "Alone?"

Lavender waved Mrs. Bickford, Marigold, and Donny out of the room.

"I don't know if you can hear me. I love you, Aiden Palmer, and don't you dare die. I wish I could hold you like you held me. I wish that every night, I'd kissed you like we did the night Tip was born. I wish I could have told you before now. And I'm going to tell you and tell you and tell you so you believe me. I don't know if I chose to or if it just happened, but I do."

Catherine searched his face. Nothing changed. The only place she could find to kiss that looked like it wouldn't hurt was near his hairline. "I love you, Aiden."

Catherine nuzzled her sleeping son, breathing in the fresh, clean smell of him. For a moment, her resolve wavered, but disappearing was the only way to keep Aiden and Tip safe. Bernard would never give up. TJ didn't need to tell her everything he'd learned from the men in his jail to know that. There would be others. Next time, Donny might not be around to raise the alarm. Aiden might not be able to yell that unearthly call to bring the men running to his aid.

She didn't know how he learned it or how he was captured and ended up working in a hospital for the Confederate Army. It was one of the many stories Aiden told her he would recount at a later time. There were so many questions she wanted to ask him, so many things to say, things she could never say if he died.

Nellie entered the room with the large basket she used to deliver food to The Rescue, her lips pressed into a thin line. "You should talk to Dr. Palmer."

"Is he awake?"

Nellie shrugged. "Lavender hasn't sent word."

"Then I need to do this. It's the only way."

The plan she'd hatched with Marigold and Nellie last night had to work. Catherine laid the sleeping child in the basket. "Tell Tip I love him every day."

"What about Dr. Palmer? What should I tell him?"

Catherine thought of the half-finished notes she'd dropped into the stove and watched burn. "Tell him—" The lump in her throat wouldn't allow the words past her lips. If she repeated the words she'd told him yesterday, he'd come to find her. He'd risked his life to save her yesterday. He'd do it again. "Tell him I wish him well."

Nellie scowled, her scars accentuating her displeasure. "He won't like it."

"But he will be alive. Don't you see?" That was all that mattered. "This town needs him."

"I see, but I don't agree." Nellie covered Tip with a cloth and placed her soft rolls over the cloth, arranged so air could still reach the baby's face. A person would have to be standing directly over the basket to notice Tip. "I should go. He'll be safe at Rose's Rescue. No one will tell where he came from."

"Thank Peony for me."

"She'll be happy to feed him, but it still won't be like having his real mother."

"But he will be safe."

Catherine closed her eyes so she didn't have to watch Nellie leave. Her fingers traced the brooch at her throat as if rubbing it would remove the pain underneath.

A half hour later, Catherine boarded the eastbound train dressed in black. The porter loaded her trunk and a tiny coffin containing a blanket-wrapped piece of wood in the baggage car. As hoped, several people were at the station to witness her departure, including a man who'd been lurking around town the past few days. He ran to the stationmaster and purchased a ticket. Could he be the fourth man the deputy mentioned, or could there be more?

Catherine covered her mouth with her hand to hide her expression. Her plan had worked.

Only Nellie waved from the platform, the empty basket hanging from her arm. She would deliver a note to Clara as soon as the train was gone.

The conductor yelled, and the train whistled and started with a jerk.

It wasn't long before the door connecting the train cars opened and the man slipped through it. He settled in the seat across the aisle. Catherine turned her head to the window and thought of Aiden holding Tip and singing to him each night. The tears she needed to continue her charade flowed freely. She dabbed at her eyes.

The train slowed for the next stop, and the man moved to the seat facing her.

"Pardon me, Mrs. Palmer, I'm—"

"The man who sent thugs to kill Dr. Palmer?"

"If he had listened reasonably..." The man let the sentence hang in the air.

"Tell the Fairlanes they got their wish. Without the doctor's help last night, my child died. Bernard doesn't need to worry about a child showing up to claim his inheritance."

"That only solves the elder Mr. Fairlane's problems. Not his son's. He still needs a wife. What of you?"

"As you see, I'm traveling east."

"And the casket?"

"I assume Mr. Fairlane wants proof."

"Will you marry Bernard?"

"As soon as I have an annulment. It should be easy enough. Dr. Palmer didn't reside in the house with me. I have the papers he didn't sign." A lie. TJ had them for evidence. Catherine wiped her eyes. "Unless, of course, you've made me a widow."

"Are you aware that if you cross the Mississippi, you forfeit the settlement from the elder Mr. Fairlane?"

"I was under the impression the contract had been broken."

The man reached into his pocket and pulled out a packet of papers. "Mr. Fairlane has been advised to honor the contract. You are not a suitable wife for his son. Now that the child is no longer alive, I need only your signature and your promise to never contact the family again."

"I have no desire to see any Fairlanes for the rest of my life." Unless she could see Bernard and his father rotting in jail. If they sent these men, weren't they also guilty?

"Sign here."

A thought that she might get more crossed her mind. "What about the suit against my father?"

"A judge dismissed it Friday, which was when I was directed to give you the money."

"Then why attack my husband?"

"Have you ever read the scripture 'No man shall serve two masters'?"

"Yes."

"I am in such a position that I work for both father and son. I was ordered to compel you back by the son, who paid me more than his father did to deliver the money to you. It's unfortunate the doctor hit his head in the altercation. I had no intention of killing the man. I won't go to jail for either of my masters. Suddenly, the lesser-paying job has more merit, so I have a proposition for you."

Catherine crossed her arms, distrustful but curious. "What?"

"Sign this. It's a receipt for the money, stating you will abide by the original contract and never contact Bernard.

I'll take it to the attorney in Fort Worth and inform him the child is dead, the doctor is nearly gone, and you have disappeared. They can decide what they want to do about the men I hired, if anything. While I am there, get on any train you want. You will not be followed by anyone in my employ. This afternoon, I will head west. I believe California is a good place to start again."

She suspected there was more to his plan. "And?"

He opened a leather pocketbook and withdrew a stack of bills. "Two thousand dollars." He counted out five bills. "Minus a small gift to me so I can disappear, leaving you with $1,500."

"Why?"

"I'm taking it because I hold the money."

He could have it. Other than donating the bulk of it to Rose's, she didn't want it—although it would help her hide until she knew it was safe to go home to Hiramsville. "I mean, why aren't you dragging me back to Bernard if he's paying you more?"

"Because the next verse is wrong. I have come to loathe both masters."

"What if I return to Hiramsville?"

"I am not the only man hired by the Fairlanes. It will be some days or weeks before they are called back to New York."

The train pulled into the Fort Worth station, and the man walked her off the train.

"Good luck, Mrs. Palmer." He disappeared into the crowd.

No one seemed to be paying her any attention. Catherine read the board for the departing trains before walking to the ticket booth. "One first class to Galveston."

"Better hurry, ma'am. It leaves in ten minutes. Do you have a trunk?"

"Yes."

The ticket master waved a porter over. She only pointed out her trunk. The coffin could stay behind. She hadn't added a tag to it, so it was likely to be buried in a pauper's grave.

Ten minutes later, Catherine heaved a sigh of relief. No one had followed her onto the train. Aiden and Tip would be safe.

rs. Bickford set the telegram on Aiden's desk, his heart
racing as he reached for it.

Twenty-two days.

He'd stopped counting the hours since Catherine left. She
promised Clara and Nellie she would send word. Marigold
and Lavender had known at least part of the plan for Catherine to disappear. He'd quizzed them all. He'd stopped short
of begging Jax to ask the Rangers to look for Catherine, but
barely. She'd purchased a ticket to Kansas City, but tele-
grams sent to the station indicated she'd never arrived.

Aiden unfolded the paper.

Arriving on Thursday westbound.
Dr. W. Newman

Wilber Newman's message was more than welcome. Aiden
had been quite literally running Lavender off her feet as he
recovered. The headaches had subsided to a dull pain most
days, and the bruising had faded. His mustache had yet to
grow back in. Lavender, Petunia, and all the other women
at The Rescue urged him to not try. But the only opinion

that mattered was Catherine's. He'd grow it out until he could ask her.

Mrs. Bickford and Lavender came to his office door.

"Not from Catherine. Dr. Newman will be here next Thursday."

"At least that's good news." Lavender sat down in one of the two chairs. "I may have some more."

Aiden waited for her.

"I spoke with Rae last night, and she wants to go to the New England Hospital for Women and Children for the nursing course with Peony. Becky is still considering the idea."

Aiden leaned back in his chair. "And what about you?"

Lavender looked down at her hands, where she twisted them in her apron. "We can make inquiries in the spring. It's likely I will have to travel to Philadelphia to complete tests. I can't go back, but I can continue as a midwife."

"Well, Mrs. Bickford, we may soon have an office full of workers." Aiden smiled as much as he was capable of.

"It's about time. I hope Dr. Newman doesn't mind living here," said Mrs. Bickford.

"I just hope he stays." Aiden put on his hat. "I'm off to Rose's to spend the evening with Tip. I'll be back at nine to handle any night emergencies."

Lavender narrowed her eyes. "Are you sure you're ready?"

"It's what I need to do." Aiden felt Lavender's glare on his back as he left.

As he neared the livery, TJ stood in the doorway of the jail, watching the street. "Got a minute?"

"One."

TJ motioned for Aiden to come in. They walked past the desk to the area that doubled as a parlor for the living quarters. "Have a seat."

"I said I have one minute."

TJ frowned. "Sit, Aiden."

"You look like your father when you frown like that. No, I haven't even been tempted to drink. I have a son to raise."

"I wasn't going to ask that." TJ sat down opposite Aiden and leaned forward, elbows on his knees. "I don't know where to start."

"Is it Catherine?"

"No. A man was found just outside of Abilene. His body had been thrown from the train. He matches the description of the fourth man who was here the day you were—" TJ swallowed. "Anyway, in his luggage he had a copy of the contract that names Catherine. There is also a record in a journal of sorts. It looks like he spoke to her on the day she left here."

"Anything else about my wife?" Aiden struggled to get the words out.

"GW has asked if they should be looking for her. I need to know what to tell him."

"Yes, please, yes." He swallowed back the tears. "I need my wife back."

⎯⎯◆⎯⎯

Holding the curtain back, Catherine watched the sea turn from calm to stormy as clouds swirled over the gulf. Her other hand toyed with the brooch at her neckline. Would the piece of jewelry protect her as it had Mrs. Reese? Each time she touched it, the memory of Aiden grew. Not that the memories ever left. Her every breath reminded her of her husband and baby.

She should move to a less expensive hotel or different city, one where Fairlane steamships didn't dock every few days. The biggest one she'd seen yet came in yesterday afternoon. All day long, smaller boats sailed back and forth, trading the steamer's cargo for goods from the south. For over three weeks, she'd watched the scene repeat itself. Had she been hiding long enough for the hired thugs to stop looking for her?

Today she should get Wednesday's paper. She paid extra for the Hiramsville papers to be delivered twice a week. The article about the men who attacked Aiden had taken two entire columns. According to Mr. Collins's article, Aiden's yell had been heard on the square. A man in the barbershop was halfway through his shave when he heard it. Like others, he'd run to help. The article didn't mention that Marigold was there or had shot one of the men. Nor did Mr. Collins mention that Aiden had been captured and forced to work in a Confederate hospital after joining the North, only that his efforts in the war saved lives on both sides. The only other news about Aiden said the doctor had returned to church without his wife and child with the insinuation that Catherine had abandoned him. Mr. Collins needed to gossip less.

The clock on the mantel above her fireplace told her what her stomach knew—her lunch was late. Catherine avoided the dining room as much as possible. Hiding in the nicest hotel in Galveston in a parlor suite had been risky, but anyone looking for her would search for her where her money would stretch. The reclusive widow would go unnoticed.

A soft tap sounded on her door, and Catherine opened it to find Bridget, her favorite maid, with lunch on a tray.

"Y-your l-lunch. It's my fault it is late." Bridget never stuttered. She walked stiffly and under the mobcap all the girls wore, her braid wasn't neat like it usually was.

Catherine held the door open and shut it after Bridget entered. "Is something wrong?"

"No, ma'am."

Catherine leaned on the door while Bridget transferred the contents of the lunch tray to the table. Something was very wrong.

"Why were you late?"

"I was just slow."

Catherine pressed her lips together. "Did one of the other people cause you a problem?"

Bridget nodded and said no at the same time.

If only Catherine had Clara's sense of people, she'd know what to say to the girl.

"I should go."

"Who hurt you?"

"He didn't hurt me." Bridget's eyes grew wide.

Catherine pointed to the sofa. "Tell me."

"I'll be in trouble if I'm late."

"I'll talk to Mr. Quinn. Tell him I needed you for the afternoon. Twenty dollars should keep your job."

"You can't pay that much. Besides, today is my last day."

"You're leaving?" Catherine studied the girl. For someone orphaned with a brother and sister to care for, there weren't many better jobs in town.

"I was offered a job on a ship, and I have to take it."

"Why?"

Tears filled Bridget's eyes. "He has Erin."

"Who has Erin?"

"The man in the other corner suite." The maid swiped at her eyes.

"What's his name?"

"Mr. Fairlane of Fairlane Shipping."

Catherine's heart froze. Lavender, ship, work. Why hadn't she seen the connection? "How old is this man? Older than Mr. Quinn?"

"No."

Bernard. "Where is Erin?"

"Tied up in his bathtub."

The girl must be terrified. She recalled the words she heard through the door three weeks ago. *You'd be surprised what a woman will do to protect her child.* And a sister her sibling. "Did he touch you?"

"He patted me," she hiccoughed, "through my clothes."

"Is Erin still there?"

"He said she would be safe until six o'clock when I brought him dinner."

The man needed to be stopped. Catherine knew exactly what kind of work Bernard had planned for Erin. Catherine didn't dare use the derringer Marigold gave her. Her mind raced, thinking of a plan. "Is your Sean working this afternoon?"

"He's not mine, but he is working."

"I'm going to go down and take care of Mr. Quinn, then I'm going to get Erin back. You are going to stay here. Eat lunch, take a bath, whatever you want. But only open that door to me or Sean. Do you understand?"

Bridget nodded.

"No one." Catherine donned her veiled hat and took her handbag and key, locking the door behind her. The steam-powered elevator would get her downstairs faster, but she had less chance of being seen on the stairs. If Bernard saw her, she might lose her chance to rescue the girl and, with any luck, put the scoundrel—no, that was too soft of a name—in jail.

Sean stood at his post near the doors. "Sean, I need you to find me two policemen, a sheriff, ranger, or even the police chief—whoever can arrest a man."

"For what, ma'am?"

"Kidnapping. Hurry."

Sean made it out the door before Mr. Quinn came. "Did you just send him off on an errand? We have errand boys for that."

"I'm so sorry. I forgot. He'll be back in a trice, which reminds me. I require Bridget for the rest of the day. You will send her brother up at half-past five? He's so reliable." Catherine used every bit of her Boston society manners when dealing with Mr. Quinn.

The man sputtered. "Normally we don't—"

Catherine drew a golden double-eagle coin from her bag. "But for twenty dollars, you can. Oh, and my lunch was not up to your chef's normal fare. Either that or I've eaten too much fish. Will you add cucumber sandwiches to my tea?"

Mr. Quinn bowed slightly before running off.

"Oh, and those delicious raspberry cakes?" That would keep him away long enough to get the law into the hotel.

Sean returned with two policemen, a man in a suit, and Hawke. His mouth dropped open when he saw her. She shook her head ever so slightly. They could catch up later.

"Thank you for coming so swiftly. Another guest has kidnapped a nine-year-old girl."

"Tell us where, and we'll get him," said one of the policemen.

"No, I'll show you. I have a plan to get him to confess to at least one other crime. A confession in front of the four of you should hold up in court, yes?"

The men nodded. "Sean, the elevator, please. And do come along. I'm afraid she's going to be frightened, and I believe she knows you."

Catherine explained her plan in the elevator. Hawke frowned at her, but she ignored him.

Bernard would never touch a woman again.

Once the four lawmen took up positions on either side of the door, Sean knocked.

"Who's there?"

"Doorman, escorting a visitor. Although you said not to allow anyone to see you, she insisted—"

The peephole slid open, and Catherine inclined her head, assuming he would recognize her as Hawke did. The door flew open.

Catherine and Sean stepped forward, Sean in position so the door remained open wide.

"What are you doing here?" asked Bernard.

"I thought you had your henchmen looking for me. Aren't you happy to see me?"

"My birthday was ten days ago. I lost it all, you little—"

"Temper, Bernard. I have a witness, and I assume anyone in the hall can hear you." She hoped they could.

"I'll kick him out."

Catherine stepped deeper into the room, which was a mirror image of her suite. "No. He stays. I only need to know if it's safe for me to return to Hiramsville."

"You signed my father's contract. You aren't to contact me." He spat the words out.

"East of the Mississippi. I ask again. May I return to Hiramsville, or are you going to have your men try to kill my husband again?"

"I told you it's too late. I don't need you anymore. My money is gone you—"

Catherine held up her hand to stop the next words from Bernard's mouth. He'd called her those things before. "So, Dr. Palmer is safe? No more annulment or making me a widow?"

"Yes, he's safe. I heard he survived. Pity." Bernard stalked after her as she assumed he would.

"And all of your men have been informed not to kill him?"

"Yes. They know my previous orders were canceled."

"And me? You intend to leave me alone?" Catherine wove her way deeper into the room.

"Since I have a signed statement that our brat is dead, yes."

The man on the train must have actually gone to the attorney's office. She was surprised he'd kept his word after taking her money. "Why are you here?"

"Because I must work, thanks to you."

Catherine glanced at Sean to remind Bernard there was a witness. "I meant at the hotel. You could have stayed on your ship."

"I needed to recruit a few more employees."

"Like you did Miss Lavender?" Catherine touched the brooch, drawing strength from it.

"Who?"

"My husband's nurse? When you visited in September, you indicated you knew her."

"You mean DD? I didn't recruit her, but she was one of our top earners. I spent time sailing with her."

Discovering her deduction was correct brought a stab of pain. She inched along the wall toward the bathroom. "She claims they forced her to work for you."

Bernard scoffed. "My father, actually. I'm starting my own ship. It's much nicer. You could work for me. You're not as bad as I claimed."

Catherine whirled on him, her back to the bathroom door. "Never."

"I'd let you keep a third. If you're staying here, my father's money will run out. And I doubt the doctor wants his charity case back." Bernard's back was fully to the door now. He seemed to have forgotten his silent witness.

Catherine turned the doorknob and pushed the door open. Erin's frightened eyes looked at her from the bathtub. Her hands were tied to the pipe, and Bernard's monogrammed handkerchief covered her mouth. "Is this how you recruit?"

When Bernard shoved Catherine out of the way and she fell to the floor, the four lawmen poured into the room, Hawke pulling his gun on Bernard. "Don't move, Mr. Fairlane."

"You are being arrested for kidnapping." One of the uniformed officers put handcuffs on him.

Hawke returned his gun to his holster and offered Catherine a hand. "If you wouldn't mind helping us untie the child."

Catherine knelt by the tub and removed Erin's gag. "Hello, Erin. I'm a friend of your sister."

"You must be the nice widow woman."

Catherine smiled and worked on the rope binding Erin's hands. "My name is Catherine Palmer. As soon as you are free, these nice men need to ask you a few questions. Then Sean will take you to Bridget."

"Sean!" The girl's face brightened with recognition.

Sitting next to Catherine on the sofa, Erin answered all the questions, sharing the details, from being grabbed and tied up to the mean man threatening her sister.

"Thank you, Miss O'Neil," said Hawke. "Is there anything else we should know?"

"He was lying. He wasn't going to let me go. I was going to work on the ship too."

Catherine hoped the child didn't understand what type of work Bernard meant. No wonder Nellie's mother had destroyed her face.

Hawke didn't react.

"If you're done talking to her, Sean can take her to my room, where her sister is safely waiting."

"He didn't get Bridget?" asked Erin.

"No, she was clever and talked to someone she could trust."

"You?"

Catherine smiled and nodded. "Me."

Erin took Sean's hand and left the room.

Hawke followed, along with the man in the suit, who was some sort of police detective.

Catherine touched Hawke's arm to stop him. "Do you have to question Bridget?"

"We do," answered the detective.

"May I be there? She's fragile," said Catherine. "Also, I suspect he has more unwilling workers on his ship."

Hawke's lips thinned, and his brows drew together. "Did I understand right? Is this the same group that had Miss Lavender?"

"Yes. I think so. That was the second confession I hoped for. Can you make arrests out there?"

The detective spoke. "Rangers can't, but that port is part of Galveston, and we can. I'm a bit behind not knowing who this Lavender person is, but I take it there have been other women pressed into the Fairlane's employ."

Catherine nodded. "Lavender was abducted."

"Here in Galveston, the law says all workers must be willing and licensed. If they are running a brothel in our port ..." The detective rubbed his jaw.

The stories her friends had shared as Catherine lay in bed during her pregnancy filled her mind. "Sir, when you talk to the women, please make sure they feel they are in a safe place. They won't tell you the truth if they think they'll be beaten or killed."

"How does a woman such as yourself know this?" asked the man.

"There was once a woman named Rose who kept a journal."

"I told you about Rose's Rescue last time I was in town," said Hawke.

Understanding filled the detective's face. "Too bad we don't have any female police officers. If some of the ladies on the ship have been forced into work, they might tell a woman the truth quicker."

Catherine bit her lip. "I can help after I know the O'Neil kids are safe."

"We'll need to hurry. It's going to be dark soon, and I want to get that ship impounded."

Hawke kept his questions to Bridget short and centered on the threat and kidnapping. Catherine saw him to the door. "I'll be out in a minute. Tea should be arriving any second."

"I told you I can't wait, especially not for some fancy woman to have her tea," said the inspector.

"Five minutes, and it isn't for me."

Patrick came up with the tea service. "Mr. Quinn said you wanted this."

"Thank you, Patrick. Come in."

Patrick nearly dropped the tray when he saw his sisters. He set it on the table. "What are you doing here?"

"Just a moment, and you'll find out." Catherine directed Patrick to the overstuffed chair. "Sean, you need to return to work. Mr. Quinn is going to throw a fit when he realizes one of his guests was arrested."

"Yes, ma'am." Sean left and closed the door behind him.

Catherine took a cucumber sandwich. "I need to go help the ranger for a while. I'll be back tonight. I want the three of you safe, and I don't know if Mr. Fairlane has any devious friends about. Please stay in my room. I will pay Mr. Quinn whatever it takes, though I know tea isn't much and my dinner won't feed all of you. When I get back, we can talk about your future."

It was almost midnight when Hawke escorted Catherine back to her door. "What are you going to do now?"

"I need to be sure it's safe to return to Hiramsville. I don't take Bernard at his word."

"I've been in Galveston for a week. How did I not figure out you were here?"

"Did you look?"

"Not here." Hawke shook his head. "I didn't think you could afford such a place."

"I can't. I only have funds for about another week."

"Do you want me to send word?"

"I'm afraid Bernard might have some telegraph operator on his payroll."

"He's behind bars."

Catherine raised a brow. "And tell me that stops all crime."

"It doesn't." Hawke played with the brim of his hat. "I'm assigned here, working on something else. May I come check on you? If something were to happen…"

"No, I'm not in any danger. But it's nice to see a friendly face. And I did miss you on my front porch pretending not to listen to our conversations."

Hawke chuckled. "Let me know if you need help with those kids."

"I'm going to send them to Hiramsville on the morning train. Will you make sure they get on?"

"I'll have someone meet them and make sure they don't get lost in Fort Worth when they change trains."

"What's going to happen to all the women who didn't want to be on the ship?"

"Most of them want to go back north or wherever home is. A few want to go to Rose's. And some …" Hawke shrugged. "They just want to be on land."

A single gas light burned from her bedroom. Patrick and Erin slept on the couch. Bridget sat up in the chair when Catherine entered.

"You're late."

Catherine crooked a finger and motioned Bridget into the bedroom. "Yes, we found other girls who had been offered the same job you were. They didn't want to work there."

Bridget shuddered.

"I have an idea that will keep all three of you safe. There is a little town west of Fort Worth called Hiramsville…"

"Still no word?" Aiden asked Clara the same question every day since he'd regained consciousness.

"No. I'll check the mail as soon as I can." Clara took Tip from his arms. "You'd better get into town. We'll have a fine day."

Clara came out to The Rescue each day for a few hours to teach and cuddle Tip. With Petunia willing to act as a wet nurse, it was best to keep his son there for the time being, since goat's milk only brought back the colic.

Jax waited next to the buggy. "I'll keep watch."

Aiden nodded at Jax. Knowing there could still be men looking for Catherine, everyone kept watch.

Still tender, Aiden winced when the buggy jolted. He drove all the way to the office. Donny came out. School started a half hour ago. "Going to school today?"

Donny shook his head. "Miss Emily is going to teach me as long as I stay out of trouble. I learn more from your books, anyway."

"I should make you write a paper on Plato—no, the Revolution … no, a list of all the Latin names for body parts."

Donny beamed. "I already have to do that."

"Tell Miss Emily I'll be out this afternoon to check on that son of theirs. I'm happy to supply you with more medical homework."

"I will as soon as I take care of your horse."

Aiden went in the front door. Mrs. Bickford sat behind her desk. "No appointments until after lunch today. Lavender is in your office, fuming—I mean reading."

Not unusual. Every day, Lavender told him he was doing too much. Aiden stepped into the office.

Lavender glared at him from behind his desk. *Fuming* wasn't a strong enough word. Anger radiated off her. She held up a newspaper clipping. "What is this?"

"I believe that's my personal correspondence you are going through."

"It's about me."

Aiden sat down in the wooden chair across from her. "Not exactly. I sent an old teacher of mine a hypothetical question. His answer is about you. Did you know people have been looking for you?"

"This newspaper article is over two years old." Lavender shook the page.

"They gave you a degree. Graduating class of 1878."

"They assumed I was dead." Her voice rose.

"It should make our inquiry easier."

"I only told you last night that I would write to see if I could get my diploma. You had no right to meddle."

"I wasn't meddling. I wanted to know what it would take to get you a degree. More patients are willing to see you each day. Even Collins let you treat his daughter."

"Only because you weren't here. He watched me like a hawk the entire time. Don't be surprised if Saturday's paper tells a different story."

Aiden sighed. "Lavender, for what it's worth, I never set out to find out your identity. You are a good doctor, maybe better than me. I just wanted to know if we could make the doctor part official."

"I'll forgive you under one condition."

"What?"

"I get to keep this"—she held up the newspaper clipping—"and you never utter my real name to anyone, ever."

"Deal."

Lavender stood to leave as Mrs. Bickford came to the door. "Reverend and Mrs. Staples are here with three new patients. They're in room one and want to see both of you."

Clara was supposed to be at The Rescue. Who was with Tip? Aiden followed Lavender into the exam room. Seven people in the room made a crowd. A wide-eyed girl of nine or so stood next to a boy about Donny's height but with bright-red hair. Another girl of fifteen or sixteen stood behind them. She had the haunted look of some who showed up at The Rescue. Aiden exchanged looks with Lavender. She saw it too.

"Hello, I'm Dr. Palmer. How can I help you?"

The boy scrunched his nose and folded his arms over his chest. "What's your first name?"

"Aiden."

"I'm supposed to give you this." The boy pulled a crumpled paper from his pocket. "And who are you?" he asked, looking at Lavender.

"Most people call me Miss Lavender. I'm a nurse and midwife."

"Then you are the three we are supposed to talk to. The widow didn't say anything about a preacher, so you can leave." The boy's protective streak ran as deep as Donny's.

Clara reached for Lewis's hand. "Reverend Staples is my husband."

The boy shook his head. "We were told to talk to only three people: Dr. Aiden Palmer, Miss Lavender—my sister is supposed to talk with her alone—and the lady that looks just like the widow."

If a stethoscope had been over Aiden's heart, it would have detected no beats. "A woman who looks exactly like Mrs. Staples."

The younger girls spoke. "Not exactly. The widow has a scar right here." She pointed to her temple.

Catherine was alive. He itched to read the message, needed to hear the story. "We were not introduced. You are?"

"Not until the preacher leaves."

Lewis shrugged and left, closing the door behind him.

"Patrick O'Neil and my sisters, Bridget and Erin. Bridget is the pretty one." This earned him a shove from the younger girl.

"And how did you come to find us?" Clara's voice was shaky.

He'd forgotten about her new condition. "If this is to be a long conversation, perhaps we should go over to my home, where we can all sit."

The children looked at each other, conversing with their eyes. Patrick answered. "Could we have something to eat as well?"

"Yes."

"We will go, but only us."

Aiden held open the door. "Use the back door. It's faster. Mrs. Bickford, will you hang The Doctor Is Out sign, please?"

Clara stopped to talk to her husband. "Lewis, will you bring us the stew and fresh bread? The doctor isn't very good at cooking."

Erin giggled at the comment, as did the boy. Bridget gave a half smile.

The air was chilly, as it often was at the beginning of December, and the children didn't have adequate clothing. Patrick carried a worn carpetbag that couldn't have contained much. Aiden started a fire in the parlor fireplace. He'd only been here a few minutes this morning, having spent the night at Rose's in the little house with Reverend Green and Jax so he could sleep with Tip. "There. It should warm right up. Now, can you tell us why you're here?"

Patrick looked to his older sister.

Bridget bit her lip. "Because of me. I am, or was, a maid in a hotel. There was a bit of trouble, and this widow who'd moved in three weeks ago told us to come here. She paid for our tickets and everything."

That story told them little. Bridget looked at her hands. "She told me I could tell the whole thing to Miss Lavender and she would understand."

Lavender stood. "Come with me to my old bedroom and we can talk."

"You used to live here?" asked Patrick.

"I was badly burned in a fire, and the doctor let me and a bunch of other people stay here after our home burned down. He's a very nice man." Lavender took Bridget to the old infirmary.

Aiden looked at Erin and Patrick. "Can you tell us anything else?"

Erin shook her head. "We can't say where we're from, and I'm not supposed to tell you about the man who tied me up."

"Erin." Patrick scowled at his sister.

"What about the woman who looked like me? Can you talk about her?" asked Clara.

"She's kind. Bridget said she sat and watched the sea a lot. She didn't take her meals in the dining room. Bridget always brought them to her room. She was very sad, like our mama was when she was a widow."

"Are both your parents dead?" asked Aiden. He'd get back to Erin's slip later.

The children nodded.

"What did you do where you used to live? Did you go to school?" asked Clara.

Patrick sat up straighter. "I did for two years. I can read, write, and do sums. Bridget's been teaching Erin."

Aiden kept asking questions. By the time Lewis came with a pot full of stew, he'd learned enough to guess Catherine was in a port town. He needed to read the note in his pocket.

"May my husband stay while we eat?" asked Clara.

Patrick gave his permission, and they moved into the kitchen, Lavender and Bridget joining them. Bridget was composed, but her eyes were now red-rimmed.

Aiden excused himself to wash up. In his bedroom, he sat and unfolded the note.

A—

I love you. If it is safe, they will tell you where I am if you give them my name.

C

It was her handwriting. He'd seen it often enough. But the words he never expected.

Aiden returned to the kitchen. "Please tell me where Catherine is."

Bridget answered. "She is in room 402 of the Lily Grand Hotel in Galveston. I'm also supposed to tell you they arrested Bernard."

Aiden looked at the clock. If he ran, he might make the train to Fort Worth.

Clara must have read his mind. "Lewis, go hold the train. Aiden needs a moment to pack, and he can't run very fast."

Lewis took off out the back door. Surprisingly, Patrick followed the reverend and passed him before they were out of the yard.

"I don't need to pack."

Clara stood. "Nonsense, you need two shirts, your shaving kit, a toothbrush, and the hairbrush my sister left."

Lavender put her arms around Bridget and Erin. "I'll take care of the children. They'll be welcome out at The Rescue."

They held the train for five minutes, which was enough for Aiden to board with the ticket Lewis had purchased.

He would see his wife tonight.

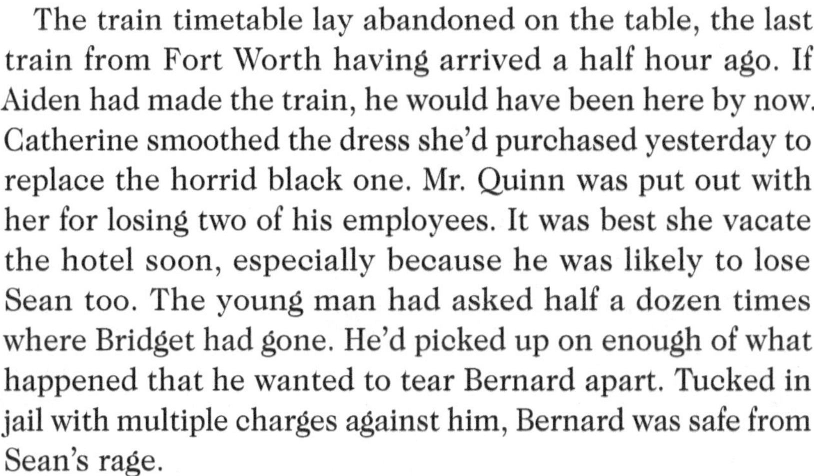

The train timetable lay abandoned on the table, the last train from Fort Worth having arrived a half hour ago. If Aiden had made the train, he would have been here by now. Catherine smoothed the dress she'd purchased yesterday to replace the horrid black one. Mr. Quinn was put out with her for losing two of his employees. It was best she vacate the hotel soon, especially because he was likely to lose Sean too. The young man had asked half a dozen times where Bridget had gone. He'd picked up on enough of what happened that he wanted to tear Bernard apart. Tucked in jail with multiple charges against him, Bernard was safe from Sean's rage.

Catherine had to calm the young man down before he figured out where the O'Neil children were. Bridget was barely sixteen and admitted during their late-night talk that she wasn't ready for marriage yet. Considering she'd been acting mother for the last year and a half, the girl needed a rest. She'd promised she'd write to Sean when she was ready.

A heavy knock came at her door. Her breath hitched. Aiden? Catherine opened the peephole and looked through it. Hawke.

She opened the door. "What are you doing here? Is something wrong?"

"Not exactly. The other ranger I sent with those kids came back with a man he was worried might be up to no good. He kept falling asleep on the train."

"Since when do rangers arrest people for sleeping on trains?" Catherine put her hands on her hips. Hawke's story was annoying; there was only one man she wanted to talk to, and it wasn't the ranger.

"We don't. But my man followed him when he got off the train in Galveston. The man would ask for directions and then walk a block or two and seem to get lost again. So my man brought him to the office."

"And so you now have a drunk?"

"Worse than that. This man is destitute."

"Being poor is not a crime." Catherine started to close the door.

Hawke put his hand out to stop her. "Listen one minute more. The man left home without any extra money. He'd been injured recently and wasn't drunk. He was in pain. He is also starving since he hasn't eaten since breakfast. So I brought him to the hotel and set him up in the restaurant. I told Mr. Quinn to put it on your tab."

"You what? Hawke, that man needs a doctor."

"He is a doctor."

"Aiden? Why didn't you say so?" Catherine threw the door open and ran toward the elevator. "I have a late dinner for two being delivered to my room."

Hawke caught her arm and spun her around.

Aiden stood in the alcove. "Mr. Quinn said you didn't have a tab."

If Hawke wasn't standing there with a stupid grin on his face, Catherine would have run over and kissed her husband.

"Do you want a tip, Mr. Hawke?"

"Sure." He held out his hand.

"Next time you bring a woman the husband she left unconscious and hasn't seen for almost a month, don't tease her."

Hawke laughed.

"You can leave now." Catherine pointed to the stairwell.

Aiden wrapped his arm around her waist. "Thanks for getting me here," he said to Hawke.

"Good night, my friends."

Catherine didn't wait for the elevator to leave to kiss Aiden in the way she'd dreamed of for weeks. He must have thought the same thing because he walked her backward into her suite without his lips leaving hers. Once inside, he dropped the bag he carried, closed the door, and turned the key.

"What time is dinner?"

"Soon." Catherine led him to the sofa urging him to sit next to her.

His eyebrows rose. "What can we do until then?"

Catherine looked into his eyes to make sure he heard her this time. "I love you. And I plan on kissing you until you believe me."

Aiden's lips captured hers in a long kiss. He broke it off and started kissing her jaw line, speaking between each kiss. "You…left…me."

"To save your life." Catherine giggled when his mustache tickled her ear.

"No…excuse."

"My plan worked. Bernard isn't after you."

He started down her neck, finding sensitive places. "He… is…in…jail?"

Catherine gave serious thought to pulling the bell and canceling dinner altogether. "Yes."

Aiden pulled back and rested his head against hers. "I heard a certain widow put him there, then helped rescue fifteen unwilling employees."

Not a pleasant subject. "Your mustache is shorter."

The hand that held her waist let go, and Aiden stroked

his mustache. "Lavender cut it off as I slept, said there was too much blood."

"There was an awful lot. And she doesn't like mustaches."

"Do you?"

"I'm still deciding. I do like the shorter length, though."

He ran a finger over the brooch at her throat, his smile widening. "You're wearing Mrs. Reese's—I mean, your brooch."

"Someone told me it would protect me." She'd even pinned it to her nightgown. Too much talking. Catherine pulled him closer for another kiss.

Aiden's mustache tickled her as he ran a line of kisses to her ear and whispered delicious words she wouldn't dare repeat. The sensations racing through her body overwhelmed her. She pushed on his chest, needing to calm the burning inside before it consumed them both. Any moment, someone would deliver the food she'd ordered. "We need to slow—"

Someone knocked on the door. "Dinner."

Catherine hopped up and opened the door to find Sean standing there. "Why are you bringing my dinner? I didn't get you demoted, did I?"

"No. On the contrary. They promoted me—something about a letter to the owner about my help in thwarting a kidnapping. I'm delivering this because Mr. Hawke added the chocolates and told me to congratulate you for not being a widow. And he gave me a hearty tip." Sean set the tray on the table and arranged the food. "Good night. We are short-staffed, so someone will get the dishes in the morning. You and your husband enjoy the evening."

Catherine shut the door behind him and turned the key.

"Did I hear him right? No more interruptions?"

Suddenly shy, Catherine nodded.

"Good. As a doctor, I've had more meals interrupted than I can count. I brought your hairbrush. You wouldn't believe how hard it's going to be to count to one hundred."

Aiden didn't finish one hundred strokes that night either. Or maybe he did. He lost count several times.

Epilogue

Six years later

Maybelle ran into the kitchen. "Mama, Tip said I was stupid."

"Tip?" Catherine turned from the bowl of frosting she stirred.

He poked his head around the corner. "I did not. I said her drawing was stupid."

"Tip..."

Tip crossed his arms. "Sorry, but the sky doesn't look like that."

Not for the first time, Catherine regretted purchasing the Dixon colored crayons. At least Maybelle wasn't coloring the new wallpaper again.

"I am sure your father will like the drawings no matter what color the sky is."

"Is he going to leave during his birthday dinner?" asked Maybelle. Only a year younger, the girl was almost as tall as Tip.

"No, Dr. Newman is covering tonight."

The back door opened, and Clara walked in with one child holding her hand and another on her hip. Dennis, Clara's oldest, followed behind, carrying a small crate. Lewis carried a larger one.

Clara pointed to the table. "Put the food there."

Tip looked up from his drawing. "May I go out and play with Dennis?"

Catherine looked at her sister and nodded. In unison, they said, "As long as you stay nearby."

The boys looked at their identical mothers, shrugged, and ran outside.

"I think we're losing our touch." Clara set her baby in the highchair while Maybelle led her cousin Maya from the room.

Lewis set his crate on the floor. "It isn't as disturbing when you try to say the same thing."

Catherine went back to the frosting. "Will you help me? Aiden will be home soon. I don't have his cake frosted, and I need to change out of my Mother Hubbard." The wrapper worked well for around the house but wasn't proper for a birthday dinner.

Catherine left Clara with the frosting and hurried to her room. A snatch of peace. It was tempting to lie on the bed and relish the moment of calm. Instead, she hung the dress on the corner of the screen and switched to her nicest corset and bustle, knowing she'd have to wash the gown in the morning because someone would smear food or something unidentifiable on the ruffles. Still, she wanted to look her best tonight. Her birthday surprise was the best. Clara and Lewis were taking the children to their house. The other doctors were covering for Aiden. And absolutely no one would search for them at Hannah's hotel. She'd even arranged to sneak in through the kitchen so no one saw them entering the building.

The bedroom door opened, and Catherine lifted her skirt to cover herself.

Aiden shut the door behind him. "Ah, my favorite look."

"Mortified?" Catherine shook out the skirt. "I thought you were the children."

"No, ravishing. I suppose Clara and Lewis would object to taking the children off now?" Aiden removed the clothing from her hands and wrapped his arms around her.

"I'm sure they would." Catherine ran a finger across the spot where his mustache used to be. Much to her delight, Aiden had shaved his graying mustache off last spring. She missed looking at it but preferred to kiss him without being poked.

"Pity." Aiden kissed her with enough passion for her to agree but not enough to climb out the window and abandon her sister altogether. He stepped back. "I should help you get dressed. The sooner we start this party, the sooner we can leave."

Catherine tapped the cleft in his chin. "You, dear, seem to be rather intent on your gift."

"What can I say? *Uninterrupted* is my favorite word. And I appreciate the lengths to which you go to arrange that."

"You should enjoy uninterrupted while it lasts because in about seven months—"

"Six."

"You know?"

"I'm a doctor. Of course I know." He kissed her again. "And I am very excited about that gift too."

THE END

Historical Notes

I may have topped my record for falling down research rabbit holes with *Healing the Doctor's Heart*. This included reading medical textbooks from 1870 to 1880. Thanks in part to the Civil War, medical knowledge grew by leaps and bounds during the last part of the nineteenth century. I have done my best to be historically accurate with the treatments and equipment that would have been available in 1880.

Even today, many medical professionals go their entire careers without witnessing a case of delayed-interval births. I found two articles of note from 1880 recording the delayed-interval delivery of twins. In the *British Medical Journal* in 1880 (1:242), a Dr. J. L. Carson reports that he utilized a wait-and-see method and the second twin was born forty-four days later. An article in the *Boston Medical and Surgical Journal* dated June 17, 1880, reports of a delayed birth of three weeks and five days, aided by cesarean section. Several scholarly works credit Dr. Carson with the first record of this delayed-interval birth; however, it's likely the possibility of delayed births was known to many midwives who lacked the scholarly credentials to document the births in the medical community. While still rare today, Catherine's twin births were not an impossibility in my imaginary 1880 Hiramsville.

In searching for medical universities for Aiden, I discovered numerous fraudulent medical schools that popped up all over the United States during the reconstruction era. I chose a legitimate one for our doctor. Established in 1819, the Medical College of Ohio merged with the University of Cincinnati in 1896. It's considered the oldest medical college west of the Allegheny.

I always knew I wanted Lavender to attend the Woman's Medical College of Pennsylvania. This was the first medical school in the world for women authorized to award them the MD. It focused on maternity; however, the women were taught all aspects of known medical practice. Reading through the theses was truly enlightening, and I learned so much about the scope and understanding they had of the human body, disease, and cures, and all before the existence of ultrasound.

The largest natural disaster in the United States in terms of death toll happened on August 27, 1900, when a hurricane devastated the port of Galveston, killing more than eight thousand. In the decades prior to the great storm of 1900, Galveston had become one of the largest seaports in the United States. By 1880, steamships were making the round-trip voyage to New York in about two weeks. In the 1880s, Galveston was known for its fashionable hotels and thriving business district. The Lily Grand Hotel did not exist and is a combination of several that did at the time.

Hairwork is one of those fascinating and slightly disturbing forms of art that was popular during the Victorian Era. *Self-Instructor in the Art of Hair Work*, published in 1867 by

Mark Campbell and located online at https://www.gutenberg.org/files/38658/38658-h/38658-h.htm, was very enlightening.

Okay, Ok, O.K. I have avoided the use of *okay* in my historical novels. While searching for a nonsense song for Catherine to sing, I found "Walking in the Zoo." The full transcript can be found at https://monologues.co.uk/musichall/Songs-W/Walking-In-Zoo.htm. The song was published in 1871, so apparently it's O.K. for Donny to use *okay*.

Author's Note

The question of the year for authors is: Did you use AI? Yes. Now, before you get all annoyed, let me explain how.

Aiden and Catherine's kisses. I have never kissed a man with a mustache and it would take longer than it did to write this book for my husband to grow one so I could experience this kiss for myself. So, I asked some of the AI bots for their input. They gave me various answers and descriptions. Not all of the feedback I received was helpful, such as shaving the mustache would be a better experience for her. However, using the AI was much faster than asking friends embarrassing questions. I wrote the kissing sections in my own words.

The mother and daughter song mash up. While playing with the limits of an AI, I asked it to write a song to the cadence of Onward Christian Soldiers expressing displeasure that the preacher was getting married. The AI generated six or seven variations that had me laughing so hard. I took a couple of the really good lines and added some of my own.

Brainstorming. As I am a discovery writer, outlines are at best a starting point for me to deviate. Since I was experimenting with AI, when I was stuck, I would put my last several paragraphs in the AI and ask it to write. More often than not the AI returned a truly awful and cliche next step, however, sometimes there was a word or a sentence which made me think of something which I hope was enjoyable. Again, the words are mine.

Editing. Technically, spell check is an AI, so all the editing software that picks up poor punctuation, wrong words, or passive voice is AI. In which case, I've been using AI for years.

Cover. I used an AI enhanced image for the doctor and applied the same filters I did on the other cover images. Now that Adobe Photoshop® uses AI technology, I suspect most photos will be manipulated using the aid of an AI.

I hope this answers your questions and keeps our author reader relationship transparent.

Acknowledgments

This book took longer than I thought because I may have needed a doctor. Although nothing major I am so thankful for medical knowledge and all the doctors who have helped me in so many ways.

As a mother of twin daughters, I am adding a disclaimer that they were not my inspiration for much other than the possibility of being mixed up by someone who hadn't seen them in a while.

As always, thanks to Tammy, Nanette, Julie, Jori, and Cami and all the others who are so willing to help make all my projects better. I would never make it through a day without Maria, and Cindy whose texts and messages keep me writing and Mara and Julie's, which keep me laughing.

Big thanks to Michele for the excellent edits. And to my excellent proofreaders who are not to be blamed for any remaining errors. Thank you all!

My family, for sharing their home with the fictional characters who often get fed better than they did. Seriously I haven't cooked in a year. And my husband who encourages me every crazy step of the way.

And to my Father in Heaven for putting these wonderful people, and any I may have forgotten to mention, in my life. I am grateful for every experience and blessing I have been granted.

About the Author

orin Grace was born in Colorado and has been moving around the country ever since, living in eight states and several imaginary worlds. She holds a degree in graphic design which comes in handy with creating book covers. Currently, she lives with her husband, and a dog who is insanely jealous of her laptop.

When not writing, Lorin enjoys creating graphics, visiting historical sites, museums, painting furniture, texting emojis to her children, and reading. Three of her books, her debut novel, *Waking Lucy* (2017), *Mending Fences* (2018), and *Not the Bodyguard's Baby* (2020) have won Recommend Read awards in the League of Utah Writers Published book contest.